MILE HIGH MAYHEM

FBI - K9 SERIES, BOOK 4

JODI BURNETT

"Dogs are not our whole lives – but they make our lives whole." ~ Roger Caras

"Some of my best leading men have been dogs and horses." ~ Elizabeth Taylor

Dedication

To all the dogs who I've loved. Fang, Gus, Joshua, Zeus, Rosie, Cocoa, Justice, Liberty, Declan, and especially Sargeant, thank you for the love, loyalty, and devotion you gave so selflessly.

MILE HIGH MAYHEM

By
Jodi Burnett

CHAPTER 1

Agent Logan Reed ran behind his K9 partner as the dog sniffed a row of lockers at Quincy High School in Denver. With utter focus, Gunner, a Belgian Malinois, stopped occasionally to investigate the interior of open cubby spaces and linger on scents emanating from a handful of closed metal doors. This was the first school Logan had ever searched for explosives. There were hundreds of places somebody could hide a device.

Logan and Gunner began their hunt even before police confirmed the evacuation of all students, teachers, and administrators from the brick school building. "*Such.*" Logan gave the dog his favorite Czech command to search.

As the partners made their way methodically down one side of a long corridor, a vague electrical scent and hum came from the fluorescent lights overhead. Logan's skin prickled with his own static electrical response. His core muscles tightened at the thought of the bulbs causing any undo friction in the air. He spoke into his radio attached to his Kevlar vest, even though he didn't like to. The danger of the radio transmission was minimal, but still possible. "Get the power to this building shut off." He left his transmitter on rather than risk clicking it off. Within minutes, the hallway dimmed.

At each classroom, Logan entered and followed Gunner's lead as he scampered along students' desks, teacher's podiums, and bookshelves. After they cleared the room, they were back out checking lockers on the way to the next. At the end of the corridor, they turned and ran up the other side, repeating the procedure.

Three K9 teams searched sections of the building. While Logan covered the main floor hallways and classrooms, another unit was upstairs doing the same. The third team inspected the gym, auditorium, and administration offices. Logan's adrenaline ratcheted up his spine. Searching for explosives was thrilling and terrifying in equal measure.

Logan adjusted his helmet before he spoke into his radio to get a situation report from the others. "K9 teams, give me a sit-rep."

"Team Prowler—ops normal."

"Team Justice—ops normal."

Logan let out a jagged breath. "Copy." None of the teams discovered anything yet, and the clock was ticking.

Gunner made his way back to the opening of the hall they had searched. He sat at Logan's left boot heel and looked up at his handler. The excited dog wiggled and licked at the drool dripping from his jaws, eager to receive his next command. Logan directed his dog down the next hallway and they repeated the search procedure.

One locker caused Gunner to sniff at length. He barked at the vent at the bottom one time, but then left it to continue his pursuit. Logan reached out with a grease pen and marked the locker to check again. There was probably a bag of weed inside or some other drug inside. Bad luck for that kid.

At the end of the hall, were a pair of closed blue metal

doors. Gunner sniffed frantically at their base. Barking with excitement, he sat down and whined. Logan reached for the lever handles, but found them locked. He spoke into his transmitter. "Need a master key for a storage closet on the west end of the downstairs hallway. Now! We've got something in here."

"On its way," a disembodied voice answered.

Within seconds, the school resource officer sprinted down the hall with a set of keys. Logan stepped aside as she shoved the metal teeth into the lock and opened the door. Gunner bolted into the small room. He squeezed behind a wheeled trashcan caddy that also held a push broom, rags, and spray bottles. The cart stood in front of a rack of shelves filled with various cleaners, boxes of toilet-paper rolls, and hand soap refills.

Gunner barked repeatedly and pawed at the tiles underneath the shelves. Logan got down on his hands and knees and peered under the shelving unit. His pulse lunged and his blood ran cold. A brick shaped box wrapped in brown paper with a small timing device taped to it sat at the rear against the wall.

He twisted his face up to the cop. "Get out of here, now!" He moved away from the box and spoke again into his radio transmitter. "We've got a suspicious package." Sweat gathered at the back of Logan's neck and trickled down his spine. "Clear the building and send a bomb tech to meet me at the front doors."

Logan jumped to his feet, resisting the urge to snatch his dog up into his arms to get him out of harm's way. He stared at Gunner, but another face swam in front of his eyes. Logan shook the image away. "Gunner, *Kemne!*"

Together, they sprinted down the hall, joining the other K9 units at the door as they all ran outside for safety.

Emergency personnel from several agencies including

FBI, local police, and firemen were swarming the parking lot, working together in a concerted effort to keep the students and staff safe. Seconds after Logan's transmission, the dark-blue FBI Bomb Squad Truck rolled up to the front doors. One tech leapt out of the back and helped another, who was wearing the ninety-pound bomb suit for protection, to step down to the pavement.

The armored tech entered through the double glass doors and approached Logan, who pointed out the room where Gunner located the suspicious device. Then Logan and his dog moved off to join the crew at the Bomb Squad truck. Inside the vehicle, Logan stood behind two agents manning computer monitors and watched the proceedings.

The suited technician waddled down the hallway to the closet before squatting down and peering under the shelves. The agent then backed away and signaled for the squad's remote-controlled robot to take over. The computer tech inside the truck maneuvered the bomb team's robot, which detached itself from a compartment on the side of the vehicle and rolled into the school on its continuous tracks like a miniature tank.

"Gorty has deployed," the controller announced.

The agents working behind the cover of the truck observed the details of the scene from one of the cameras mounted on the robot as the tech remotely lowered a mechanical arm with a pincer-type device attached to the end.

"Take cover, Thorne," the remote driver spoke into his microphone. "I'm going to reach under the shelves and pull the package out and lay it on the floor."

The suited bomb tech gave a thumbs up and backed out of the room. Gorty's robotic arm unfolded and the metal, finger-like extensions reached forward, gently clamping around the box before lifting it.

Logan's eyes burned from staring hard at the computer screen. His shallow breathing had him feeling light-headed so he forced himself to draw in a lung full of air. He shook his fingers out of the tight fists he'd curled them into and focused on relaxing his muscles.

The tech reversed the robot and carefully maneuvered it until the mysterious package lay flat on the ground. He spoke in a monotone voice. "Okay, Thorne. Proceed with the x-ray."

Agent Thorne approached the package and scanned it with a black-and-yellow, hand-held x-ray machine. The images flashed across the computer screens. Logan leaned closer, looking for an improvised explosive device, an IED, packed inside the box. While he studied the image, Logan reached his hand into his front pocket and grasped hold of a thin metal disc. He rolled the quarter-sized object over and over in his fingers while the scene unfolded before them.

One of the tech's monitoring the images shouted, "Looks like it could be a brick of C-4 plastic explosive. Thorne, return to the truck, now!" Everyone in the truck held a collective breath, praying the tech would escape in time.

Without hesitation, the suited-up tech moved away. The robot operator gently lifted the suspicious package and waited. Another tech deployed an automated containment vessel. A slow smile spread across Logan's lips as he watched the technical ballet of the robot taking further x-rays of the explosive device and then lifting the package and placing it inside the bomb-proof vessel. As soon as the robot secured the box inside the twelve-inch-thick steel, bomb-proof ball, Logan breathed out a sigh of relief.

By the back door, Agent Thorne unclipped the helmet and pulled it off, shaking a head of short, glossy black curls free. She smirked as her gaze took in the truck's occupants. "Who's the gorgeous dog?"

Logan rocked back, surprised. All the bomb techs he'd known were big burly men.

Reaching in the compartment toward Gunner, Agent Thorne's hand froze in mid-air and she glanced up at Logan. "Can I pet him? Or will he bite?"

"You can pet him," he sputtered. "His name is Gunner."

The woman's hazel eyes held a knowing look, as if she could read his admittedly sexist thoughts. "You're the hero of the day, aren't you, Gunner?" She stroked his head. "Good boy."

Agent Thorne climbed aboard the truck. When she stood, her full height had her looking Logan straight in the eye. "You can close your mouth, Agent." She grinned. "I'm guessing I'm not what you expected?"

"Honestly, no." Logan held his hand out to her. "I'm Logan Reed, the new guy. I joined the Denver K9 Unit last summer."

"Addison Thorne." She shook his hand with a firm grip. "I'm sure we'll be seeing a lot of each other. You've met the rest of my team?"

"Not by name." He nodded to the crew as they introduced themselves, all shaking hands.

Thorne, wearing black leggings and a long-sleeved Under Armour shirt, slid into a black leather jacket. "Let's get this bomb to the detonation sight," she called out before glancing at Logan. "You coming with us?"

"No, ma'am. I have my K9 vehicle here."

She nodded, then spoke to the driver. "Have we received an all-clear yet?"

"No. Apparently there's another suspicious locker. ATF's truck is handling it though."

"Okay, let's roll."

Logan and Gunner made their way to the rear exit of the truck.

"Reed," Thorne called out. "There will be a debriefing today at 3:00. Be there."

"Yes, ma'am."

"Bring Gunner too. He makes a welcome addition to the team." She smiled, and Logan nodded at her as he hopped down to the street with his dog.

CHAPTER 2

Addison watched Reed and Gunner through the window of the bomb truck as they made their way to his specialized K9 SUV. She'd worked with K9 bomb teams before, but this was the first pair that the FBI had assigned specifically to their squad. Reed seemed nice enough. Professional. Gunner was a sweetheart and obviously good at what they trained him for.

One of the other agents closed the truck's back door. Addison buckled herself into her seat, musing further about their new team members while the heavy 32,000-pound, tank-like vehicle jerked and heaved. She was pleased with the idea of a permanent K9 attachment to their squad. Dogs took much less time detecting explosives, which made their mission much safer all around. The driver shifted through the first gears, and the massive engine roared.

"Bring up the x-ray images, I want to see what we're looking at. Was the device C-4?" Addison bent toward the monitors.

"From the outside, the brick looked like C-4, but the x-ray shows the package to be hollow inside." Miller, one of the computer techs, clicked on his keyboard and several black-and-white images came on screen. "I'm not convinced we're seeing an actual bomb at all."

Addison peered closer, the muscles in her neck straining as all her senses focused on the screen. "I agree. This looks like something a kid could make."

"Yeah, something that Wile E. Coyote and the Road Runner ordered from ACME."

Addison nudged Miller's shoulder. "Still, as soon as we get out to the field, we'll have Gorty check it out. Don't get me wrong, I love our robot—but not as much as my own skin."

"You don't trust me?" Miller flashed her a grin.

"You know I do, but..."

The FBI Bomb truck surged east on I-70 toward the detonation site on the Colorado plains out in the middle of nowhere. Once there, the mechanical waltz orchestrated by Miller's nimble keystrokes began once again. Gorty detached from the truck, followed by the remote-controlled containment chamber. Miller maneuvered them a safe distance away before he released the sealed lock of the compartment holding the suspicious box.

Gorty's arm reached inside and removed the package. It's delicate and precise finger like pincers held the suspicious brick up to the remote camera.

"Is that a timer?" Addison watched as Miller directed Gorty to hold the device up for digital inspection.

Miller zoomed the image in. "It looks like one, but there is no connecting wire." Gorty turned the apparatus over. "There's no igniter either."

"Let's open it up." Addison stood back and watched the robot remove the false timing mechanism and pull the brick apart. It was hollow. "Hey, zoom in again. Is that writing?"

The image zoomed large. A cardboard carton, with a

stone taped inside giving it weight, was covered with what looked like plastic explosive material. Someone had scrawled red lettering on the interior walls of the box.

"False alarm." Miller directed the robot to spread the items out on the ground. "Has the ATF team reported in?"

The second computer tech removed his headset. "Yeah. The K9 alert ended up being for drugs in a locker, not explosives. Bet that kid never imagined he'd get busted during a bomb threat."

"So this is it?" Addison reached for her explosive protection gear. "I'm going out there. I'll suit up, just in case, but I want to read the message our pretend bomber has for us up close." She tugged on the heavy outer covering and grabbed a pair of thin, blue rubber gloves and a handful of evidence bags before exiting the truck. Addison stepped out onto the barren, wind-swept plain and plodded to the spot of land scraped clear of vegetation for fire prevention.

"A clay-like substance is covering the cardboard, but I don't think it's C-4. We'll have to see what the lab can tell us about it, but there's some black material rubbed into the surface. I'll buy the first-round if there isn't a trace amount of black powder explosive in this putty. That's probably what the dog smelled." Addison slowly flipped the box over and opened it just enough to read the words inside. "*Who's ashamed now?*" She slid the cardboard into the evidence bag. "What the hell does that mean?"

Miller spoke through the speakers inside her helmet. "Who can understand psychos?"

"The profilers at HQ can. Thank God." She put each piece of the fake device into its own bag before sealing them. She removed her headgear and returned to the truck. "Let's get this over to the CBI lab. The sooner we know what all this is and if we have any trace evidence to work with, the better." Addison shed her heavy suit and climbed into the rig.

Miller brought the robotic devices back to roost on the truck, and the team drove to the city—to Lakewood and the Colorado Bureau of Investigation Lab.

Addison stretched her legs out and leaned back in her seat. "The question remains, how did someone get into the building with no one on the staff noticing? School security is tight these days."

"The call could have come from anyone," Miller scratched his chin, "but it is highly probable that the bomb threat came from a student or staff member."

By the time they dropped the evidence bags off for examination, the squad had barely a few minutes to grab a greasy fast-food lunch before the debrief meeting at three.

Benjamin scratched at one of the many scabs on his thinning scalp as he watched the dwindling news coverage of the bomb threat at his old high school. As soon as the media discovered the threat was a false alarm, the talking heads moved back to their incessant analysis of the upcoming political election. They didn't bother to mention the note he'd left for targets inside the box.

They'll never get my point now. Not if they don't hear the words on the news. Familiar acidic pressure flared in his chest and up his throat, burning his tongue. He squeezed his skull between his hands, curling his fingers into fists. He hit the side of his head until lights flashed across his vision. Another migraine pierced the back of his right eye, darkening his peripheral view. *The FBI removed the package too fast. Now, no one knows what it said. I failed! One job and I failed. Again.*

He clapped both his hands hard against his ears. The vibration sent stabbing shock waves through his brain. *Idiot. Idiot. Stupid driveling idiot! They think the whole thing was just a prank. A* kid's *prank! The money I used to bribe the boy to hide the package in the closet—wasted.*

His fingers flew over the keyboard of the computer on the card-table that served as his desk. In the dark room, the image of a man in his late twenties glowed brightly on the screen. *Time to up the ante.* He clicked the return button.

Next to the table, on a TV tray, a printer came to life, running through its pre-printing gyrations. The photo paper slowly scrolled through the machine and printed an 8 x 10 portrait of one of his tormentors. After removing the photo from the tray, he breathed in the scent of the fresh ink before he blew across the paper to dry it. He taped the picture next to a ten-year-old printed flier depicting his personal ruination, and a recent photo of the janitor's closet. Above the fresh print-out was a copy of the man's senior high school yearbook photo. He stared at the images on the wall above his monitor and focused on the man's tanned face. The guy looked the same after all these years, except he carried about twenty extra pounds around the middle. He'd recognize this guy anywhere. He'd remember all their faces laughing and leering at him for the rest of his life.

They'd remember him too—in the final seconds of theirs.

CHAPTER 3

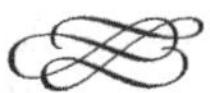

It was a deceptive type of day. The kind that picked at Logan's carefully woven plans, unravelling them long before he realized he was exposed. Technically, it wasn't supposed to be a workday for Logan, though he'd learned long ago that for K9 handlers and their dogs, there were no proper days off. They had called him in for the bomb-threat at the high school, but regular K9 training was a constant thing, and Logan had Gunner with him almost twenty-four hours a day, seven days a week. The FBI provided high-tech custom kennels for their K9 officers, and whenever Logan got around to buying a house, the agency would build one for Gunner in the yard. For now, his dog had the run of Logan's apartment.

Logan drove home for lunch and as soon as he and Gunner walked through the door, he clicked on his 60-inch wall-mounted TV to watch the news. The only living room furniture he had was a pair of worn-out reclining chairs he had positioned to face the screen. He listened for what the reporters were saying about the morning's bomb threat. A glance at his watch told him he had two hours before Agent

Thorne expected him to report for the Bomb Squad debriefing. Just enough time to go for a run and grab a shower and a bite to eat.

With one ear on the broadcast, Logan went into the bedroom and poked through a pile of clean laundry stacked on the floor until he found some gym shorts and an old sleeveless Army T-shirt. He looked around the room and sighed as his gaze flitted over the too short queen-sized mattress laying on the carpet. He hadn't taken the time yet to settle in and make his apartment homier. Buying furniture felt permanent, like he was moving away from his past, and he wasn't ready for that. He didn't deserve it.

Logan tied his running shoes and reached for Gunner's lead. "Ready to run?"

Gunner hopped up and spun around in a circle, his tongue hanging out the side of his mouth. A loving warmth tried to seep into Logan's heart at the sight of his partner's excitement, but he clamped down on it immediately. Gunner was his partner. They worked together. That was it. Logan clenched his molars as he focused on keeping his relationship with Gunner purely professional.

"Let's go." Logan jogged down the three flights of cement steps to the street level before bending into a few preliminary stretches. Today he'd run the five-mile northern track up around the Dick's Sporting Goods Park and into the Rocky Mountain Arsenal open space.

He stepped off with Gunner at his side, when he heard a jumbled crash and an accompanying groan. Fifty-feet behind him, an older woman struggled with a broken bag of groceries she'd spilled in the street beside her car. Logan pivoted and ran back to her.

"Need some help?" he asked as he bent to pick up several cans of soup.

At first the woman stepped back and narrowed her eyes

at him. She took in the dog and when she saw Gunner's FBI collar, she smiled. "Yes, thank you." She reached down for a dented box of Triscuits. "I've seen you around here. We're neighbors. You work with the FBI?"

"Yes, ma'am. This is my partner, Gunner."

The lady held her hand for the dog to smell and then ran her fingers over his head before asking, "I hope it's okay to pet him?" She scratched under Gunner's chin. "Too late now, I guess." She peered up at Logan with clear blue eyes that sparkled with mischief.

He grinned. "He seems to like you."

"I'm Harriet Loomis. I live on the second floor." She thrust her hand out toward Logan.

"Nice to meet you." He gently pressed her gnarled, arthritic fingers. "I'm Logan Reed. I moved in last month, but you're the first neighbor I've met."

"Are you the guitar player?"

Logan cocked his head. "Yeah, I play sometimes. Have I been bothering you?"

Harriet waved her fingers dismissively. "Not at all. I enjoy it. I think you live in the apartment right above me."

He looked up at his building and then back at the woman. "Let me help you carry these groceries up."

"That's okay, I can manage." She didn't sound convinced as she considered the broken bags and cans scattered across the pavement.

"It's no problem at all." Logan dispersed the cans he'd retrieved into several of the still intact bags, and after telling Gunner to stay, he ran them up the stairs. After two trips, he had all the groceries next to Harriet's door. She finally accomplished the climb and was breathing hard when she pushed her key into the lock.

"Thank you, Logan. Let me pay you something." She opened her door and then riffled through her purse. The sweet scent of cinnamony baked goods floated out of her apartment.

"No, ma'am. I'm happy to help."

"Call Gunner up here. At the very least, I want to offer you some banana-nut bread. I made it fresh this morning." She touched his arm. "I won't take no for an answer."

Logan glanced at his watch. He'd never get his run in at this rate, so he called down to Gunner. "*Kemne.*"

The dog bounded up the stairs and scampered right into Harriet's apartment like he lived there. Logan's brows shot up.

Harriet laughed. "Looks like Gunner wants a treat too."

"No banana bread for him." Logan shook his head and gathered the groceries to take into the kitchen. The old woman had decorated her home with comfort in mind. An overstuffed couch and matching loveseat nestled around a coffee table. Quilts and afghans lay draped over their backs, ready to warm a guest's lap. Random knick-knacks covered every surface, and she proudly displayed a collection of teacups on a rack designed for the purpose.

Logan followed Harriet into the kitchen. She took her time slicing the bread and plating it. "Tea?" she asked as she turned the burner on under the kettle.

He figured the old woman was lonely and hesitated only a few seconds. "Sure, thank you."

"You're a nice young man." Harriet pointed to a chair at her kitchen table, and Logan sat. "I'm glad we're neighbors."

"Me too." He smiled at her and reached for the butter. "How did you end up here, Harriet?"

"In Denver? Or at these apartments?"

"Both, I guess."

"The complex had an immediate opening and a good signing bonus."

"Same for me, but couldn't you get a first-floor apartment?"

Harriet sighed. "I tried, but this was all they had left. It works... mostly." Her gaze panned over the groceries sitting on the counter. "Thank you again, for your help."

"Any time. In fact, I'll give you my cell number. Let me know when you get back from grocery shopping, and if I'm home, I'll be happy to run down and help. Anytime."

The kettle whistled and Harriet poured the boiling water over the tea leaves she'd measured into a flowered teapot. She set the microwave timer for three minutes and then sat down across the table from Logan. "You're a good boy." Harriet patted his hand. "Where did you grow up?"

He swallowed a bite of the moist, spicy banana bread, licking the remains of crumb topping from his lips. "Wyoming. My family has a cattle ranch up there."

"You seem like a country boy. How did you end up in the FBI? Were you in the service?"

"Yes, ma'am. Army." Time to change the subject and get the focus off of him. "Do you have any kids, Harriet?"

The timer buzzed, and the old woman struggled to her feet to pour the tea. "No. None of my own. I have a niece and two nephews." She returned with their mugs of tea and pushed the sugar bowl toward Logan. "You must have a girlfriend, though I haven't seen anyone? In fact, I never see anyone coming and going from your apartment besides you."

Logan chuckled, certain the woman had been spying. "No, ma'am. I just moved to Denver a couple of months ago. Still getting settled, and work keeps me busy."

A smile hovered over her mouth as Harriet spread jam on her nut-filled bread. She stirred a spoonful of sugar into her cup and slowly lifted her gaze to Logan. "I moved here from Phoenix to be near my niece. She lives over in Stapleton, and she is single too..."

The banana bread turned into sawdust on Logan's tongue. He swallowed it with a gulp of hot tea. "Thanks for the treat, but I've got to get going. Gunner and I have a mandatory meeting this afternoon." Logan drained his cup and stood. "Don't forget to call me if you need help. Anytime."

Harriet rose and followed him to the door. "I will. Maybe you'll come down for dinner sometime soon?"

"I'd like that." Logan figured Harriet would conveniently invite her niece for the same dinner. He didn't mind helping Harriet out whenever she needed a hand, but that was as far as he planned to let this acquaintance go.

CHAPTER 4

Agent Reed slipped into the briefing five minutes late, his dark-brown hair wet as though he came straight from the shower. The meeting was already underway, and Addison stood at the front of the room giving her report to the team. She darted her gaze to Reed as he entered and then glanced at the clock above the water cooler to check the time. She drew her mouth into a disapproving line, hoping he got the message. She insisted her team be on time. Wandering in late was a sign of disrespect.

Reed acted as though he didn't notice her scowl and leaned against the wall in the back with his dog.

"Thanks for showing up, Agent Reed." Simmering, she gestured to him, and the other agents turned to look. He raised a hand in greeting and nodded to the group. "Agent Reed and his partner, Gunner, are two new members of our team." She asked everyone who had not been with them that morning to introduce themselves by name and job title before she continued her briefing.

"Agent Reed and Gunner located the fake bomb in the downstairs janitorial closet at the school this morning.

Though the explosive-looking device ended up being a dummy, it appears there was some black powder residue on the outside of the package. Gunner sniffed out a small amount of the real thing.

"Whoever planted the fake bomb went to a lot of effort to make it look authentic. When we opened it up, we discovered a note written in red marker on the inside of the box." Addison pasted a photo of the message on the evidence board. She passed an additional copy of the picture around to the team and read the words out loud. "Who's ashamed now?"

Miller leaned back in his chair. "I'm still trying to figure out what that means."

"It's obviously a note to someone specific." Addison angled her head to ease the tension in her neck and shoulders. She sipped the last drops of her watery soda left over from lunch.

The driver of the bomb truck handed the photo to the guy on his right. "Do we know who the prank-bomber addressed his note to?"

"Not sure." Addison tossed her empty cup into the trash can in the corner of the room. "Could be the janitor, a teacher, or an administrator. Even though the news speculated about it being a disgruntled student, I don't think so, because the explosive material found on the outside of the package would be difficult for a kid to get their hands on. Of course, we can't rule that out. My guess is the bomber wanted to see what the reaction to a bomb threat entailed, and now he knows. I'm afraid we can expect another incident soon, only the next one is likely to be the real thing."

Reed's deep voice sounded from the back. "The message could be to anyone the unknown subject thought might be watching the news, too. It's too early to tell." He rolled what looked to Addison like a silver coin back and forth across his knuckles while he spoke.

Miller slowly bobbed his head in agreement. "We may have to wait until the unidentified subject claims responsibility or, unfortunately, until he strikes again."

"There's always the hope that the unsub is just a prankster and the whole thing blows over—so to speak." The other computer tech leaned back in his chair and tapped his pen on the edge of the table.

Additional photos of the fake bomb and the location where Logan found it hung on the board next to her. Addison stared at them for a few seconds before taping a copy of the school's floor plan beside the pictures. She pointed to the closet in question. "Agent Reed, will you please give the team your account of the incident?"

"Sure." He stuffed the disc into his pocket and approached the board, followed by his dog. Starting from the time he arrived on scene, he walked the squad through the morning's events. When he finished, he looked to Addison. "How was the bomb threat delivered?"

"By phone. In fact, the call was made with a mechanized voice, and we originally thought it was a prank. We've had several incidences of this type of swatting lately—mostly kids seeing if they can get a significant police response called out on a joke. However, none of those calls resulted in finding any actual suspicious devices."

"No trace?"

"Unfortunately, no. The call came from a burner phone, and I.T. couldn't trace it."

Gunner's nose swiveled back-and-forth between the volley of questions and answers like he was watching a tennis match. He was hyper-alert to every move his handler made.

Reed continued. "Have any witnesses come forward? Did

anyone see anyone suspicious hanging around or inside the school? Any strange packages or backpacks sitting abandoned anywhere?"

"No, not yet, but the student interviews are still underway. Unfortunately, the bomber didn't park in the parking lot, at least not as far as we can tell from the first pass of security footage. If he wasn't a regular at the school, he must have snuck in from the side. Of course, it's possible he was aware of the location of the surveillance cameras. The camera set on the front doors was on the fritz. So, at this point, we have nothing other than the fake device itself to go on."

"No hallway cameras?"

"Not that show anything out of the usual. There is no direct view of the custodial closet in question."

Agent Reed sighed. "What about the explosive residue? Has the lab been able to identify it and find where it came from?"

"They agree with my assessment that it's black powder explosive. Preliminary tests show it to be GOEX, but that is such a common brand it's impossible to trace where it came from."

Reed frowned. "Damn."

"Yeah, my thought exactly."

"What do we do from here?" Reed asked before he made his way back to his position against the wall and resumed his coin trick. Gunner moved when Reed did, sat down when he stopped, and watched every roll of the disc.

"We'll wait on the lab to send over its conclusions and hope for something to pop up, like a finger-print or a hair, or some other trace evidence." Addison pressed down a surge of frustration. "We need to figure out how someone got all the way inside a school—into a locked custodial closet—without being seen."

One of the team asked, "Has anyone claimed responsibility for the incident?"

"No." Addison slid on a boxy pair of black framed readers and scanned a report. "We have heard nothing since the unsub phoned in the warning and as I said, the call came in from a burner. No way to trace it." She removed the glasses and tapped her front teeth with one of the stems. "That's all for today, guys. I'll keep everyone up-to-date with any additional information as we get it. Other than that, all we know is we have a potential bomber out there somewhere. Hopefully, he doesn't escalate, but it's highly likely he will. Stay alert and be careful out there."

The squad gathered their things and made their way out of the room. Reed remained.

"Sorry for being late, Agent Thorne."

"Had something better to do?" Tardiness spelled unprofessionalism to her. Especially since this was Reed's first team meeting. It didn't bode well.

"No, ma'am. I got caught up with a woman who lives downstairs from me. She—"

Addison held up her hand. "I don't want to hear about your trysts, Reed. Don't be late again. Got it?"

His brows shot up and something that bordered on dislike settled in his eyes. "Got it."

"Good. See you Monday—at 8:00 a.m. sharp."

CHAPTER 5

The following week, on a particularly beautiful autumn morning, Logan ran through the daily sniffing drills with Gunner at the FBI K9 training facility. He hid Gunner's favorite toy in the trunk of a beat-up car they used for simulation. He stuffed it under a bag of dirty rags, an old suitcase, and several other smelly decoys. To earn his breakfast, Gunner first had to find his toy.

"*Such*!" It took less than five minutes of sniffing through the fallen leaves and other obstacles around the training yard for Gunner to focus on the trunk of the car. He barked at it until Logan opened it for him. Within seconds, he discovered where his handler hid his Kong chew toy and gained the reward of some playtime along with his frozen-beef breakfast.

Once Gunner tore through the meat, their exercises continued. Logan placed various scents of explosive materials randomly in identical empty tin pails around the yard, and commanded, "*Such*!"

The word sounded like 'sook' and meant 'search for explosives.' For Logan's Belgian Malinois, the work command was like giving him the go ahead to play. Each time Gunner found the correct substance, Logan said, "Yesss!"

The head of the K9 Facility, Agent Clay Jennings, leaned his forearms on the top rail of the chain-link fence surrounding the training yard and watched them work. Jennings, a former Marine, ran a tight ship and oversaw all the ongoing K9 training. He was the one who provided Gunner with his initial training and he continued to take a particular interest in his progress. Logan endured his boss's derogatory, but playful, jokes about being in the Army with the good humor in which he intended them.

"Looking sharp, G.I."

Logan raised his chin in greeting and jogged to the fence with Gunner. "He's a great dog, sir."

"He is." Jennings's piercing sky-blue gaze stabbed into Logan. "He'll do anything you ask, but I expect he could use more encouragement from you."

"Sir?" Logan didn't really want to hear what his boss was going to say. Agent Jennings had partnered Gunner with Logan a mere three months ago, but their pairing proved to be a great fit. Gunner worked and played hard and was fast becoming a trusted co-worker. Though, he'd never replace the spot in Logan's heart held by Lobo. Logan couldn't go there. Ever again.

"No one around here thinks it's odd if you show your approval of Gunner with exuberance—like he was a puppy. We're not ashamed to love our dogs here, Reed. I know it might have been different in the Army, but we believe spirited play and praise are essential in forming a powerful bond with our K9 partners."

"Got it," Logan said, and he did. Only, he couldn't afford to open himself up to that kind of relationship with Gunner. Besides, Gunner did everything commanded of him with energy and ease. He seemed just as comfortable keeping things clean and professional as Logan was.

"What's the skinny on that explosion yesterday up in Firestone?" Jennings bent over the fence to give Gunner a friendly head rub.

"The one at the construction site? Speculation is there was a gas leak. The power company's shut down the area, but they're still trying to find and repair the leak."

"Did I hear right—it killed a man?"

"That's what I understand. He was the supervisor of the development. That's why he was there so early. It's fortunate none of the rest of the crew was there yet."

"No kidding." Jennings's phone buzzed, and a smile formed across his face when he looked at the screen. He glanced at Logan before attending to the text. "Take some time to play with your dog. Have some *fun* together."

"Yes, sir." Logan unclipped the Kong from his web belt and threw it for Gunner to retrieve. The dog took off after it.

Jennings returned his phone to his pocket. "It seems to me like you're keeping your dog distant from you, Reed." Jennings slid a pair of mirrored Oakley sunglasses over his eyes and watched Gunner chase the toy. "I know you're still grieving, but Gunner doesn't understand that. You need to find a way to forgive yourself and move forward. For Gunner's sake, as well as your own."

Heat flushed up Logan's neck and over his face. His chest compressed, making it hard to get a full breath past the sudden lump clogging his throat. He glared at Jennings and gave him a quick nod, but didn't trust himself to speak.

"Why don't you take a break from training for the remainder of the day. I only want to see the two of you playing, eating, or resting. Got it?"

Logan cleared his throat. "Yes, sir."

Gunner brought the toy back and bumped Logan in the

thigh with it before bouncing backwards and spinning in a circle. He nudged his leg again—an invitation to play tug-of-war.

"Pust." Logan ordered, and Gunner immediately dropped the toy, but his hope-filled eyes never left Logan's face. Logan reached forward and rubbed Gunner's soft head. Forcing a false brightness into his voice, he praised, "Good, boy. Good dog, Gunner."

Some of Gunner's excitement left him, and he sat down awaiting Logan's next command.

Jennings's phone buzzed again, and he scanned the screen. He returned his mirrored gaze to Logan. "You might fool others, but you're never gonna fool your dog. Don't make Gunner pay for your past." He pressed on his phone and lifted it to his ear as he strode back to the K9 offices, leaving Logan with a dog that could see into his soul.

Logan threw the toy again to give himself some breathing room. Jennings was right, and he knew it. But knowing something and making it a reality weren't the same thing. His mind drifted to memories of Lobo, and his heart fisted in pain as he absently ran his fingers over a smattering of burn scars on his forearm.

An alarm blared across the yard, and all training stopped. Jennings's voice echoed over the out-door speaker. "All bomb-dog teams report to the ready room immediately."

Logan and Gunner sprinted to the building. They met three other pairs in the briefing room, prepared to receive their assignment.

Jennings stood at the front of the room. Ranger, his all black Belgian Malinois, sat at attention beside him. "We've just received a report of a bomb threat for two different malls in the metro area. Our suspect called into the reception desk at the FBI headquarters minutes ago using a mechanized voice. They are reviewing the audio feeds now to see what they can find. Unfortunately, they could not trace the call. However, the threat is for both the Cherry Creek Mall and the Park Meadows Mall. Both sites are evacuating as we speak."

The K9 director ordered the different teams to their locations. He assigned Logan and Gunner to Park Meadows, which was a good half-hour away, even at top speed. Stopping at his locker, Logan strapped on Gunner's protective gear before securing his own. "Let's go, Gunner."

"Reed." Jennings's voice shot through the tension in the air, and Logan stopped mid-stride. "I have every confidence in Gunner—and in you, too." His boss's mouth quirked into a half grin. "Even though you are just an Army puke." His eyes remained serious. "Trust your partner, Reed. Gunner will not let you down."

Logan nodded. "I hope I never let him down either, sir."

Jennings clapped a hand on Logan's shoulder and squeezed. "You won't. Today is the day you leave the past in the past. Now, get out of here and try to come back in one piece."

"Yes, sir." Logan sprinted toward his service SUV. Gunner leapt into the kennel compartment in the back. Logan's heart pounded with each second as they sped down the highway—lights and sirens blaring. He prayed they'd get there in time. The longer it took, the more likely they'd be dealing with an explosion.

CHAPTER 6

During his research, Benjamin found out that Nicole Grey was the store manager at *Sophistications,* a high-end woman's fashion shop in the mall. He'd been sitting in a chair opposite the entrance to her boutique since the shopping center opened. Occasionally, she traipsed across the showroom with the same haughty confidence she'd had in high school. His mind wandered back to images of Nicole in her cheerleading uniform, her long smooth legs —tanned even in January—jumping and kicking under her short red skirt.

He'd been overcome with wonder when she cast her attention on him. It was a well-known fact that she was dating Tyler Brookes, wide receiver on the football team and debate team captain. He couldn't believe she'd set her eye on him—Benjamin Sykes. The night Nicole smiled and waved at him from the cheer-line at the football game, he'd glanced behind him to see who she was waving at. No one acknowledged her, and when he returned his gaze to her, she waved again. What a fool he'd been. Benjamin could still feel the sparkling heat of elation flooding through his body. He'd had a drooling crush on Nicole since the fifth grade, and she had finally noticed him.

After a week of tempting him, Nicole passed him a note asking him to meet her after school at the door of her math class. Her honeyed voice still echoed inside his head.

"Benji." She'd walked her fingers up his chest and placed her hands on his shoulders. She rose to her tiptoes and whispered, "Meet me in the janitor's closet." Her sweet floral perfume engulfed him, and he became dizzy when Nicole licked the outside of his ear before plunging the tip into the canal. She'd sucked his lobe into her mouth and nipped it. Then, she left him with a soft, sultry laugh as she bounced off toward the end of the hallway. His heartbeat tormented him in time with the swish of her impossibly short skirt. She looked back at him over her shoulder and blew him a kiss as she opened the closet door and disappeared behind it.

He couldn't believe this was happening. His chest had swelled with hope and love for the girl who occupied his fantasies. Looking both ways, he had seen no one watching, so he jogged to the double doors and followed Nicole inside. She had switched the lights off, but her luscious shape stood out among the shadows. He closed the door behind him.

In a flash, she was there. Her arms had encircled his neck, and she pressed her soft breasts against him. His body responded heartily. Though he had tried for a little space, she noticed his erection and emitted a sexy giggle. Before he knew what was happening, her hand had clasped him. She rubbed his bulge through his jeans, up and down. He had kissed her then, and she tasted like bubble-gum. Nicole undid the button and zipper and drew him out.

"Hold on a sec," she'd said.

He was dizzy with intense adolescent lust and hadn't noticed what she was doing until it was too late. The doors flew open, and the light snapped on. A group of her friends,

Tyler at the forefront, buckled over laughing, pointing, and shooting pictures of Benjamin's engorged humiliation.

Again today, sitting there in the mall, his heart stung like a pin-cushion run through with needles and he couldn't breathe. Same as that day, when he had dropped to the floor and huddled in a ball, the self-protective move only increasing the laughter of his classmates. Emotionally, he had shrunk into himself to a place only he could reach. A secret spot that he would retreat to more and more as his life imploded at the hands of these kids he'd gone to school with for years.

With re-kindled rage, he marched into the store where Nicole worked. On his way to the back, he ran his hand along a display of angora sweaters, knocking them to the floor. Benjamin found her on the phone in her office behind the cash registers. He slammed her door open against the wall. Her huge brown eyes stared at him as he scratched his arms. The sores on his face itched. God, he needed a fix.

"What do you want?" Certain fear rang in her voice.

"Remember me?"

Nicole's perfectly plucked brows drew together, and confusion covered her features. "Should I?"

Boiling hot rage poured over his head. He'd thought about her every day for the last ten years, and she couldn't even recall who he was. He rushed her then and clamped his fingers around her delicate throat. Nicole's eyes bulged as she grasped and clawed at his hand, but she had no hope against his fury. Her terror thrilled him, and he yanked one of her hands away from his and forced her to feel his growing excitement.

"Remember me, now?"

Her eyes grew larger and her pupils dilated. She opened her mouth to scream, but before she could, he slapped his palm across her lips. He booted the door shut with his foot and reached into his hoodie pocket for a roll of duct tape. He pressed the tape to her cheek and unwound the roll over her mouth and around the back of her head four times. He tore the strip with his teeth and then bound her wrists together. She kicked and bucked as he wrapped her ankles. Indulging his memory of her long teenage legs, he ran his hands up under her skirt, up her thighs to where they met her pelvis. Nicole screamed behind her silver gag, but the sound was ineffective. She jerked her legs and desperately tried to escape from his grip.

He laughed and tore the skirt along the seam, flinging it from her body. Her body quivered seductively with her sobs. Taking his time, he opened his backpack and pulled out a knife. He pressed the side of the blade against her bare thigh, and she stilled. Slowly he slid the face of the knife up to her black lace thong. Benjamin slipped the tip under the silky fabric, and jerked the blade, cutting it through. He repeated the action on the second leg before yanking the lace free—exposing Nicole completely. Benjamin tucked the lace into his pocket, then shoved her against the leg of the desk and duct taped her to it.

She curled her legs into herself and helplessly tried tugging her blouse down to cover her nakedness. He laughed at her then, a deep satisfying laugh. He pointed at her and guffawed.

He reached into his pack and removed three pipe bombs strapped together in a pyramid. Their braided fuses attached to a timing device that would ignite them when the seconds ran out. He placed the mechanism on the floor in front of Nicole just outside of her reach and clicked the timer on. One hour.

The sheer terror in her eyes stirred his excitement once again. "I wish I had more time with you. I would do all the things I've dreamt of over the years."

A pool of urine formed under her. *Exquisite.* He drew his phone from his backpack and snapped several photos. "These pictures can join the ones your boyfriend took of me. Your humiliation mingled with mine. A perfect marriage." He crouched next to her and ran his fingertips through the tears and snot running down her face. "I once believed you were all that mattered in the entire universe. Look at you now. What did I ever see in you?"

He stood then and packed the tape and knife back into his bag. Peace wrapped around him like a fur blanket on a cold winter night. He slung his pack over his shoulder and opened the office. She serenaded his exit with garbled screams and he smiled as he closed and locked the door behind him.

Whistling, he made his way out to his car.

CHAPTER 7

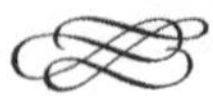

Early shoppers frantically trying to escape the mall as fast as possible inevitably tied the parking lot into knots in their rush. Horns blared angrily. Logan screeched to a halt in front of the plaza doors to the food court after maneuvering against the traffic stream racing toward the exits and frenzied pedestrians running across the pavement. A minimum of two police vehicles blocked each mall entrance. The FBI Bomb Squad truck was on its way, along with multiple fire engines and ambulances.

Snatching his visored helmet, Logan jumped from his K9 SUV and opened the door for Gunner. He had compartmentalized his mind and focused on the danger at hand. Logan and Gunner reported in with the site commander and he gave them their assignment. Since bombs threatened two major Denver malls at one time, they divided the four pairs of FBI Bomb Sniffing Units between locations. Logan joined in with a handful of local police K9 teams from Greenwood Village, Douglas County, and Castle Rock. They divided the mall into sections and began their search.

"Agent Reed, you and your K9 will move through the

food court and then search the upper level on the east side, travel north from there, and complete your inspection with the whole top floor of Dillard's."

"Roger." Logan knelt down next to Gunner and spoke to him. "We got this, Gunner. Let's go."

Gunner plied a wet lick to the side of Logan's head and ear. Anticipation crackled off his dog like an electrical storm.

"Okay Gunner, *such!*"

Gunner sprang forward, pulling Logan with him. They ran a grid pattern through the seating area and storefronts in the food court, careful to cover every square foot. It was too early for the restaurants to be cooking, but the aroma of previously brewed coffee and sweet pastries waiting for customers that weren't coming filled the air. They searched each kitchen and the delivery hallways behind them. After running through the great dining room once more, checking each trash can and planter, Logan guided Gunner out of the restaurant area and turned to the right. They entered the first shop along the walkway. Music strummed through speakers, echoing against the walls of the empty store. Gunner padded between table displays of shirts and jeans on his path toward the back. He made quick work of the register counter before dashing into the dressing rooms. Logan sprinted to keep up, watching his dog for any sign of explosives.

Finding nothing, Gunner retraced his steps, and double checked for scents on the way out. Shop one—down. Logan followed Gunner through every store with the same detailed attention. Each time they turned up no explosives, it gave Logan a sense of relief, but the overall tension elevated. The longer it took to find the explosive, the less time they would have to disarm it. He wondered how the teams at the other mall were progressing in their search. The situation of two simultaneous threats was overwhelming. He swallowed hard and sharpened his focus. Gunner entered the next shop, a shoe store filled with merchandise on shelves and racks in the front, and stacks of boxes in the back. The smell of leather and shoe polish permeated Logan's nose, and he was thankful for Gunner's ability to filter through thousands of scents.

Logan pulled down boxes stacked high, while Gunner sniffed the ones within his reach. As if a clock ticked in his head, Logan's pulse throbbed a count down. The effort took too long and valuable time raced by.

The next search location was the entire top floor of the Dillard's department store. Logan and Gunner ran their grid pattern through each section, stopping to inspect all the dressing room spaces and storage rooms along the way.

Gunner's speed increased, as though he too sensed the seconds slipping by. His paws slipped on the slick tile surface of the aisles as they raced through the perfume and cosmetics department. The cloying scents there were so thick, Logan tasted rather than smelled them. Gunner remained unaffected as he hunted for the bomb.

Addison gulped a cold drink from her water bottle. She bent into a few stretches before going inside to cool her heated muscles. Her legs hummed from the exertion of pushing herself an extra mile on this morning's run. She checked her watch. If she hurried and ate breakfast in the car, she'd still make it to work on time.

The stream of hot water she stepped into showered down into the curtained tub. Someday, she wanted to have a shower stall put in and get a claw-footed bathtub. Someday—but there were many other renovations that needed to come first. She loved her old turn-of-the-century house, but fixing it up was a slow and costly venture.

Addison ran her razor over her legs as fast as she could without nicking herself. She sudsed up, rinsed off, and bolted from the shower to her closet. The nice thing about her short hair was it took hardly any time to style it. A dab of matt-fiber product massaged into her roots to give her a tousled look, and she was done. She dashed to the kitchen, grabbed a protein bar and a mug of coffee to go, and she was on her way.

Addison drove into the parking garage next to the FBI Headquarters building three minutes before her scheduled meeting with the Behavioral Analysis Unit. She hoped to gain some solid information to take back to the bomb squad about the person who planted the fake bomb at the high school yesterday.

Double automatic doors opened for her at the entrance of the blue-glass building, but before she could put her cell and wallet in the tray for security, her phone rang.

"Agent Thorne, here."

"It's Miller. We just received another bomb threat. This time it's at the Park Meadows Mall."

"Have the mall evacuated. Right now!"

"Already underway. Good news is, it's early on a weekday. Mostly only employees and an estimated less than a hundred shoppers on site."

"Good, get them out. I'm leaving HQ now."

"We'll pick you up on our way. Stand by."

Addison called upstairs to let them know she'd miss the meeting and ran out to the drive to await the bomb truck. When they arrived, she jumped in the back door and they took off again, heading south with lights and sirens. "Did you get a hold of Reed?"

"Yes, ma'am. He and the dog are already on their way. I suspect he'll beat us there by a good fifteen minutes."

"Excellent. Tell me about the threat. How did it come in?"

"Phone call. Same mechanized voice as yesterday's bomb threat."

"Any trace?"

"Nope. Another burner."

"So, we're going on the assumption it's the same guy?"

"We haven't had a voice analysis done yet, but I'm guessing it's the same unsub."

"Or a copycat." Addison added thoughtfully.

Miller shrugged. "Wonder if it's another false alarm."

The adrenaline pumping through Addison's body was acting on the possibility that this time the bomb was real. It was an imperative assumption. Every. Single. Time. Silently she sent up a word of thanks that the early morning threat meant far fewer people were at risk. They raced down the highway toward the upscale shopping center, weaving in and out of traffic. Absently, she wondered why some drivers didn't see the need to move out of their way.

She gripped a handle next to her seat when the huge vehicle made the sharp turns necessary to get them to the food court entrance on the east side of the massive mall complex. Addison leapt from the truck in search of the agent in charge of the scene.

"Have they evacuated everyone?" she shouted at the scene commander.

"Yes, we believe so. The K9-units are searching for explosives now, and they'll also do the last sweep for people." The lanky uniformed officer crossed his arms and stared at the building. "Thank God, the threat came in before the mall was full."

"Agreed." Addison returned to the truck to wait for developments. "Get Reed on the radio."

Miller tapped into the frequency and called for him.

"Reed here."

"Reed, this is Thorne. What is your location? Closest exit?"

Fine china and crystal—a department no dog ought to be welcome in—was next on their search path. Gunner raced between racks of the delicate glassware. He stopped so suddenly, Logan almost tripped on him. Muzzle to the ground, Gunner sniffed like mad. He followed his nose up the side of a counter with glass shelves holding expensive knick-knacks. He leapt up, bracing his paws on the display and knocking two cut crystal vases to the floor. They shattered into a sea of diamonds on the tile. Gunner barked repeatedly and Logan scanned the items on the shelves.

He saw it. *Clever bastard.*

Logan grasped Gunner with both arms around his chest and lifted him away from the crystal shards. He carried him to a clear spot, and setting his dog down, he pressed the radio. "I've got something. Dillard's, top floor near the north entrance in the fine china department. The bomber wired a Waterford clock with plastics."

"FBI Bomb Techs on their way. Stand by."

"Roger."

Within minutes, a bomb tech followed by the robot entered the mall doors. Logan pointed to the device, and the tech gave him the thumbs up. That was his signal to get the hell out of Dodge, so he and Gunner raced out the door to take cover behind the bomb truck.

Before long, one of the techs inside the vehicle poked his head out and called to Logan. "False alarm. The bomb is a fake."

"You've got to be kidding me!" Logan's adrenaline drained out of his system, leaving him weak-kneed and shaky.

Addison clunked around the corner in her protective suit and unclipped her helmet. "Looked like the real deal, but it wasn't. Keep searching."

Logan nodded. "Come on, Gunner. We're still on. *Such*!" The partners started near where they'd left off with their department-by-department patterns. They were halfway through the lingerie department when an announcement broadcasted over the radio.

"A bomb in the Cherry Creek Mall has detonated. I repeat, there was an explosion on the east end of the Cherry Creek mall. No word on casualties at this point. Keep searching and be careful."

Icy blood flushed from Logan's skull to his feet. His ears rang with muscle memory of other explosions he'd been near. An image of Lobo shot through his mind's eye, and he sucked in a breath. Gunner cocked his ears at him and barked in question.

Logan gave his head a shake. "I'm okay, boy. Let's go. *Such*!"

Gunner hesitated a fraction of a second before turning to obey the command. Logan kept pace as they continued to search the section of the department store assigned to them. Painful memories clamored for entrance to Logan's consciousness, but he marshalled them back, and fiercely compartmentalized his thoughts. His focus had to be one hundred percent on the job at hand.

Hours later, they cleared the mall of all threats. The fake bomb Logan and Gunner found was the only suspicious item discovered in the entire complex. The hours of constant strain and adrenaline had taken their toll and exhausted Logan. He sat outside, perched on a cement pylon at the entrance to the food court, propping his arms against his knees.

Addison and one of the bomb techs who worked the robotics approached him. "Long day, huh?"

He glanced up at them, but then hung his head again. "You could say that."

"You and Gunner did an outstanding job in there. I'm thankful the device you found was another fake."

"Yeah, but the Cherry Creek team wasn't so lucky."

Addison squatted down so she could see his face. "No, they weren't. Did you know anyone who was injured?"

Logan shrugged. "I don't know. Have you heard a final report?"

"I heard one of the local K9 teams was hurt, but not critically. Thankfully, no other people were on that side of the mall."

"Thank God."

"For sure. From what the linguistic specialist has determined, they are as certain as they can be that the same guy called in both bomb threats."

"No surprise there."

"No, but now there's an official Bureau investigation into whether this is an act of terrorism. We have a pow-wow with SAC Sanchez and his crew over at headquarters tomorrow at 10:00 am."

"Got it."

She placed a hand on his shoulder. "Listen, the squad is going for a beer when we're all through with our part of the search. It's important to decompress, to talk these experiences out and laugh a bit."

"Thanks, but not this time."

"I think you should. It'll be good for you."

"I'll see you all tomorrow at the meeting, but have fun." The walls Logan built around his emotions were closing in.

He stood abruptly, forcing Addison to step back to keep her balance.

She steadied herself on the pylon. "What's up with you, Reed?"

He had to get out of there fast, before his memories engulfed him. Before the darkness came. "I'm good. See you tomorrow, okay?" He broke into a jog toward his SUV with Gunner on his heels.

"Wait!" Addison yanked up her gear bag and ran after him. She caught up as he was loading Gunner in the back of the car. "We're not yet done for the day. I want you to come with me to the Cherry Creek explosion site. You and Gunner. We need all hands and paws on deck to sniff out any other secondary explosives that might still be in the rubble."

"You think there's more than one?" Logan's jaw tightened at the thought of rescue workers in danger.

"I hope not, but I'd like to be sure."

"Gunner and I will head over there now."

"Great. I need a ride." Addison opened the passenger door and tossed her bag in. "Let's go!"

CHAPTER 8

Reed's knuckles were white on the steering wheel, and his jaw muscles bulged. He was pissed, but she didn't care. Addison needed to get to the other mall and didn't want to wait for the bomb truck and team to finish up at Park Meadows. Plus, this would give her a chance to learn a little more about the new guy. She was uneasy about him for some reason and wanted to dig into what caused her to react that way.

"Do you know how to get there?" Addison asked as she clicked her seat belt in.

In lieu of answering, Reed punched the name of the mall into the navigation system in his car and the directions popped up on the map.

"Okay, let's go. I'll light us up." Addison switched on the siren and the hidden lights inside the grill of the SUV and they took off, speeding toward the downtown ground zero.

Twenty minutes later, they signed the scene access control log and pulled into the lot set aside for emergency vehicles. They parked next to the ATF's bomb truck. Addison clutched her equipment bag and leapt out of Reed's SUV before he came to a full stop. She approached the officer in charge. "I'm Agent Thorne with the FBI Bomb Squad. I've brought one of our K9 teams with me. How can we help?"

A bomb tech pointed in the direction of the blast. "We have teams going over the explosion site, but we can always use another dog. Even though there was a warning, the location hadn't been fully evacuated at the time of the blast, so we are not only looking for secondary explosive devices, but survivors—and of course, victims."

"We're on it." Addison stood at the edge of the scene and removed a pair of binoculars from her bag. She scanned the blown apart mall. In a matter of seconds, an explosion made an upscale shopping center look like the deserted shell of a war zone tenement. Gone were all the beautiful, shiny cars in the lot. High-dollar clothing, jewelry, and gadgets were shredded and strewn throughout chunks of broken concrete and brick. They had shut down the electricity in that section of the city, but wires and rebar poked out haphazardly from the rubble.

Reed and Gunner approached her side. "Holy shit."

"That about sums it up." Addison pointed to the other K9 teams on location. "Let's find out where they can best use us."

"Us?" Reed canted his head at her, but she couldn't see his eyes behind his mirrored aviators.

"I'm not just going to sit around doing nothing. Get your gear and let's go." She drew a hardhat, respirator, and leather work gloves from her bag before stalking off toward the search teams. Reed seemed to hesitate a fraction, and Addison wondered again what made him tick.

By the time she approached the nearest team, Reed had geared up and was right behind her. He'd clipped Gunner's flack vest on, and they were ready to go.

They ducked under the perimeter rope. "FBI bomb tech, Agent Thorne." She blurted out at the man in charge of the hunt. "This is Agent Reed and his K9 partner, Gunner. Where do you want us?"

The officer suited up in military style utilities gestured to the far-right side of the destruction. "My team has just finished setting up grid markers in that quadrant." He pointed to their right. "Start there."

"On it." Addison tossed her head in the direction he indicated. "Let's go." Reed followed her there.

"Find 'em, Gunner," Logan commanded. "*Such*."

Gunner trotted ahead with his nose to the ground. Pacing five steps before turning back to check a scent and then continuing on. Reed kept pace, and Addison remained right behind them. They focused on the grid pattern, marking the area with flags showing the space they had covered and any potential evidence. Logan spotted a sign directing shoppers to the Mandarin Grill.

"Thorne, look at the angle this metal is bent and how the edge melted." He ran a heavily gloved finger over the rough side.

"Looks to be a restaurant logo. Must have blown clear out here from somewhere near the seat of the blast."

"Like a missile."

She shuddered, thinking of the power of an explosion. If a bomb could do this to a steel sign, what would it do to a soft-tissued human being?

Reed's dog was excited. The search was a game for him. He surged forward to a pile of broken bricks where he barked several times and sat down.

"Good boy! Yessss!" Logan reached for Gunner's reward toy clipped to his belt and gave it to him. He called out to Addison. "Over here. I think he's discovered a body. Call the extraction team."

Addison spoke into the radio on her shoulder and waved so they could locate her quickly. "We've found someone."

Reed chucked bricks away, not waiting for the equipment and team to get there. "I see a hand. Thorne, help me!"

Addison raced to his side. Together, they moved loose stones off the pile, not wanting to disturb any potential evidence. A bloodied arm led to a crumpled body. There was no movement—no response to their shouts. When they arrived, the extraction team took over, pushing Addison and Reed away.

Reed's eyes methodically clicked to a spot further along the grid. "Let's keep searching. Where there is one person, there's likely to be more." He tugged on Gunner's toy playfully before he asked him to drop it. Clipping it back on his belt, he told the dog to search again.

Reed took off behind Gunner, and Addison remained hot on their tail. This was not her usual job. Normally, Addison was attached to the bomb truck. Her uniform was the heavily padded bomb proof suit, and her expertise was dismantling explosive devices. This task, the tracking of explosive scents and finding victims was new and exciting on a different level. Addison was used to being in situations where the greatest risk was to herself. They generally evacuated all the people before they called her in. And more often than not, they sent the bomb robot in to retrieve the device and dispose of it. Somehow, this felt more hands on and less secure. If there was another device, she didn't know where it was or what type of explosive they might be dealing with. For that, they relied on Gunner.

Addison noticed other FBI K9 teams showing up. Everyone wanted to help locate the people covered under the crumbled building. Hoping against hope to find them alive. They came up to a team covering the grid section next to theirs. Reed nodded at a female agent with a dark brown ponytail hanging from the back of her FBI cap following a chocolate Labrador.

"Hey, Dean. Good to see you and Annie here."

"Hi, Reed." The woman stopped. "I heard you and Gunner found a fake device over at Park Meadows?"

"Yeah. Can't figure what's up with this bomber. Presuming these are all the same guy. Why the false alarms?"

Agent Dean shrugged. "Maybe trying to divide the rescue teams? God knows." She thrust her hand out toward Addison. "I'm Kendra Dean. Reed and I train together at the FBI K9 facility sometimes."

"Addison Thorne, bomb tech. Agent Reed is new to our team." The women shook hands. "He pretty much keeps to himself, so you'll have to give me the skinny on him over beers sometime."

Dean offered a slight smile and glanced at Reed. "He's good people. I'm sure he'll tell you everything he wants you to know." She nodded at Reed and then looked back at Addison. "Nice to meet you. Be careful out here, you guys." Dean refocused on her job. "Find 'em, Annie." The pair continued down their section.

Reed moved off at a brisk clip. "Something you want to know about me, Thorne?"

"Yeah." Addison wasn't one to shrink back. "What's with you? Why don't you want to hang out with the team?"

Gunner barked and dug in the rubble with his front paws. He barked again and sat down whining, and looked at Reed expectantly. "He's got something." Reed held up a hand, signaling Addison to halt. "We may have a secondary bomb. Fall back!"

CHAPTER 9

Memories of the collateral damage from explosions he'd experienced before pressed in on the edge of Logan's mind. One particular image refused to be ignored and stabbed its way into his brain—Lobo's face, the second before the blast. The reassurance, the love, hell... the *trust* in those eyes was what fueled Logan's unmanageable guilt. But now was not the time. He shook the painful remembrance off, swallowing the bitter emotions, and forced himself to focus on the task at hand.

Logan cleared the area and called for the ATF bomb squad on site to investigate the location Gunner keyed in on. The rubble was too rough to send in their robot, making this mission one of extreme risk. Their tech ambled over in his bulky protective suit.

"Agent, you and your dog need to get back."

"Absolutely, as soon as I show you the exact location Gunner indicated." He pointed to the spot where Gunner had tried to dig. If there was a bomb, it could explode any second. Logan's heart ticked like a stopwatch and sweat trickled into his brow. "I don't believe the explosive is deep down."

"Thanks, brother. Now get out of here."

"I'm gone." Logan raced back over the rubble toward the safety of the bomb truck. He found Thorne there and stood next to her behind the rig, watching the monitors she had streamed to her phone.

"I can't help but think of survivors buried under beams and cement chunks having to go through another explosion." The strain on her face echoed the tight muscles across Logan's neck and shoulders. "Good find. Hopefully, their tech can get to it in time."

Logan blinked away the knowledge of what would happen to the guy if the bomb blew. The padded suit could only offer so much protection. Techs kept their fingers bare so they could work with delicate wires, meaning their unprotected hands remained completely vulnerable to explosions. Not to mention, the suit couldn't keep them from being crushed under heavy blocks of concrete.

"What makes someone want to become a bomb tech, anyway?" Logan murmured more to himself than to Thorne, but she answered.

"People think we're all adrenaline junkies with a death wish." Her breathing was shallow, and her eyes did not leave the screen.

Logan regarded her. He had never known a female bomb tech, though he'd heard of a few. He couldn't reconcile why such a lean woman would choose this profession. Most techs were big, bulky men whose bodies had at least some chance of surviving an explosion. Agent Thorne was tall and thin. She was in good physical shape—fantastic, in fact—but still. His gaze traveled up her delicate neck to a firm jaw. She wore her short dark hair in layers flipped up in the back. Her eyes, a blue-ish sea green, pivoted to meet his perusal.

"What?" Her question jerked Logan back to the situation at hand.

"Nothing. I'm just wondering how you became a bomb tech and thinking I'm glad that's not you out there facing the possibility of a second device."

She rounded and faced him fully. Her eyes sparked as they narrowed. "Why? You don't think I could handle it?" Thorne pressed a fist against her hip. "I'll have you know, I've been a bomb tech for five years and in that time I've been sent flying my share of times."

Shit, Reed. Way to screw up being part of a new team. "That's not what I meant. I don't doubt you know what you're doing, and can handle it. I'm just glad you don't have to."

Her eyes narrowed further. "Hm." Thorne turned back to her phone and Logan figured she didn't buy it, even though he was sincere. "Look. I think he found it!"

Logan leaned over her shoulder and watched the ATF tech lift a duct-taped device from under fifty pounds or more of debris. Keeping one eye on the screen, he reached for Gunner's toy and gave it to his dog. "Good boy, Gunner. You did it again." Gunner bit down and tugged. Logan yanked back. "Yes! Good dog!" Logan let Gunner take his toy and returned his attention to the phone.

"That's it… easy…" Thorne spoke to the image on the screen. "It looks like an IED with a timer. The clock shows forty-five seconds. You've got this. Come on, Stan." Together Logan and Thorne held their breath and watched as the ATF tech opened his small tool-box and remove the wire snips. He carefully slipped the red wire between the blades and clipped. Logan's breath caught, and he clamped his jaw tight as the tech repeated the action with a blue wire.

The timer stopped with thirteen seconds to spare, and a collective cheer went up throughout the bombed-out area. "Way to go, Stan!" Addison yelled.

A pent-up breath rushed out of Reed's mouth. "You know that guy?"

"Yeah, he may be ATF, but it's a small community. As you'll see, we do a lot of training together." Thorne reached down and ruffled Gunner's fur. "You did it again, boy." She peered up at Logan. "The jury is still out on you, but your dog has proven himself in spades."

He deserved the dig, so he didn't bite back. "Yeah, he's a great dog."

"You two are new to each other, right?"

Logan nodded. He did not want to talk about this. Her question was one that invariably led to more about other dogs he'd worked with. "I better head back out there. I'll have Gunner focus on explosive scents. There are plenty of K9s here that can search for survivors." He called Gunner to heal, and after praising him once more, re-clipped his dog's toy to his belt. "Let's get back to work, Gunner."

"Hey, Reed. I've heard a rumor or two about you."

Logan darted a glare at her.

"You may as well talk to me." She smirked. "I'll find out whatever you're hiding, one way or the other."

"Maybe you should have been an analyst rather than a bomb tech. Seems more your style."

That barb hit its target. Thorne drew herself up to her full height. "You know nothing about me." A storm brewed in her sea-colored eyes.

Smug, Logan replied, "Likewise." He jogged back to the grid he'd been searching and started where they'd left off. "Gunner, *such.*"

Reed jogged off and Addison wondered exactly what he was running away from. She was aware of a few whispers about him—conjectures about what he'd faced while he was still in the Army. Though there was likely some truth in what she'd heard, Addison was not one to listen to gossip. She wanted to hear about his life from the man himself.

Sharing their pasts, as well as their current experiences, was what bonded a team like hers together. Ultimately, that's what gave her the niggling at the back of her neck about Reed. He didn't want to share. It didn't seem like he cared about becoming part of the team—and that was unacceptable. When you worked in an occupation where the lives of your team members were constantly in each other's hands, trust was imperative.

The site of the explosion sounded like a construction zone. Once searchers cleared an area of secondary explosive devices, chainsaws cut through beams, opening up pathways inside. Jack-hammers and sledge hammers pounded against large blocks of concrete as emergency personnel rushed to find survivors. Cement dust clouded the early evening sky and settled like paste on Addison's tongue.

Addison watched as Reed and another searcher hauled several crumbling chunks of rubble from one place and stacked them to the side. He stuck his arm down into the hole they made. After a minute, Reed shook his head at the other man. Together, they both reached down into the space and lifted the lifeless body of a woman out of the rubble.

Reed kept all of his emotions shuttered as he scooped the woman's corpse into his arms. He carried her gently to a tent constructed specifically for casualties. Both Reed's confidence in directing his knit-together-on-site crew, along with his respect and compassion for the deceased, impressed Addison. Still, she wondered what drove him, and she was determined to find out.

The padded ATF tech shuffled past the truck to the spot where they had deployed the containment device for the disabled bomb. Even though he'd defused the device, they wouldn't take any chances. Once they sealed the explosive inside, the tech unclipped his helmet.

Addison approached and held his heavy headgear for him while he shucked his armored suit. "Nice work out there, Stan."

"Yeah—thanks. I'm worried now, though. More than one bomb could mean any number. Have you heard any word on who they think did this? Any groups taking responsibility?"

"I've heard nothing yet, but I've been out in the field too. We were over at Park Meadows this morning. There was a fake bomb planted there. Makes you wonder what the motive is. Homeland Security is currently working to determine if this was an act of terrorism."

"Maybe domestic terrorism, but either way, the bastard effectively split the response teams."

"Do you think that was his intention?" Addison helped Stan stow his gear. "I heard most all the people got out of the mall before the explosion. God, I hope so."

As if her words had magical powers, a dog's excited barks filled the air. Addison and Stan strained to see where the alert came from. The Lab with the agent Reed had introduced her to barked again and pawed at the rock-strewn scene.

"We've found someone!" Agent Dean shouted. "Get an excavation team here. Now!"

A crew of diggers ran toward the woman and her dog, followed closely by two paramedics. Hope-filled energy laced with tension ballooned inside Addison's ribcage. It was such a precarious situation. The very weight trapping survivors could also be what kept them from bleeding out. Removing people from blown apart structures was risky at best and could be as difficult as neurosurgery.

Reed had completed his grid search and ran to help dig the survivor out. He and another man lifted a beam that must have weighed 500 pounds. The K9 handler sure didn't shy away from pitching in. He worked well with the group of strangers. Addison observed him as he took charge and gave clear direction to the crew. *So, why does he have a hard time connecting with his own team?*

CHAPTER 10

Moments after hoisting the beam off the one victim, Logan's gaze snapped toward a gaping hole in a section of the structure left standing. Addison's skin prickled with cold apprehension.

"I think I hear someone!" Logan yelled as he darted inside the dark opening with his dog at his side.

"Reed! No!" she screamed. "Stand down!" It wasn't safe to run headlong into a bombed-out building. The structure wasn't stable, and there was still the possibility of another bomb. He should know better. "Logan!"

Addison ran to the truck and listened to the radio chatter. A firefighter reported he also heard someone calling out. She watched helplessly while a member of her team disappeared into what could be a death trap.

She grabbed the arm of one of the ATF bomb techs entering the rig. "What is the likelihood of there being another explosive device inside there?" Addison pointed toward the yawning opening strewn with blasted apart clothing, wires, and twisted rebar.

"No telling. You know that." A grim expression settled on his features.

"Yeah, but what does your gut tell you?" She knew he couldn't answer, but she wanted him to reassure her anyway.

The tech canted his head. "That your K9 guy who just ran inside?"

Addison nodded and chewed her bottom lip.

"Well, if there's another explosive device, let's hope his dog finds it before it blows."

Her eyes closed, and Addison lowered her chin to her chest.

"Hey, this is the job. But, if it makes you feel any better, my gut tells me there aren't any more bombs. From what I can tell, the bomb-maker isn't too sophisticated. His devices are effective, but smaller in scale than someone with a grander plan."

Addison bobbed her head and met his eye. "That's what I think too. That, and I can't help but wonder if we can connect this bombing with the threat at the school last week."

"Why do you think so?"

"Type of explosives. Multiple bombs. Three of them were false. This whole thing feels like one guy who's trying to say something."

"Like what?"

"Don't know. We'll have to see if there is any physical evidence left. We couldn't find any prints on the fake devices, but hopefully we'll get a hit on where the materials were purchased. And maybe someone will claim responsibility for this."

Logan's voice came over the radio, calling for extraction assistance. "Gunner found someone. They aren't speaking, but they are tapping. Whoever it is—is still alive!"

. . .

By nine p.m., they considered the bomb scene secure from further explosives. Exhaustion settled in Addison's bones. Logan located her in the evidence tent where he appeared as tired as she felt. His brown hair was gray from dust and debris. She probably looked the same.

"Did the person you found survive?" Addison propped herself up against an evidence table.

"He was still living when the ambulance drove away."

"That's good." She offered him a weary smile. "I think it's time for us to go get some rest." Addison bent down to run her fingers over Gunner's soft muzzle. He licked her once in response, but he too was worn out. "Can I ask you to give me a ride?"

"Sure." Logan's eyes, when they met hers, looked black and bleak. It may have been a trick of the light, but it was as if Addison glimpsed into his soul for a brief second. He ran a scuffed and slightly bleeding hand over his face.

"It's been a helluva day. Let me buy you a drink."

His deep, dark eyes studied her for a long moment. "Thanks, but I'm beat. If you don't mind, I'd rather drop you off wherever and just head home."

He's as hard to pin down as a watermelon seed. She was exhausted too, though, so she didn't argue.

Logan settled Gunner in the back of his vehicle. The dog hopped in, circled twice and laid down in the corner. "Good job today, Gun."

Gunner's tail flopped one time in acknowledgement of the praise before he tucked his muzzle between his front paws and closed his eyes.

"He looks as tired as I feel." Addison hugged herself and rubbed a chill from her upper arms. "My car is at headquarters."

"Good. That's on my way." Logan unlocked and opened the passenger door for her.

"Really? Where do you live?"

He side-eyed her. "North of there."

A sharp laugh burst from her belly. "I can easily look up your address, you know. It's not a state secret. Why don't you ever answer questions about yourself?"

Logan slid in behind the wheel. "I guess if you want to know about me that badly, you can read my file." He drove on back roads, through some older Denver neighborhoods on his way to the Stapleton area and the FBI building.

Addison gestured toward the steering wheel, which he gripped with both fists. "You should have your hands looked at. You're bleeding."

Logan released his right hand and stretched his fingers open, as if noticing their state for the first time. "Just skinned up a bit. Nothing a hot shower won't fix."

"You defied my order today."

"I didn't hear you."

Heat flared in her mind but fizzled out with fatigue. "Yes, you did. I could write you up."

"You could, but since we found more survivors, I doubt much will happen to me. Maybe a slap on the wrist."

He was right, but she wasn't finished. "You put yourself in a lot of risky situations today." Addison stuck her proverbial toe in, hoping he'd talk to her. "Not just yourself, but Gunner too."

Logan flashed a glance at her but remained silent.

"Do you have some kind of death wish?"

"It's my job to find explosives, Thorne."

"Yeah, but there are safer ways than to run headlong into a recently bombed out shopping mall."

"There were people inside, crushed under debris. I'm sure they didn't want to wait while we figured out how to get the robot to roll over chunks of building." His tone hardened, and his knuckles whitened on the wheel.

"No doubt you saved lives today, Logan." She hoped the use of his first name would let him know she wasn't chastising him professionally. "But if you or Gunner would have been hurt, you couldn't have helped anyone else."

The muscles in his jaw bulged, but that was the only response he gave her. She wondered why he took such risks when he didn't have to. The man was a mystery. Addison rolled down her window. Brisk air cooled her irritation. They rode in silence, both too tired for idle chitchat.

Her eyelids bounced open when Reed's SUV thumped over the speed bump at the entrance to the FBI parking garage. She peeked at him out of the corner of her eye to see if he'd noticed she dozed, but his eyes were on the road.

"It's the blue Mustang on the right." Addison adjusted her posture, sitting straighter in the seat.

"Nice sled. What year is it? '69?"

"'Yes. I'm impressed." *So he knows his muscle cars. Interesting.*

"So am I. How long have you had it?"

"About five years. I love all things vintage."

"Well, you've got great taste in cars."

"Thanks." They sat in silence. Addison considered her words before she spoke. On one hand, she respected Reed's decisive actions and his selfless bravery, but on the other hand, she worried he was a loose cannon. "We're both too tired tonight, but I'd like to talk with you about why you took such risks today."

Reed closed his eyes and pressed his head back against the headrest. "I told you already. It's my job." He swung his head to look at her. "You're not the mother-hen type, are you? How do you expect to get anything done?"

"No. I'm a follow-the-regulations type. I want to keep my team safe *while* they're getting the job done." Defensiveness and irritation flared hot in her chest. Now was not the time to have this conversation. "We can talk tomorrow morning after the brief."

"Yes, ma'am."

"I'm keeping my eye on you, Reed. Your actions today may have helped victims, but they could also have potentially put your team members in danger. I won't have that."

Reed stared straight ahead. "Sure you're okay to drive? You were snoring pretty good there for a bit."

"I don't snore."

His smart-ass expression said he knew otherwise, and Addison experienced a moment of self-conscious doubt. Fortunately, anger rushed in to save her. "Shut up, Reed." She pushed her door open. "See you tomorrow."

"Yeah. By the way, while you were sawing logs, we got a unit text. SAC Sanchez wants us at a briefing here at HQ tomorrow morning at ten."

"Good to know." Addison frowned. She'd slept harder than she thought if she missed a text. It would be hard to fall asleep again now. "Sure you don't want to grab a drink with me, or get something to eat?" Right now a big, greasy, bacon cheeseburger would hit the spot, and the last thing she wanted to do was go home and lay in bed wide awake. She could call her boyfriend, but Matthew didn't like her to phone him after ten.

Reed seemed to consider her offer, but then shook his head. "No thanks. I'm beat, plus I need my beauty rest."

She rolled her eyes. "Thanks for the ride." Looked like she was in for another night of keeping the demons at bay by binging Netflix.

~

The ten o'clock news glowed from the TV screen, intensifying the migraine pain behind Benjamin's eyes. A ghostly white and blue light flickered across the scabs and raw sores on his arms. Absently, he scratched and reached for his glass pipe. He lit the peezo, pursed his chapped lips around the tube, and sucked in. After two tokes, the stabbing headache that had been threatening evaporated and rose to the ceiling along with the meth smoke.

The newscaster interviewed a sobbing woman at the scene of today's bombing at the Cherry Creek Mall. His groin twitched, and he grew hard as he enjoyed his front row view of the damage he'd caused. Still, there was no mention of Nicole's death in the news. The pleasure he had experienced in the midst of her agony was fleeting.

At least they're paying attention now, but still no one gets it. No one knows why I must do this. A sneer slid across his mouth as he unzipped his pants. He reached for the photo he had printed earlier. He'd kept it next to him on the threadbare couch. The arousing image of Nicole in the horrific and humiliating last seconds before he blew her into pieces caused him to ache in ecstasy.

Later, after he was spent, he moved to his desk and taped the picture of Nicole's terror to his wall of accomplishments. Her senior photo grinning above the new one displaying the elegance of her fear.

Two down, two to go...

CHAPTER 11

Logan entered the conference room on the third floor of the FBI building. A stocky agent with reddish-blond hair was dividing the glass evidence board at the front of the room into three columns with a broad blue marker. He'd posted the information they had on the fake bomb Logan and Gunner discovered at the high school, including a photo of the strange note found inside, on the left. All the details regarding the imitation explosive at Park Meadows Mall were in the middle, and the right column contained everything the FBI had discovered involving yesterday's bombing of the Cherry Creek Mall.

"The ballistics report confirms that both of the false explosives had trace elements of C-4, and both had the same black powder residue, presumably so a bomb dog would locate them." Special Agent in Charge, Ricardo Sanchez, spoke from the podium next to the board. His commanding presence demanded attention. "We are certain the same suspect planted all these devices. Now, our questions are: Where is the unsub acquiring the explosive materials? What is his motive? And is he finished, or is he planning more mayhem?"

Another agent asked, "Has anyone claimed responsibility for the bombing yet?"

"Yes," Sanchez lifted a slip of paper from the table in front of him. "The usual suspects. ISIS and ISIL have both piped in. And of course, the inevitable rumors of a Taliban influence. Agent Cameron," he addressed the stocky agent to his left, "have we determined the credibility of these claims?" Sanchez stuck the note to the top of the clear board.

"Yes, sir. We're certain none of those claims or rumors are credible. First off, these groups all jockey for credit every time there is a terrorist incident, and frankly, sir, if they were responsible, they would have done a more thorough job. There would not have been warnings or false alarms, and there certainly wouldn't have been a note about someone being ashamed."

Sanchez panned his gaze over the faces in the meeting room until they found their target. "Reed, you are the agent of record who discovered both of the fake bombs, aren't you?"

Logan stood tall, but reached into his pocket to feel the comfort of the metal discs. "Yes, sir. I found the first false explosive planted at the high school, and the second fake bomb hidden at the Park Meadows Mall. I did not arrive at the Cherry Creek Mall until after the actual detonation. However, my dog located another bomb after the fact in the same general area. It resembled the previous two false devices, only this IED was live and set on a timer. The ATF bomb tech on site defused it before it blew."

"Excellent work, all of you. From your experience, would you say the same person made all these bombs?"

"The first two were the same, sir. Both fakes made to look like bricks of C-4 with a small amount of black powder rubbed into the clay. The two at Cherry Creek were pipe-bombs, both real. Forensics will tell us if the detonated bomb also had an ignitor attached to a timer. All that to say, I agree with Agent Cameron. These bombs lack sophistication and yes, were likely built by the same unsub."

"Thank you, Agent." Sanchez bounced his fingertips on the table surface. "Agents from the FBI, ATF, and Homeland are currently looking into where this particular explosive material came from and who might have access to it. For now, let's discuss what other similarities there are in these threats and then possible motives for the bombing. Is there reason to believe there will be further bombings and if so, where should we expect an attack?"

Logan's skin puckered like someone was watching him, and he searched the faces in the room. Addison had her full attention directed on him rather than on the investigation. *What is her deal*? He raised a brow at her in question, and she responded by narrowing her eyes. She was going to be a pain in his ass. Logan refocused on Sanchez and the small amount of evidence they had gathered so far.

Halfway through the morning Sanchez gave the agents a breather. Logan made his way to the break room in search of water and a protein bar. He took a bite of the sweet-and-salty peanut-butter snack, and as he bent to fill a cup from the water cooler, fingers wrapped around his elbow.

"Good morning, Reed."

He side-eyed Agent Thorne.

"Have you met Agent Reynolds?"

Logan stood and studied the face of the man standing with Thorne. "I don't think so." He stuck out his right hand. "Logan Reed."

"Andy Reynolds." They shook hands. "Nice to meet you. I think you might have known my brother while you were in the Army."

A cold knot formed in Logan's belly, and he forced his breath to remain even. *Please don't let this be a grieving family member.* "Who's your brother?"

"Sergeant David Reynolds. Ever heard of him?"

Air gushed out of Logan's lungs with relief. "I don't think so, but the Army has a vast sea of soldiers."

"I think he knows you, though. He told me some story about a Lieutenant in the K9 unit who was the only survivor of a personnel carrier explosion near his base. I'm pretty sure he said the guy's name was Reed."

Logan's gaze darted between Reynolds and Thorne's speculative stare. His heart jumped to double-time, but he kept his expression passive. "Doesn't sound familiar. Probably some other guy named Reed."

Thorne leaned in. "In the K9 unit? Wouldn't you know if there was another handler named Reed?"

"Did you serve in the military, Agent Thorne?" Logan leveraged his tone with condescension.

Her chin shot up, and she narrowed her eyes at him. "Yes, in fact, I spent four years in the Navy after I graduated from the Naval Academy."

Shocked, Logan struggled to keep his surprise from his face. "So, not on the ground then?"

"No—but I definitely served. I was a naval EOD tech."

"Well, the area the Army covers in Afghanistan is extensive. There is no possible way for me to know all the K9 handlers serving in-country. Sorry to disappoint you." Logan chugged his chilled water and crumpled the cup in his fist. He tossed it in the trash-can and nodded to Reynolds. "Nice to meet you." He hustled back to the crowded briefing room before Thorne could continue her interrogation.

Why can't that woman just let me do my damn job?

The investigatory meeting continued for the rest of the morning. Fatigue nibbled at the edge of Logan's consciousness. He wanted nothing more than to go home and take a long nap before helping coach the football practice at the middle-school that afternoon. He pitched in with the team whenever his schedule allowed. As the minutes trudged by, Logan occupied himself by rolling the silver disc back and forth across his knuckles. He caught glimpses of Agent Thorne staring at him. *What is her problem?*

No matter, Logan planned to slip out of the room seconds before Sanchez dismissed them so he could avoid her nagging questions. When the time came, he casually made his way toward the door. He overheard Thorne speaking to Agent Jennings.

"I tried reading his file, but it's seriously redacted. More black line-outs than print."

Jennings leaned down. "Why don't you just try talking to the guy? I'm sure he'd rather answer a few questions than have you digging around in his past."

Not likely. Logan pressed forward toward the door.

"I've tried. He isn't talking. Listen, I just want to know what I'm dealing with—for the safety of my team."

"Well, he passed the FBI psych exam, so I'm confident you're worried over nothing."

Logan was thankful Jennings had his back and without a glance, Logan slipped out the door and made a quick escape.

CHAPTER 12

Addison drew in a huge gulp of the crisp, cool air of the autumn morning. She could almost taste the sweet tang of the dying leaves. Without the heat of summer weighing her down, she ran faster and further than usual. Her feet flew like Hermes as she sprinted north up Pennsylvania Street. Sunshine winked at her through a veil of orange, red and yellow. At the corner, she jogged in place at the red light on Speer. Her six-mile loop took her up through Capitol Hill and on further to Park Avenue. From there she planned to jog across to Coors Field and back home along the Platte River path. It was the perfect way to start the weekend.

Matthew, her boyfriend—she supposed—was probably still in bed. He'd left her house late the night before. Generally, he didn't like to spend time at Addison's place. "Too Bohemian," he had said. *Whatever that meant*. He preferred his glass and concrete apartment in LoDo where he could control his environment. But he'd probably be awake and out by the time she got home. Matthew worked out on Saturdays at the Denver Athletic Club with his personal trainer. There were days when Addison wondered why they stayed together. They didn't have much in common besides their physical attraction.

He was beautiful to look at with his tall, blond, Nordic structure, and he was smart. Matthew was an architect. One who never had any dirt under his carefully manicured fingernails. Addison admitted to herself that he made a nice 'plus-one' when necessary, except that he had a strict exercise, diet, and rest program which meant he didn't drink or like to stay out past ten.

Addison was completely different and wanted to believe the old adage that opposites attract, but was finding little evidence to back it up. She loved to grab a beer with friends and didn't enjoy sitting still. There was too much life to live. Bed-time came only when she was too tired to do anything else. For her, the worst period of the day occurred between laying her head on the pillow and falling asleep, so she kept those moments short whenever she could. Her remedy was to push herself to exhaustion.

The traffic light turned and Addison sprinted ahead of a group of pedestrians, north up Lincoln. The homeless population in Denver had exploded recently. Addison dodged people who had camped out on the sidewalk. Running past the Capitol depressed her these days. Graffiti blanketed the once beautiful limestone walls of the grand building with its gold-plated dome and garbage covered the lawn. *Maybe I should choose a different route.*

The downtown sky-scrapers blocked the sun, and the colder air had her speeding up. Addison cut across the 16th Street Mall, avoiding the MallRide shuttle-bus as it rattled past her on its tracks. She jogged down the sunny side of the street toward Broadway and drew up short. Was that—?

"Logan?"

Logan's head snapped toward her and he slipped the

silver coin he had the habit of fiddling with into his pocket. He appeared equally surprised to see her. "Agent Thorne? What are you doing here?"

"Do me a favor. When we're not at work, call me Addison." She stopped at his side, and catching her breath she added, "Please." She sucked in a drink of water from her gator pack. "I run a loop that brings me up here every Saturday." She gave him a once over. He wore basketball shorts and carried a gym bag, but hadn't yet broken a sweat. "What about you? You don't live around here. I know this because your home is somewhere vaguely 'north of HQ.'" Addison made air-quotes and smirked.

"I'm just going to the Y."

Addison propped her hands on her hips and kept her feet moving out of habit, trying to keep her heart rate up. She peered up at the building in front of them. "The YMCA? You know that if you don't have your own gym membership, there's a decent facility at work, right?"

"Uh…" Logan glanced both ways up and down the street. "Do you live downtown?"

He was evading again, but she chose not to call him on it. "Not really. My house is on Pennsylvania, south of Speer. On Saturdays I have time for a longer run, so this is part of my weekend route."

"That's a pretty hefty jaunt. What is it, five miles?"

"Six."

Logan nodded. "I'm a runner too, but I prefer cleaner air." He chuffed and shifted his bag into his other hand and swung it up on his shoulder. "Well, I—"

"Hey, coach!"

Addison turned toward the voice of a young man in his mid-teens. The boy's hooded sweatshirt was two sizes too big and hung low over his baggy red and white basketball shorts. He grinned, first at Addison and then Logan.

"Nice to see you're on time for once, Tyrone," Logan teased.

The boy shot a bright smile at Addison. "Hello, pretty lady. I'm Tyrone." He held his hand out to her.

She laughed and placed her palm in his. "I'm Addison. Nice to meet you."

Like a prince of old, Tyrone bent and kissed the back of Addison's hand. Humor lit up his eyes. "Are you Coach's girlfriend?"

"Ha! No." Addison choked out.

Logan playfully shoved Tyrone's shoulder. "Agent Thorne is my boss, you lug-nut. So be good. Go on inside—I'll be right in."

"Well, if you and Coach aren't a thing, maybe you'll give me a call?" Tyrone waggled his eyebrows at Addison.

She shook her head, grinning. "Yeah, maybe in ten years."

"Oh—" Tyrone pressed his hands onto his chest. "You're crushing my young heart."

"Okay," Logan laughed and steered Tyrone's shoulders toward the door. "Go inside, Romeo."

"Okay, okay. Good bye, Ms. Addison." He glanced back at Logan. "Don't be late for practice, Coach."

When Logan chuckled, Addison realized she'd never seen the man laugh before that moment. Usually, he wore a stoic expression, but the sudden levity brought a certain light to his mahogany eyes and Addison was momentarily taken aback. Covering her impulsive quiver of awareness, she asked, "You're a coach?"

He dropped his gaze to the sidewalk, and his long dark lashes shuttered her glimpse of his emotion. "Basketball. Just on Saturday mornings."

"Really?"

"It's no big deal. Just trying to help."

"Hm. I'm surprised, but I guess I don't know you well

enough to be." Addison noticed a group of kids about the same age, dressed for the court, enter the Y.

"Hey, coach!" one boy greeted. All of them took a long appraising look at her before they went inside.

Logan raised a hand in greeting. "I'll be right in."

"Take your time, coach. You still got game." The teens laughed and disappeared behind the doors.

"Sorry about that. You know how boys are."

"No problem. I get the boys. *You,* however, continue to be a mystery. One I find intriguing." Addison grabbed onto his arm for balance as she pulled one ankle up to her backside for a quad stretch. Then the other. He flexed to accommodate her and she couldn't help but appreciate his solid strength. "Thanks." She shook out her legs. "How did you end up coaching basketball all the way down here?"

Logan shrugged and checked his watch. "Well, I don't want to keep you from your run..."

Addison laughed. "You're an interesting cat, Logan Reed, and you should know I'm far more persistent than you can fathom."

"There's not much to know. No mystery here."

"Yeah–right." She bounced on her toes. "You better go to practice. When I get home, I'm gonna do some digging. I'll figure you out. Count on it."

Logan sighed and shook his head. A flicker of irritation snapped in his eyes. "See you Monday." He ran up the steps and through the door.

What is it he doesn't want me to know?

So much for having my work and personal lives remain separate. Logan jerked open the glass door to the YMCA. He'd thought keeping his business to himself would be easy in a city the size of Denver. Apparently not. When he entered the gym, his team of inner-city middle-schoolers stood in a loose circle by the stands, still in their warm-ups, joking and laughing together, the soles of their shoes squeaking against the floor.

"Hey coach!" one of the boys called. "Where's the dime you was chattin' up? She with you, man?"

Logan stifled a laugh. "The *lady* you're referring to is my boss. Show some respect."

The shortest team member threw his arms up. "We got nothin' but respect, man. She fine!"

"Dude! She's your boss? Does she order you around and shit?"

"That's kinda hot." The boys laughed, high-fived, and elbowed each other in the ribs.

"Okay, sounds like you guys have tons of energy to burn. Start running. Ten laps, then we'll do layup drills."

The team shed their extra layers into a heap and took off around the perimeter of the gym, running the well-worn boards of the basketball court—and their mouths. Logan knew by the time they finished with the warm-up drills, they'd be ready to focus on practice. He loved working with middle-school and high-school kids, and it was a perfect means of giving back. He couldn't change the past, but he could affect the future. Logan poured his hours and energy into kids just getting started in their lives as his way of making up for other lives that had been cut short. Way too damn short. No matter how much he gave, coaching or teaching guitar lessons, it would never be enough to make up for that.

He shook off the encroaching memories and jogged to the middle of the court, blowing his whistle. The boys gathered around him, each youthful face eager to hear his next assignment. The scent of rubber swirled together with adolescent sweat created an aroma that sent Logan back to his own school days. He squeezed the nubbed basketball between his spanned hands and passed it hard to the team's center. "Let's see those layups."

He watched as the team split into sides and took turns practicing the drill. These boys were ready to bolt into their futures with enthusiastic promise. They gave Logan the hope he needed to face each day. Without the kids he worked with, his own stilted life would be unbearable.

CHAPTER 13

Logan spent Monday morning at the K9 training facility. The first hour, he practiced with Gunner to keep his dog's chemical-explosive sniffing abilities sharp. They dedicated the rest of the time to physical training. Logan's private goal was to beat the facility's obstacle course record set by Agent Jennings and his stellar K9, Ranger. They were still 3.4 seconds short.

"Nice run, Reed. Of course, your dog is making you look good." Jennings leaned against the fence by the rope climb at the end.

Logan tossed his chin at the needling. "Yeah, we're coming for you, Jennings." He unclipped Gunner from the harness he used to carry him up the rope climb.

"Good luck. I've never known an Army puke to surpass a Marine, but I admire your gumption." Jennings grinned. "Hey, how's the bomb investigation going?"

"Slow." Logan and Gunner jogged up to the chain-link. "Hopefully, the lab will shed more light on where the explosives came from. Agents are interviewing every employee from the school and both malls, and all the high school students. So far we've found nothing conclusive."

"If Sanchez is running the investigation, you can expect some long days and nights. He's relentless."

"Must have been in the Army." Logan's mouth tipped up on one side.

"Nope, sucker! He's a brother from the Corps. Best of the best, man. You can't fight it." When Jennings straightened, he stood at least two inches above Logan. "Just follow his lead. You'll be fine." He crossed his arms over his broad chest. "All kidding aside, you and Gunner look good together. How's the training going from your perspective?"

"Good. Real good. Gunner's a terrific dog." Logan glanced down at Gunner sitting next to him.

"Glad to hear it." Jennings took his sunglasses off and met Logan's eye. "But I'd like to see you play together more. His technical discipline is razor sharp, but I want you building your friendship."

Logan crushed his molars together and swallowed hard. "Yes, sir."

Jennings regarded him for an uncomfortable moment before he nodded once and slid his glasses back on. "Take the next hour before lunch to play."

Logan respected Clay Jennings. He was one of the best, but he needed to mind his own business when it came to Logan and Gunner's relationship. They were fine. Logan didn't doubt Gunner's loyalty or ability for one second.

After the forced play-time and a quick bite to eat, Logan and Gunner drove to HQ for the day's bomb investigation briefing. They entered a conference room crowded with people from several different agencies. The FBI investigators had filled evidence boards at the front of the room with site sketches, architectural schemes, and floor plans for the mall. There were two employee lists coded by each store—one of those working the day of the explosion, and another of employees that were not. Pinned to the wall next to the boards were four full-color aerial photographs of the bombed-out mall.

Logan's neck bristled at the tense atmosphere in the conference room. It was taking way too long to find any meaningful evidence, and a bomber on the loose made everyone edgy.

Once everybody had settled, SAC Sanchez started the meeting. "Thanks for coming, people. I know the slow speed of this investigation is frustrating, but we do have some recent developments to report on today. Our investigative team is currently talking with the incident commander and the first responders to determine what exactly happened, and they're assessing the current situation."

Agent Cameron stood next to Sanchez and flipped open a file. "For those of you who don't know me, I'm Agent Burke Cameron. I'm presenting the information we've gathered so far, after talking with all on-site personnel." He held up a stapled packet of papers. "We have lists of victims and another list of potential witnesses divided into groups by the priority in which to interview them. We'll start with survivors and employees before moving on to delivery and service staff, first responders, neighboring businesses, and passersby. Local police departments are assisting with these interviews."

Cameron slid the papers back inside the file and bounced its edge on the table. "We've documented all the evidence discovered so far, and it is currently going through forensic investigation."

Sanchez tapped on some keys on his laptop and dual images appeared on the Smartboard at the front of the room.

"We've pulled video from security cameras from both malls at all entrances and in the parking garage at Cherry Creek. We also have video tape from nearby ATMs and other businesses with useful angles. This is what we have so far." He clicked on the initial image.

Logan narrowed his eyes to focus on the grainy, black and white images. The first video showed a Caucasian male, average height—maybe 5' 8" to 5'10" with a slight build. He couldn't weigh over 150 pounds. The guy had a backpack slung over one shoulder. He wore a baseball cap with the hood of a sweatshirt over the top and sunglasses. The camera captured him as he approached the elevator in the parking garage.

"The reason this man is a suspect is that he showed up at the Park Meadows Mall a half hour later. He entered the doors at the food court." Sanchez tapped again and the second video played depicting a man with the same build. He was no longer wearing the hoodie, but the hat was the same and he carried the same backpack. He kept his face down as he walked through the door. "This is all we have so far, and it's not much. The tech lab is working on facial recognition as we speak, but they have little to work with."

"Even if they can identify this guy, going to two malls on the same day isn't a crime." Logan crossed his arms and leaned back. "Do we have anything else to go on?"

"You're right, Agent Reed. It's all circumstantial at this point. We're also working to identify the type of explosive material that the bomber used. From that we'll determine who might have access to the specific substance and where they got a hold of it. Hopefully, we'll find a connection."

Addison stepped up to the evidence board at the front of the room. "Good afternoon, everyone. I'm Agent Addison Thorne. I'm one of the FBI Bomb Technicians." She pointed to the larger map hanging on the wall. "This map marks the locations of the victims the search teams have found so far." She touched a second print. "This one notes the location of the many witnesses at the time of the blast. We are studying the types and degrees of injuries to help establish the nature of the explosive device and the circumstances of the incident. Once the investigative teams have a chance to assimilate all the information, we'll have a much stronger idea of where to hunt for our bomber. We expect he will strike again, so the faster we can work this investigation the better."

"Thank you, Thorne." Sanchez nodded to Cameron to re-run the surveillance videos. "Let's watch these one more time to solidify this guy's image in our minds. We need to find him. Even if he isn't the unsub, he was at both locations on that day. He may have seen something important."

On her way back to her seat, Addison caught Logan's eye from across the room. She nodded at him in greeting before mouthing some unintelligible words.

"What?" He mouthed back.

Her lips flew through a string of words completely lost on him, and Logan couldn't keep from chuckling.

When she smiled at him and rolled her eyes, a tiny fissure tongued through the iron barricade he kept bolstered around his emotions. The warmth that seeped in startled him, and he snapped his gaze away from the woman whose smile had caused the breach. Reaching for the disc in his pocket, Logan pressed the thin edge into his palm as a sharp reminder for why he needed to stay away from Thorne. He pretended an intense focus on the board at the front of the room while he concentrated on steadying his pulse and pasting on an unaffected expression.

The short videos ended, and Sanchez gathered his files. "That's it for today," Sanchez continued. "Lucinda will email each of you your assignments. If you have any further questions or thoughts, I'm available here until five.

After that, you can reach me on my cell." Sanchez remained at the front of the room, fielding immediate comments.

Addison edged her way around the table, and Logan stood, hoping to make it through the door before she caught up to him. No such luck.

"Hey, Coach." Addison poked his back, sending electric tremors up and down his spine. She wore some sort of cool, languid scent that floated over his shoulder. He breathed it in before he glanced back at her to answer.

"Thorne. What's up?"

"Glad you asked. The bomb squad is headed over to the pub for a couple of beers. First round is on you, so I'm making sure you're coming."

"What?"

"That's the way it goes. If the new guy refuses to show up the first few times we meet for beers, then he has to apologize for the slight by paying for a round of drinks." Her tone was mock serious. "I tried to save you, but you wouldn't have it."

"I can't. I have Gunner and everything. You know." Logan filed out the door and moved off to the side of the flow of agents.

Addison followed him. "Great news! The Irish pub we go to is only a couple of blocks away and they love dogs from the FBI K9 Unit. So… guess you're still buying." A black brow arched under her bangs.

Shit. Logan couldn't see a way out of this. He may as well go, have one drink, pay for ten others, and get it over with. Then maybe Addison Thorne would leave him alone. *Yeah, right.* "Okay. I'll go—but I can only stay for one beer."

"Finally!" Addison yelled down the hall to a few agents from their team. "He's coming guys! Today is expensive beer day!"

"And nachos!" Another bomb tech called back. "You told him he has to buy munchies too, right?"

Addison patted Logan on the shoulder. "I don't feel sorry for you at all. You could have avoided this." She crouched down. "Ready to go get some treats, Gunner? Let's go, boy."

CHAPTER 14

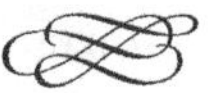

A guy whom Logan guessed probably went to Harvard or Yale with his light-blue button down and tortoise-shell horned rims stood up from the bar when Logan followed Gunner and Addison inside. The man's cultured gaze held steady on Addison as he approached her and kissed her cheek.

"Hi Matthew. I'm so glad you came." She pecked his cheek. "This is Agent Logan Reed. He and his dog, Gunner here, are the newest members of our team."

Icy blue eyes assessed him as he shook the guy's hand. "Reed. Matthew Todd—I'm Addison's *boyfriend*." His grip tightened as he made his claim. Logan got the message. Addison was a strikingly beautiful force of energy bobbing amongst a sea of hardened, mostly military-veteran, federal agents. *The guy probably feels like he has to stake his claim every time he goes out with her. He must not realize Addison Thorne can —and does—take care of herself. Her boundaries are self-imposed and self-defended.*

"Good to meet you. What do you do?" Logan noted

Matthew's smooth hands and his buffed fingernails. Interesting type difference from the men Addison worked with on an everyday basis. He couldn't help but wonder about that. Maybe Todd was easier to control than her squadmates?

"I'm in architecture. I have a firm down on Seventeenth Street." Matthew wiped his fingers on his drink napkin.

Is it the dog, or me? Logan had to turn away to hide his smirk. He reached down and rubbed his hand over Gunner's muzzle, receiving a juicy lick before he responded. "Residential or commercial?"

Addison jumped in. "Commercial. Matthew's firm designed the Plaza Buildings. Do you know them?"

"No, sorry. But I'm new to town."

"What kind a beer do you want, Logan?" Addison moved toward the bar. She wasn't one to stand still long enough for small talk, which was one of the things Logan appreciated about her.

"I'll come with you." He didn't want to get stuck listening to this guy's list of accomplishments. Logan nodded to Matthew and followed Addison. They both ordered Avery IPAs.

"I'm glad you came." She leaned her elbow on the wooden surface and faced him. "As soon as we get our drinks, let's go hang out with the guys. They're in the back room where the pool tables are."

"What about Matthew?" Logan observed the man in his peripheral view. He didn't fit in with the FBI crowd. Even Sanchez, whom he'd only seen in an impeccable suit and tie, fit in better than Addison's boyfriend. The SAC stood next to a table filled with agents. He'd loosened his tie, and his sleeves were rolled up. He kept one arm draped around Kendra Dean, Logan's fellow K9 handler, as their group laughed off the office stress.

"He'll be fine. Of course, he'll want to leave early." Her mouth dipped into a slight frown as she reached for their beers, handing a glass to Logan.

He took a long sip, enjoying the crisp floral hoppiness, before pointing his chin toward the corner of the pub. "What gives with Sanchez and Dean?"

"They're married." Her eyes sparked with mischief. "I'm surprised you didn't know that. You work with her, don't you?"

"Yeah, but it's not like we're best friends."

Addison moved away from the bar and headed to the back room. "It isn't a deep, dark secret. Seems like something you'd know if you spent any time with the K9 team at all."

"I'm with them all the time—when we train."

She glanced back at him and pursed her lips. "I mean socially. Are you shy?"

"No, I just have stuff to do." Addison was looking for buttons, and he wasn't going to show her any. He took two long gulps. Logan had only promised to stay here for one beer, and he intended to make it quick.

She spun around to face him so suddenly, he almost ran into her. "Like coaching inner-city kids?" Her eyes held excitement, as if she'd just caught him in a trap.

"Yes, like that." He chuckled. "Listen, I'm outta here as soon as this beer is gone, so..."

Addison gave him a teasing glare and turned to lead him to their team. "Hey, guys! Look who I found. Anyone recognize this guy?"

The two men who monitored the computers in the truck and dispatched the robot and containment device sat next to each other playing a video game on an iPad. The one whose turn it was didn't break his concentration, but the other man raised his beer in greeting. "It's the new guy!"

Another agent reached out his glass to touch Logan's. "We have a new guy? Never seen him before."

Addison laughed. "I had to threaten his job to get him here."

"Do we smell?" A short but muscle-bound bomb tech sniffed his arm-pit.

"Okay, okay. I'm here, aren't I?" Logan grinned through the flash-freeze sealing his heart. He appreciated the teasing and knew this group would welcome him into their fold, but he couldn't risk it. He'd been part of a team that felt like a family once before. Not something he ever wanted to experience again.

"Only for one beer, though." Addison rolled her eyes before fixing them on the short guy. "And, yes Miller, you do stink. Take a shower, for God's sake." The group laughed and went back to their conversations. Someone pushed a chair out from the table with their foot, and Addison tilted her head at it. "Sit. Come on. You can stay for one more beer." She leaned in to him and spoke into his ear. "These are the times that matter. We all want to know we can rely on you. Don't you want to know we're gonna have your back too?"

"Can't I just trust you to be professional? Good at your jobs?" he murmured back.

The look Addison gave him was a mixture of confusion, hurt, and speculation. He wasn't winning any points.

"Okay, one more beer, but then I really do have to go." Logan took the seat that was offered and Gunner laid down next to him. The server brought his dog a bowl of whipped cream.

"Is it okay if I give this to your dog?" The young woman wore her tawny hair in braids she flipped over her shoulders as she bent down.

"Sure, thanks. And—" He handed her his credit card. "Next round's on me."

She took his card and retrieved a pen from behind her ear. "Okay, everyone. This guy said he was buying." She wrote down all the orders. Another server carried a tray of nachos by, and the cheesy smell caused noses to rise.

"Better bring out four orders of those too, while you're at it." Logan tilted his head down toward Gunner. "Don't get spoiled, Mister. This is a onetime deal."

Gunner sat drooling politely, watching Logan for any sign that he could indulge.

Logan gave the nod. "Okay." His dog dove muzzle first into the bowl.

Matthew moved up behind Addison while she shared a joke with another tech. He slid his arm around her and pulled her backwards against his chest, interrupting her conversation. "Let's get out of here."

She pushed his arm away. "Not yet. I'm having a good time."

"We have dinner reservations, remember?" The guy's hand gripped her shoulders tight, and he lowered his voice, "And you know I hate coming to these things."

Addison jerked away, turning to face him. Gunner stood and inched in between Addison and Matthew's legs. "Cancel them. I want to stay for a little while. We can order food here."

Matthew looked down to see what was pressing against him and noticed a gooey smear of cream on his pressed trousers. Angry eyes found Logan. "Damn it! Can't you keep your mangy mutt away from me? Are you planning to pay for the dry cleaners?"

Addison's jaw dropped open. "Wow, Matthew. It's just a little whipped cream. *I'll* pay for the frickin' cleaners." She stepped back and stumbled on Logan's boot. Losing her balance, she almost ended up in his lap.

Logan caught her by the waist and steadied her. Heat

spiked his veins as he rose to his feet behind her and reached into the pocket on the side of his utility pants. Opening his wallet, he drew out a twenty. "Sorry for the mess, but my dog doesn't like it when guys are assholes to women." He stuffed the bill in Matthew's breast pocket. The man was too stunned to respond, and the voices at the table grew still—the quiet before a storm.

Matthew glared at Logan, then shifted his angry gaze to Addison. "I'm leaving. Are you coming with me, or not?"

Her hands curled into fists before she folded her arms in front of her. "Not. I'm staying." She tossed her chin up at him.

His sky-blue eyes scanned Addison's team, each member ready to leap to her defense. He let out a sigh and murmured, "Fine. Don't bother calling me when you get home, though. I'm planning on having an early night."

"Come on, Matthew. Don't leave angry." Addison ran her hand down his arm with a conciliatory squeeze. "Let's just stay here for dinner. You'll still be able to get to bed early."

"Not tonight."

Without saying anything to Addison's co-workers, her boyfriend spun on his heel and made his way to the exit.

The server returned to the suddenly subdued group carrying a drink-laden tray and hesitated. Logan brushed away the uncomfortable moment. He took his pint and raised it to the team. "Cheers."

"Welcome aboard, Army." Miller tapped Logan's glass with his, and the loud jocularity roused once again amongst the bomb squad.

After he gulped down his second beer, Logan stood. "I've got to go, Thorne," he turned to include the whole table which had gone quiet. "See you guys tomorrow."

The group shouted out a myriad of see-ya-laters and teasing comments. Logan needed to get out of there. The way Addison's boyfriend had treated her pissed him off—

more than it should have. He was already getting too close to this new team. "Come on, Gun. Let's go home."

"Okay, but just so you know," she gave him a self-satisfied grin. "I have discovered *exactly* where 'vaguely north of HQ' is…"

CHAPTER 15

The 428 Cobra Jet engine rumbled contentedly under the hood of her Mustang as Addison rolled up to the curb of the address she'd copied from Logan's employee file. She studied the modern-style gray-brick apartment building with its bright orange acrylic accents and tried to imagine Logan living there. He didn't seem like the ultra-hipster type.

It was October, but the day had been warm. Windows were open to the last gulps of fresh air before winter crept in. Comforting, Saturday dinner smells wafted on the early evening breeze and tangled with the strumming of a guitar. Addison's belly gurgled as she slung her purse over her shoulder, reached for the six-pack she had brought along, and climbed out of her car. She checked the address again to be sure she was at the right building, then panned her gaze up to the third floor.

Addison mounted the stairs and found that Logan's apartment faced the street, and the vibrating musical chords came from behind his door. Surprised, she raised her eyebrows and rapped her knuckles on the entrance. The music stopped and complete silence followed. Addison knocked again, and a dog barked. Gunner.

A shirtless Logan yanked open the door and greeted her with a suspicious scowl.

She tried not to ogle his muscled chest. "Hi. I hope it's not a bad time?"

He stared at her, saying nothing.

Addison cleared her throat and pressed on. "I told you I figured out where you lived and I thought I'd surprise you." She held her arms out akimbo and making a silly face she sang, "Surprise!"

"Isn't this some kind of co-worker stalking?" One side of his mouth twitched in what could have become a smile, but didn't. He stood back and held the door open for her to enter. "Or harassment?"

Addison wasn't entirely sure he was joking. She pressed the six-pack of beer into his six-pack abs as she walked into his living room. Gunner wagged his tail and spun in a circle. "Hi, Gunner." She knelt down to pet him. "At least you're happy to see me."

Logan skirted the kitchen bar and yanked open his empty fridge. He set the beer on the shelf before crossing the living room and disappearing into the bedroom. Addison moved so that her gaze could follow him, and she quickly scanned his personal space. The man had no decorations other than a single framed photo on his nightstand. A lightning fast glimpse told her it was an image of Logan in his Army uniform kneeling next to his service dog. She swung her gaze to him when he returned wearing an old Army t-shirt.

"So, what brings you here?"

"Curiosity, mostly." Addison shoved her hands into her jeans pockets, suddenly nervous. Jitterbugs danced in her gut as she glanced around at his barren space. "Can I sit?"

"Oh, shit, yeah—sorry." The speculations left his features

as he rushed to move several sheets of chord music and a hoodie off a dining chair he was using as a music stand. He gestured for her to take a seat. "I don't usually have company."

"I can see that." Addison sat, clasping her hands between her knees. "So—you play the guitar?"

"Uh—yeah. A little."

"I wouldn't have guessed that. But there's a lot about you I wouldn't have presumed. Like the coaching."

"What *did* you presume?"

She shrugged. "Honestly, I can't get a feel for you. I suppose that's really why I'm here. We all have to trust that everyone on our team has our backs. It's hard to give trust to a guy who's so tough to get to know—so elusive."

Logan spread his hand through the air, indicating his apartment. "Well, this is me. Not much to it."

"Doesn't look like you plan on staying." She stared into his eyes, challenging him.

He shrugged and looked away. "I just don't have a lot of stuff."

"I see that. You're kind of like an onion Logan, and with each layer I peel back I find something unexpected."

Logan smirked. "I prefer to think of myself as an artichoke. Lots of leaves and they taste better than onions."

"Okay, I'll go with that. They also have sharp tips at the end of their leaves and can be a little prickly." Addison smiled and her eyes flickered to the guitar. "Will you play me a song?"

Resistance stretched across Logan's face. He cocked his head sideways and the muscle in his jaw flexed. "I—" Before he could refuse her outright, another knock sounded behind him. He glared at the offending sound. "Who the hell…" Logan yanked open the door.

Addison peered around his trim waist to see an older

woman standing at the threshold. His body relaxed, and he stood aside to let the woman enter. "Hi Harriet. Is everything okay?"

Harriet trundled in. She set a casserole dish on the kitchen bar and then closed her cardigan over her chest. She spotted Addison, and a brilliant smile wreathed in soft wrinkles brightened her face. "Well, hello. You must be sweet Logan's girlfriend." She shuffled forward and Addison stood to greet her. "I'm Harriet Loomis. Logan's needy downstairs neighbor."

Before Addison could correct the woman about her girlfriend assumption, Logan placed his hand under the woman's elbow. "You're not needy, Harriet." He glanced at Addison. "Harriet is the object of the tryst you counseled me about at my first team meeting." Laughter sparkled in his eyes and caused the skin at their corners to crinkle. He held out his other hand toward Addison. "Harriet, this is Agent Addison Thorne. She's definitely *not* my girlfriend. She's my boss."

"Is that so?" Harriet chuckled and reached out her hand. "Well, good for you, dear. I'm happy to meet you. I bet you're glad to employ such a hard worker." She beamed at Logan, whose coloring deepened.

Addison took Harriet's hand in both of hers. She adored the woman instantly. "It's nice to meet you, and yeah, Logan's alright." She winked.

"Thank you for dinner," Logan interjected. "You didn't need to do that, but I'm grateful. Do you need help with something, Harriet?"

She looked momentarily startled. "Me? No." She patted his shoulder. "No, I just wanted to bring you the casserole. And well, I guess I do have a few bags of groceries in my car too, if you don't mind."

The rare grin that changed Logan's face from stern to

heart-fluttering handsome appeared. "Not a problem. Do you have your keys?"

"Both the car and my apartment are unlocked."

"Harriet," Logan's voice lowered. "We've talked about that. This is not the kind of neighborhood where you can leave things unlocked. I want you to be safe."

"I know, but I am completely safe with a secret agent living right above me."

Addison barked out a laugh, and Logan rolled his eyes. "Harriet, I'm *not* a secret agent. How many times—"

"Well, of course you deny it. If you told me, it wouldn't be a secret."

He looked sideways at Addison. "I'll be right back."

Logan took three steps at a time, his footfalls echoing in the stairway. The last thing he wanted was the two women in his life gossiping about him behind his back. *Why is Addison here? I can't believe she just showed up, sticking her nose into my personal life.* He looped all six grocery bags over one arm before locking Harriet's car doors. He sprinted back up the flights to his neighbor's apartment and let himself in. After setting the sacks on Harriet's kitchen table, he bounded up the stairs to his own place.

At the door, he heard Harriet expounding on his social life—or lack thereof. "Logan never has any company over. I worry that he's alone too much."

Addison reasoned, "He has Gunner. That's like living with his best friend."

"It's not the same. That boy needs a woman in his life."

Embarrassed, Logan's cheeks prickled, and he pushed through the door. "I do have a woman in my life, Harriet. I thought *you* were my girlfriend." He placed his arm over her shoulders and gave her a gentle squeeze.

Harriet batted her hand at him. "Stop your nonsense." Her smile broadcast her pleasure at his attention, and he was glad to give it to her. "There is way too much food for just one person in that dish, Logan. Why don't you invite Addison to stay for dinner?"

She may as well have punched him in the gut. The last thing he wanted was dinner company, but there was no way out of inviting Addison to stay now. *Harriet is determined to find me a wife, but she is nowhere near as determined as I am not to find one.*

He sighed and raised his eyebrows in question. "Casserole?"

Addison laughed a jaunty sound and embraced Harriet. "It was a pleasure to meet you, Miss Harriet."

"Yes, you too, dear. I hope I see you again soon." Harriet stepped out the door and then turned. "Oh, and Logan, I forgot to ask you if you would mind watching my Prissy. I have to go to University Memorial for a minor procedure, and I'll be away overnight.

Concern squeezed Logan's heart. "A procedure? Harriet, are you alright? What kind of procedure?"

"Yes, I'm fine. It's nothing. No reason to worry. My niece will drive me there and bring me home. I just need someone to care for my kitty."

"Of course, I will. Happy to. You'll let me know if I can do anything else?"

"I will, dear boy. Thank you."

"Take care on those steps."

Harriet patted Logan's cheek on the way out.

"Good night, Harriet, and thanks for dinner." He kept the door open, hoping to be rid of both women at once. He met

Addison's gaze. "Thanks for stopping by, Addison. And for the beer. I guess I'll see you on Monday?"

She perched her hands on her hips. "No way, Reed. I was invited to stay for casserole, and I'm not passing something up that smells that good."

His breath rushed out as if someone kicked him in the chest.

"Harriet said there was more than enough for two, and I brought a six-pack. Plus, there's a Broncos game on tonight. What do you say we hang out?"

Bowled over by Addison, Logan shut the door. "Sure, I guess." He didn't want to become friends with Addison, but he had to admit it would be nice to have someone to share a meal with. At times, she was challenging to be around, but Addison had a sharp sense of humor and her warm energy comforted him somehow.

Addison made herself at home. She set the casserole in the microwave and pushed the buttons to heat it before she removed two bottles from the refrigerator. After rummaging through his drawers for an opener, she popped the tops and handed him a beer.

She clinked the lip of her beer on his. "Here's to surprise visitors." Her smiling lips curved around the mouth of her bottle, and Logan's abdomen tightened. He turned away to find the TV remote.

They settled in front of the football game with their cheesy pasta and chicken dish. Addison sat in one of the recliners. He leaned back in the other and extended the footrest. It was the first time he wished he had a couch.

Addison swallowed. "I'm not generally a casserole fan, but this is pretty good."

Logan laughed. "Yeah, I think Harriet's trying to single-handedly fatten me up."

"She loves you."

His chest expanded. Logan had come to love Harriet too. He took another bite.

"You said you like to think of yourself as an artichoke, right?"

Uh-oh, just when he was relaxing into this having dinner company thing…

"Well, I happen to love artichokes. My problem is I'm impatient to get to the heart." She glanced at him from the corner of her eye. "I am persistent, though."

"I can see that, but you should be careful. Artichokes are much pricklier than onions."

"But they taste better, especially dipped in a buttery lemon sauce." She licked her lips, double-raised her eyebrows, and grinned.

Logan lowered his feet to the carpet and braced his forearms on his knees. "Are we still working the analogy?" His pulse ricocheted inside his chest.

Addison's eyes flew open wide. "Oh, God. Did it sound like I was flirting? Did you think I was coming on to you? Cuz, I absolutely *was not.*" She jumped up. "Want another beer?" Her cheeks flamed and Logan noticed a vein fluttering in her neck. *Interesting.*

He stood and took the plate from her hand. "I didn't think that. I just got lost in the analogy, that's all." They stared at each other for a second without breathing before Logan shook himself out of the moment. "I'll get the beers. Want popcorn?" He abruptly escaped the ten feet to the kitchen, putting what little space he could between himself and any ideas his body was having.

This is not good. Not good at all.

CHAPTER 16

The afternoon light filtered in through the thin window covering and splashed across the table where Benjamin studied the floor plan of an office building. He'd finally found Jacob Price working as a hospital administrator. Price was still someone's little helper—always someone else's lackey. Swallowing his rage and humiliation, Benjamin focused on mapping out his next attack.

His finger-nails ran over the rough surface of the scab he picked on his cheek as he settled himself on the thread-bare couch to suck his pipe and think. His mind nibbled at the edge of the memory that fueled his obsession. Even after all these years, the shame slithered through him, causing him to squirm, his degradation bitter on the back of his tongue. Together, Jacob and Tyler had ruined his life. But, since their actions were not the same, it made sense they should suffer their consequences separately for their brutality. He'd save the worst for last.

Benjamin hoped the cops would discover the identities of the bombing victims soon and release them. He wanted the others to figure out what was happening—to make the connection. *Then they'll live in fear for their lives, wondering if they'll be next.*

He clicked on his computer and searched for the local news website. There was a list of missing persons from the area around the Cherry Creek mall posted. The FBI asked anyone with information regarding any of those people to contact them. Briefly, Benjamin entertained the idea of calling in to report that one person on their list had definitely been killed in the bombing, and then explain his mission. Why the bomb was necessary, and why Nicole Grey was at the epicenter of the explosion.

Everyone in that old gang is so stupid. It's taking far longer for them to figure out my purpose than I expected. My message is simple enough for a preschooler to understand. They hadn't even made the connection between the school, Ryan, and Nicole yet. He scratched his face until his sore bled. *Guess I need to give them more clues.*

He sucked in one last hit of the sweet smoke that smelled like melted-plastic and went back to his map. With a red pen, he circled Jacob's office around and around again. "I'm coming for you, Price, you son-of-a-bitch. You're going to know what it feels like to be helpless—to be at the mercy of someone who could save you but chooses not to." Benjamin opened a file on the computer titled REVENGE. He clicked on an image, and the printer clunked and hummed into action, coloring in the face of a man who had once been the boy who enabled the worst hours of his life.

The memory of the youthful version of Jacob laughing and pointing at him, super-imposed itself across the print-out trembling in his fingers. Bile charged up Benjamin's throat, and he ran to the toilet to spit it out. After all these years, events of that day still had the potential to bring him to his knees. Once his stomach was empty, Benjamin wiped his mouth with the back of his hand. He returned to the printout and taped Jacob's current photo underneath the copy of his senior picture.

Once they are all dead, their power over me will evaporate. At least that had been the case with his mother.

CHAPTER 17

It was the end of a long work week, but Friday, without deviation, was date night. Addison sighed as she dabbed her nose with powder and avoided her own gaze. Matthew was due at 6:30 p.m. He would take her to one of the three restaurants he liked, and he'd order a grilled chicken breast with steamed vegetables. Red wine by the glass was acceptable, but never a bottle, even though they drank the same vintage. Dessert was never an option, and they'd be home by nine. How they ended up in this monotonous routine was beyond her, but Matthew was a good guy so she didn't argue.

Dinner was uncomfortable from the get-go. Matthew spoke only to answer direct questions and after a bevy of yes's and no's, Addison stopped trying. She glanced at the others in the dining room of the Table 6 restaurant and noticed couples leaning toward each other, chatting or laughing at some private joke. Her gaze returned to their own icy table void of conversation or jocularity.

She poked at a bite of her pork and smeared it around in the tangy Chevre cheese and mustard sauce. "What's going on, Matthew? If you weren't planning on talking to me, we should have just stayed home."

"You *never* want to stay home. That's part of the problem. You constantly prefer to be out socializing, running from one event to the next."

"What's wrong with that? I've always been that way. I thought it was one of the things you liked about me." An ache formed deep within her chest and radiated outward, scraping against her breastbone.

"I did—at first. But, are you ever going to settle down and want to spend time hanging out at home? Maybe make dinner and—."

"And what?" Several faces swiveled her way, and Addison realized her voice was louder than she intended. She took a breath and let it out slowly. "And sit next to you while you play your video game or watch TV?"

"Most couples settle down, Addison. I'm not asking for the world." His eyes glinted with polar ice.

"You are to me. I don't like to sit still."

Matthew wiped his mouth with his napkin and spread it back across his lap. His gaze never left hers. "Exactly. Why is that, do you think?"

When did being active become a crime? Heat rose up her neck. *Why is he grilling me?* "What's wrong with wanting to live my life? I don't want to turn into a boring old fart."

He raised his eyebrows but said nothing in response to that. The waiter approached and asked if they wanted to see a dessert menu. Addison lifted her wine to her lips and escaped into the dark plum and black cherry aroma. Without looking at her, Matthew answered for them both. "No, thank you. We'll just have coffee, please. Decaf." When the server left, Matthew crossed his arms on the table and leaned forward. "Is that why you dress like some seventeen-year-old hipster? Because you're afraid of becoming an old fart?"

Addison's mouth dropped open, and she gaped at him. "I don't even know how to answer that," she hissed. "First of all, my style is preppy punk—not hipster. Second, I have dressed this way since way before you met me. If you didn't approve, why'd you ask me out in the first place? Third, you are already becoming an old fart, and you're only thirty-two!"

His face pinched into a condescending expression that a middle-school teacher might paste on for a mis-behaving adolescent. "Nice to know what you think of me."

Addison sighed. Her temper had run away with her tongue again. "Matthew—"

"Don't." He held his palm up.

Their coffee arrived, and Addison tilted her head up at the waiter. "You know, I think I'll have dessert after all. Will you please bring me whatever your chocolaty-est option is?"

The server flipped open his order book. "We have s'more beignets? We stuff them with chocolate and marshmallow cream."

"Perfect." She smiled at him, but she couldn't force any joy into the expression.

The waiter nodded and avoided Matthew's eye, clearly aware of the tension at the table. He raced off toward the kitchen.

Matthew's condescension thickened. "And now you're acting like a petulant teenager."

"Because I want dessert?" *What the hell?*

"The only reason you ordered dessert is because *I* didn't."

"I don't care whether or not you have dessert, but you never asked me what I wanted. You just decided for me."

"Now you're going to whine about dessert?"

Frustration lost ground to anger. Addison had no idea what was causing Matthew to behave like a petty asshole, but it pissed her off. "Are you trying to pick a fight?"

"No, but it sure seems like you are."

Addison closed her eyes for a moment and attempted to swallow her ire. "What's this all about, Matthew? Why are we fighting over stupid stuff?"

His jaw tightened, and he wadded his napkin up and tossed it on the table. "I've met someone else."

She blinked and stared at him, waiting for a wave of pain to come. Waiting for at least some emotion to overwhelm her. Instead, she felt… empty. "Who? Where?"

"I had hoped we could talk about this outside. Now, apparently, we have to discuss it over your dessert."

That set her off. Addison stood so fast, her chair toppled over backwards. Without bothering to right it, she dug around in her black-leather backpack, yanked out a twenty-dollar bill, and dropped it on the table. "That's for my beignets. I'll meet you outside where you can tell me all about your other woman." All eyes in the dining room were on them. No one even pretended they weren't watching the scene unfold. *Good. I hope he's embarrassed down to his socks.* Addison marched out of the restaurant.

Several minutes later, Matthew followed her. His fair cheeks were bright red, and his eyes blazed. "Your behavior in there was humiliating."

"Good. You deserve to feel humiliated. Why the hell did you take me to dinner if you are seeing another woman? How did you see this playing out? Did you think I'd be sympathetic?"

"I thought you'd be a grown-up."

"Screw you!"

"Not anymore."

Her hand flew out so fast the sting on her palm registered well before the thought to slap him did. They stared at each other in silence. She clenched her teeth together and drew air in through her nose.

"Goodbye, Matthew."

"Don't you want to talk about this?"

"Ha!" she barked. "What's there to discuss? Where you two met? What you find so attractive about her? Where you first slept together?" Addison flung her pack over her shoulder and turned toward home.

"At least let me drive you home."

"No thanks. The walk will do me good." The autumn evening was darkening, and the crisp air bit at her cheeks. She was a little more than three miles from home, but the walk would feel much better than being cooped up inside Matthew's car with him. She needed to clear her head and think about why she wasn't sad. She was pissed—which came from the raucous combination of her pride and Matthew being an ass. But where were the tears? The pain? Oddly, it was a sense of freedom that flooded through her veins and had her breathing deep, reveling in the cool night air.

After a fitful sleep, Addison stumbled into the kitchen before the sun woke and make a pot of coffee. Strong coffee. She'd spent the night re-living the good times—the early days—of her relationship with Matthew. He was handsome and seemed sophisticated. At first, she'd thought he was a little out of her league. They'd gone to museums and galleries, even traveled together to cities where some of his building designs were constructed. There were parties and business outings...

Looking back, though, she admitted to herself that Matthew had always acted bored whenever they were with her friends. He didn't like to talk about her work. *Was he only happy when I entered his arena and we talked about him? Is my job an issue? Or is it just me? Am I too much... or too little —something?*

Addison slammed a cast-iron skillet onto the stove-top

and drizzled olive oil into it. She lit the gas underneath and leaned against the counter to wait for the pan to heat. A sip of rich coffee burned the end of her tongue, so she blew across the dark surface. *Why can't I hold on to any of the men I date?* This six-months-of-effort only to get dropped routine was getting old. The fact that it was a routine worried her.

She knew what Matthew had said about her always wanting to go and do was true. Sitting still for too long made her anxious. Addison didn't like the spotlight to shine too brightly on her for any length of time. Too much study would reveal what little she had to offer. Sure, her job was exciting, but that was all she had. If she stayed active, the focus could remain on the interesting activity rather than on her. *What is so bad about that?*

The oil on the stove popped and stung the skin on her forearm, yanking her back to the task at hand. Addison cracked two eggs into the skillet and dropped a slice of bread into the toaster. The truth was, she just wasn't all that compelling. Her parents, both academics, had always told her she should read more. "The more you read, the more you have to share." But Addison didn't like to read. She had always preferred action.

It wasn't that she didn't have the intellect. She was a Naval Academy grad, for heaven's sake. You had to be smart to get through the FBI Academy too, but she had never acquired the knack for telling her adventures in a way that sounded interesting to others. She was too direct, and that never seemed to go over well with the male ego.

The toaster dinged, and she loaded her breakfast onto a plate, the smell of warm bread causing her stomach to rumble. With her coffee mug re-filled, she took her food out to the backyard. The trees rustled their autumn reds, yellows, and oranges. The morning held a nip in the air. Winter would soon blow in, but for now, Addison snuggled under a quilt in the comfort of her favorite spot and waited for the sun to rise.

After she ate, Addison thought about going for a pre-dawn run, but with so little sleep the night before, she decided instead to go back to bed. She climbed under her rumpled covers and buried her head under her pillow. She wasn't sad about Matthew specifically, but still, she didn't have the energy to face the day.

What was the point of her life, anyway? She had never been someone who desired to get married or have kids. She couldn't imagine it. *But do I see myself growing old alone? Is that what I want?*

Addison punched her uncomfortable, uncooperative pillow before burying her face into it and screaming her frustration and confusion into its stuffing.

CHAPTER 18

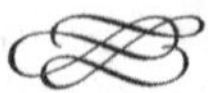

Logan's phone rang before the sun peeked over the eastern horizon. He jabbed the green dot on his screen. "Yeah? Reed here."

"Good morning, Logan. Did I wake you?" Addison—sounding more chipper than he'd ever heard her. Brighter than anyone should be so early in the morning. Downright perky, in fact.

"What's wrong?"

"Why do you think something's wrong?"

Seriously? "Okay. What's with the 6:00 a.m. wake-up call?"

"I wanted to see if you'd like to go on a hike with me this morning? I know it's early, but it's good to get an early start."

Logan scratched his head, leaving his hair sticking out in all directions. He must have given Addison the wrong message when she was over the other night. She seemed to think they were friends, and now he'd have to ease out of the mess he made. "I uh—I've got plans today. Sorry."

"You sure?" There was a vulnerable quality to her tone that reached in and yanked a handful of strings inside his chest.

"Are you sure there's nothing wrong?"

"Yep. Okay, well. Never mind then. See you on Monday." Addison ended the call.

Logan sat on the edge of his bed and rubbed his eyes with his thumb and middle finger. He wanted to go back to bed, but it was too late now. He was up. May as well start the day.

After his morning run, he and Gunner ate a quick breakfast. During the run and in the shower, Logan couldn't keep his mind from mulling over the tone he'd heard in Addison's voice. Something was wrong, and he'd been an insensitive jerk. His basketball team had their first game today at the YMCA, but after that, he'd call her back to check in.

His team didn't win their game, but they only lost by four points. Not bad for a band of newbies. Out on the street, Logan waved at the boys as they left the gym, then reached for his phone to call Addison. It rang three times before sending him to voicemail. He clicked off and tried to shrug off the concern climbing onto his shoulders. Addison was a strong woman, fully capable of handling her own problems. *So, why is the tone I heard underneath her way too cheerful voice this morning, haunting me?*

He reached down and stroked Gunner's silky ears. "Want to see if we can figure out where Addison lives?"

Gunner barked and wagged his tail.

This dog understands more than I thought, and after all, one surprise visit deserves another. "Okay boy, let's go." Logan loaded Gunner into the SUV and drove south to Speer. The street Addison told him she lived on was one way going the wrong way, so he continued down to the next road and squared the block. Some of the homes lining these neighborhood streets were over a hundred years old. They were small, but many of them had been renovated and held a certain charm.

Logan spotted Addison's Mustang. It stood out, lined up on the curb between all the newer model cars. Presumably, her house was one of six nearest her parking spot. He hadn't thought this part through. Was he going to knock on doors until he found hers? "What am I doing here, Gun?"

Gunner's tail slapped the floor encouragingly. Logan chose a place to park and eased his car between two others on the street. *What if Matthew's there? I'll look like a total chump.* He tried to talk himself out of it, but before long, Logan found himself walking up the sidewalk, studying the houses on either side of Addison's hot-rod. A couple in their fifties came out of one house with their wiener dog and walked toward Logan and Gunner. They waved and smiled as they approached. The dogs sniffed each other politely.

"Excuse me. Do you know which house belongs to Addison Thorne?" Logan asked.

The woman glanced across the street. "You mean the FBI lady?"

Logan chuffed. "Yeah, that's her."

"Her house is right there. Directly across from ours."

Logan's gaze followed her pointing finger to a two-story, red brick structure with a large front porch and lawn that sloped down to the walk. "Thank you." He and Gunner jogged across the street and up to the front door. He knocked and waited before he rapped again.

"Well, boy, I guess nobody's home." Logan turned to leave when he heard what he thought was a 70s ballad unsuccessfully disguising someone's tears. He stopped and focused on where the sniffles were coming from. It sounded like the backyard, so Logan went around the house to the gate and peered over. "Addison?"

She still had a powerful hold of the strings she'd tugged

on earlier that morning, and now they yanked him right over the fence. He vaulted into the backyard with Gunner at his heels. They both rushed to Addison's side. Logan sat on the bench next to her. She held her face in her hands, her shoulders rocking with her quiet sobs.

"Addison? What's wrong? Are you alright?"

She lifted her eyes and stared at him for half a second before she buried her nose in his chest. Automatically, his arms wrapped around her and drew her in. That was the moment he knew he was in over his head. He had somehow gone way past the point of keeping himself distant—from not caring. He breathed in the ginger scent of her shampoo and dove deeper.

"What happened?" He murmured into her jet curls.

Addison sat up and scrunched her brows together. Her red-rimmed eyes took him in. "How did you find my house? Why are you here?"

"You mentioned your street, I saw your car… your neighbor—"

"Why am I asking an FBI agent how he found my house?" She laughed and hiccupped at the same time. Then tears filled her eyes again.

"Hey, don't cry. Tell me what's wrong." Logan was desperate to fix whatever made her so sad. If it was that jerk-off she was dating, he'd bust his jaw.

Addison swallowed and worked to get control of her emotions. "Matthew is seeing someone else."

"That bastard!" Logan jumped to his feet.

Addison smiled at his reaction and took his hand, pulling him back down to the bench. "He is that, but that's not why I'm crying. The break-up was long over-due. We are completely different people."

"Anyone could see that."

She glared at him, and guilt crept up his throat. "Sorry."

Addison sighed. "I suppose everyone saw it but me."

Logan held his tongue this time. He'd only seen them together for about an hour and wondered what she saw in that prick.

The autumn afternoon sun warmed his shoulders and a cool breeze rattled the dry golden leaves in the trees and shrubs in her small backyard. Gunner laid down with his chin resting on Addison's feet. Logan soaked in the moment, waiting for Addison to continue.

"Anyway, it made me mad that he was seeing someone else, but that's just a dented ego. I'm not sad about the break-up. The two of them will get matching cardigans and watch sitcoms in the evening and wither away in grayness, happily ever after. That's not what I want."

"No, I can't see you wearing a cardigan." She smiled and Logan's chest expanded. "So, what is it that has you in tears on such a perfect afternoon?"

Addison took a moment to look at her surroundings. "It is perfect, isn't it?" She twisted toward him and raised her eyebrow. "We should be hiking." Light darted into her eyes and lit her features. "Want to drive up and see the aspen tomorrow?"

Logan felt the outline of the round metal pieces in his pocket, but didn't reach for them. *To hell with worrying about getting hurt.* "I'd love to. But you're avoiding the question. What caused your tears?" He reached forward and wiped her cheek with the side of his thumb.

She shrugged. "It's just that I don't want to grow old all alone. I'm no good with relationships. Guys never stick around. It's either because my job scares the crap out of them, or they become lazy and dull. Why can't relationships stay the way they start? You know, exciting and active? Why do guys always end up wanting to lie around on the couch watching TV. Boring!"

Logan chuckled. "Uh—this feels like a talk you should have with your girlfriends. If I answer you honestly, I'd be a traitor to my own gender."

Addison rolled her eyes. "Do you lie around doing nothing on your days off?"

"My life is different. I have a high-energy, too-smart-for-his-own-good dog, who keeps me running." Gunner lifted his head and barked. "I swear he understands English too."

Laughing, Addison framed Gunner's face with her hands and kissed his wet nose. "You do, don't you, boy? You're the smartest one here." Gunner rewarded her comment with a juicy dog kiss that made her giggle. The sound filled a long-left empty spot deep inside Logan's gut with pure joy.

"Don't encourage him. He already has an enormous ego." Logan chuckled when Gunner drew the corners of his mouth back and let his tongue hang out the side. He looked as if he was smiling.

"I'm serious, Logan. Are all guys like that? Do they all turn boring once they're comfortable?"

"I can't give you an answer, but I hope not. Maybe everyone wants to be comfortable, but that looks different to different people."

"Comfortable to me is going and exploring. Trying new things." Addison peered at him from the corner of her eyes. "What's comfortable to you?"

Logan leaned forward, bracing his forearms on his knees, and stared at the ground between his feet. "Honestly? For a while, I thought comfortable meant not letting anyone in. Not getting close to anyone."

"And now?"

"I don't know."

Together, they sat side by side, quietly enjoying the ebbing afternoon. As the sun relinquished its hold on the day, the air grew chilly and Addison shivered. Logan opened his arm to her, and she snuggled in to him. "Want to stay for dinner?"

"I'm not sure. Can you cook?"

She pinched his ribs. Hard.

"Ow!" He laughed and jerked to the side. "How about I take you out?"

"I have been wanting to try a new place over in Highlands."

"Let's do it."

"What about Gunner?"

"He likes to go on adventures. Don't you, Gun?"

CHAPTER 19

During supper, they had agreed not to talk about Matthew, or any other past relationships. Addison relaxed and laughed more than she had in a long time. After relishing a leisurely dinner from a trendy nouveau menu, they topped their meal off with a chocolate confection that looked like a fancy bird. The cream and cocoa melted in her mouth, but the dish was so elaborate it was almost impossible to eat. Finally, they crushed the artistic arrangement down to the plate and scooped up the delicious remains.

Logan and Gunner drove Addison home. He opened her door for her, and she swung her legs around to get out. She didn't want the night to end, but she didn't want to be stupid either. Logan technically worked for her and, well... that complicated things.

He took her hand to help her out of the car and heat zipped up her arm, giving her pulse an extra charge. Addison wasn't used to men behaving as gentlemen. Most of the guys she hung around treated her like one of their own—and that was how she liked it. Usually. But it was nice to have a good-looking guy open doors for her and buy her dinner. Matthew was polite, but had never gone out of his way to make her feel special.

"Thanks again for dinner. You didn't have—"

Logan pressed his finger against her lips to stop her. "I told you, I wanted to."

He was so close, it seemed natural to lean into him. To kiss him, to…

A chill brought her back to their conversation when he and his body heat moved away from her. Logan kept her hand in his and led her up the front steps of her porch, but then he released her and stepped aside. She was a little let down but smirked at herself. Logan was a nice guy, simply being a good friend. A teammate—finally. *Don't screw that up.*

"I had fun tonight. Cool restaurant. I'm glad you suggested it." Logan stuffed his hands in his pockets. "I'd never been over to that neighborhood. There were a lot of cool little places to eat."

"Yeah, it's the go-to local for a fun meal, for sure." Addison rummaged in her bag for her keys.

"You know, Addison, you're going to be okay. Better, without that douche bag anyway."

A laugh bubbled up from her chest. "I think you're right."

"I'm always right." He grinned.

She rolled her eyes and shoved her key in the lock. "Want to come in?" *Shut up, Addison!* Logan held her gaze for an uncomfortable moment. She'd have paid a nice sum to know what was going through his mind.

"Nah, thanks. I gotta get Gunner home, and…"

"Of course." She glanced back at his car. "What are you up to tomorrow?"

His wonderful but rare full smile lit his face. "Trying to hide from Harriet. She always wants me to come down for dinner on Sundays if I'm around." He rubbed the dark stubble starting to shadow his jaw. "It's not that I don't like to spend time with her, but every Sunday is a little much."

"Want to go on a picnic with me instead? I'd like to drive up and look at the aspen before it's too late."

His eyes took on the same thoughtful look they had before when she had asked him to come in. She'd overstepped again. *Why can't I keep my big mouth shut?*

"Yeah. That sounds nice. I don't remember when I last made the time to view the aspen. Probably not since I was a kid. My mom loves to go every year."

"Does she live in Denver?"

"No. My folks have a ranch up in Wyoming."

"Do you see them often?"

"Not as much as my mom would like." A wistful look brushed across his features.

"Do you miss it? Ranch living?"

"Sometimes. My brother runs the place now."

"Just you and one brother, then?"

"No, my sister lives up there too. A big happy family… minus me." He smiled, and his words flowed without an edge.

"I didn't see any photos of your family in your apartment. Do you have any?" The only photo she'd glimpsed in his apartment was the framed picture of Logan in his Army uniform kneeling next to a dog.

His arms stiffened, and Logan took a step backward. "I'm not really a sentimental guy." His eyes darted toward his car. "Well, I should go."

"Okay." There it was. She had discovered his invisible line. And she'd tripped on it. "So, tomorrow… how about I pick you up? If it's warm enough, we can drive through the mountains with the top down."

He moved toward the steps. "I don't know. Do you mind if Gunner rides in your car?"

"He'll be fine. I can lay the thick picnic blanket down on the back seat. Say ten?"

Logan didn't answer right away. He seemed to consider all the angles. "Sure, okay. See you then." He nodded his head once, then turned to go down the stairs.

Addison let herself in and pressed the door closed by leaning against it. "What is the matter with me?" She asked the house. "He probably thinks I want to jump his bones." She strode across her small living room to the kitchen and grabbed a pen and pad of paper to make a grocery list for the next day. *He doesn't know, I just hate being alone.*

The next morning, Addison was up and at it early. On a Sunday, that meant 8:00 a.m. She raced to Whole Foods and filled her basket with tasty finger snacks for their outing. She'd brought a blanket and a pack that held plastic plates and wine glasses. When she had everything she needed for the humans, she grabbed a box of dog treats and a bottle of water for Gunner on her way to the check-out stand.

It was ten-thirty by the time she arrived at Logan's apartment. Harriet called down to her from her small balcony on the second floor. "You-hoo! Addison! Good morning."

Addison waved. "Hello, Harriet."

"Logan told me you two are going on a picnic date. Beautiful day for it."

Heat bloomed up Addison's neck. Hopefully, Logan didn't hear Harriet say 'date.' *Unless Logan told her it was a date.* Her heart mule-kicked her ribcage at the thought. She needed to get a grip. It had been less than forty-eight hours since Matthew broke it off with her. She shouldn't be thinking about another man so soon. Plus, she and Logan were co-workers and friends, and they both wanted it to remain that way.

Logan opened his door and stuck his head out when she was halfway up the stairs. "You're late." He flashed her a teasing grin. He and Gunner bounced down the steps toward her. "Let's go."

"Good morning to you too." Addison chuckled and reached to scratch Gunner's chin. "I got you some treats too, buddy."

They loaded into the Mustang and were heading west on I-70 within minutes.

Addison tapped her fingers on the steering wheel. "How did Harriet feel about being stood up?"

Logan turned his face toward her, but she couldn't see his eyes behind his dark sunglasses. Still, his smile warmed the pit of her belly. "She was thrilled. Harriet thinks there is something going on between us. I've told her a hundred times there isn't. Anymore, I just let her think what she wants."

"She's sweet, and she loves you."

"Yeah. I like her alright too."

"King of understatements."

Amusement played on his lips as he leaned back against the headrest and canted his face toward the sunshine.

As they climbed in altitude, the temperature cooled and the trees turned brilliant yellows and golds. Addison filled her lungs with the pine-tinged mountain air as she sailed past Idaho Springs on her way up to Breckenridge, where she knew of an excellent place for their lunch. They enjoyed the beautiful drive with long stretches of companionable silence. Perfect.

Addison pulled onto a dirt road that led to her secret spot. She parked to the side of a flat clearing that boasted a breath-taking view. Together, they unpacked their supplies and lay a quilt on the dry grass. From their blanket they glimpsed a lake through the trees and took in the vast expanse of Colorado's bright blue firmament. No other sky shared such brilliance.

Logan pushed up the sleeves of his sweatshirt and poured wine while Addison set out the spread. "There's enough food here to feed a platoon." He passed her a glass.

She winked at him over the rim of her crisp, white wine. "I wasn't sure what kind of appetite you'd have, and I didn't want you to go hungry."

"This is great, Addy." His gaze warmed. "Thanks."

Her hand stilled. No one but her dad ever called her Addy. She didn't allow it. Yet somehow, she liked the sound of her shortened name coming from Logan. *I'm in trouble.* She coughed to cover her discomfort and sputtered. "You're welcome."

Logan reached across for the Castelvetrano olives, and Addison noticed mottled burn scars on his forearm. "What happened to your arm?"

He drew his hand back, shoving his sleeve down to his wrist. He popped three olives in his mouth before turning away. Gunner, sensing a change in the air, wiggled closer to him and rested his chin on Logan's leg. Logan rolled away from his dog and got to his feet. He walked to the edge of the hill and stared down at the lake.

"Nice view."

After that awkward moment, they never recovered the light-hearted mood they'd shared at the beginning of the picnic. The silence between comments during lunch, and on their way home, crackled with tension. Logan had retrieved the silver disc from his pocket and focused his attention on rolling it over his knuckles for most of the drive. Addison parked at the curb in front of Logan's building. "I'm truly sorry if I said something that offended you. I know you like to keep your history to yourself and in the past. I shouldn't have asked about your arm."

"I told you it was no big deal." He brushed off her apology, and he and Gunner hopped out of the car. They stood on the sidewalk and Logan lifted his hand in goodbye, leaving Addison no choice but to drive away, feeling like a jerk.

CHAPTER 20

Days later, Logan continued to be distant. It wasn't that he didn't speak to her, but when he did, his words were clipped and void of the warmth he'd shown her before.

Addison knelt down and stroked the top of Gunner's head. "Hi, buddy." He lay on the floor next to his handler's boot. She peered up at Logan. "How are you this morning?"

Logan dipped his chin. "Good." He stood and walked across the room to stare at the evidence board. Gunner followed him, but glanced back at her with eyes filled with a canine wisdom she wished she understood.

During Logan's first weeks with the bomb squad, Addison had poured over his file. There were a ton of blacked-out lines of redacted information, so she hadn't learned much. But, from the pieces she could put together, she discovered Logan had signed with the Army for a second four-year tour of duty. After a page and a half of the thick black lines, she learned he spent time in a hospital in Germany, and that he received a medical discharge.

Obviously, he'd been burned. She assumed there had been

an explosion. But there was no official documented information regarding any of it. That, along with Logan's current behavior, was like a loose stitch in a sweater that Addison could not leave alone. She'd pick at it until it came unraveled. Curiosity killed the cat, but not until after the ninth life. She figured she still had a few more of those to go.

Her desk phone rang and went to her desk to answer it. "Thorne."

"Agent Thorne, this is Agent Cameron over at HQ."

"Hey, Cameron. What's up?"

"We got a call from a woman who told us her best friend was one of the victims killed in the explosion at Cherry Creek. She said she had some information that might be helpful to our investigation, and she's on her way over here now. Thought you'd like to be in on the conversation."

"Did she say what kind of information?"

"No, I didn't press. It's better to interview her in person."

"Okay. I'll be there. Mind if I bring a couple of my guys?"

"No problem."

Addison hung up and scanned the room to see which of her team were present. "Miller, Reed, I'd like you two to come with me to HQ. A woman claiming to be good friends with one of the bomb victims has stepped forward. I need you both to help determine if what she has to say jibes with the bomb investigation. Be ready in five."

When they arrived at the FBI conference room, Cameron and Sanchez sat across from a well-dressed couple. Purple half-moons hung under the woman's eyes and tears smudged her make-up. The man, presumably her husband, held her hand and patted it encouragingly.

Addison pushed through the door. Cameron stood and introduced her and her team to a weepy but attractive woman in her late twenties. "This is Megan and Zachary Carlson. Mrs. Carlson had been close friends with Nicole Grey ever since they were in high school."

Addison took a seat next to Cameron and propped her arms on her knees, leaning forward. "So, you have some information you think will help our bomb investigation?"

Megan sniffled and wiped her eyes with a crumpled tissue. "Nicole worked for *Sophistications* and died in the explosion at the mall."

"I'm sorry." Addison's throat ached as she witnessed the woman's obvious pain.

"Thank you." Megan's breath tripped on a sob before she continued. "My husband and I were discussing the several bomb incidents that have occurred in Denver over the past weeks. You see, the school that evacuated—where you found the fake device? That was the high school I attended. Then there was the explosion at the construction site up in Firestone. The man who was killed—the foreman—his name was Ryan Long. I went to school with him, too. He was in our group of friends." Megan's eyes sought her husband, and he rubbed her shoulder.

"Go on, Mrs. Carlson," Addison encouraged.

Her red eyes closed briefly before she continued. "Then there was the bombing at the mall that killed Nicole." Her gaze bore into Addison's. "I can't help but see a connection. It's too much for it to be a coincidence."

Miller folded his hands on the table. "There are tons of kids who graduated from that high school who work or shop at Cherry Creek mall, and the explosion in Firestone was an accident. A gas leak."

Megan shifted her swollen eyes to consider him. "Was it?"

Addison sat back in her chair and exchanged a look with Cameron. "All of this is still under investigation, ma'am."

Cameron opened a file and turned it toward Agent

Sanchez. "Can you think of anyone who might want to hurt your friends?"

"I'm not sure."

"Did Ryan Long and Nicole Grey stay in touch over the years?"

"As far as I knew, they weren't in touch." She wrung her hands and everyone waited for her to continue. Megan drew air in through her nose. "But, there was a boy who hovered around our group..." She stopped and shook her head at her husband.

"Honey, you were all just kids. They need to know. If it isn't anything, then it doesn't matter, but if..."

"Okay." Megan drew in a huge breath. "This is so embarrassing, but the group of friends I hung around with in high school liked to tease and make fun of a certain boy. He had a terrible crush on Nicole. She was dating someone else, and the two of them tormented the boy about it all the time."

Classic. Addison clamped her teeth together and cleared the dry ball of cotton from her throat. Personal opinions aside, they needed this woman's cooperation. "What was the boy's name? Do you remember?"

"Yes, his name was Benjamin Sykes. Benji."

Cameron scrawled the name in the file. "Was there a particular reason he was the target of your group's bullying?"

"I'm not really sure. He was odd, you know. He tried too hard. An easy target."

Agent Sanchez tapped his pen on the table. "What made him odd?"

Megan shook her head, and her eyes darted up and left, looking as though she were thinking back over the years. "His looks, I suppose. He was skinny, his eyes bulged out, and he had acne. He didn't shower often enough... but it was more than that. He badly wanted to be a part of our crowd and would stand near us at games or show up where we hung out. He never got the hint that he just didn't fit in."

Sanchez pinned the woman with his almost black eyes. "What form did your teasing take, exactly?"

"It wasn't *my* teasing, Agent Sanchez." Megan sat up imperiously and leveled her chin at his challenge. "Mostly, it was Ty. He was the varsity quarter-back and captain of the debate team. He and Nicole were dating. I think it angered him that Benji had a thing for his girl."

"But it was Ryan Long who died in the accident, not Ty." Sanchez scribbled on a pad of paper. "Ty—short for Tyler? What is his last name?"

"Yes. Tyler Brookes."

"What did Long do to trigger this level of rage—this anger still boiling ten years later?" Sanchez leaned toward the woman. "Exactly what incidents do you remember that prompted your visit with us today?" His question cracked the air like a whip.

Note to self—never try to hide information from Ricardo Sanchez! Addison admired his no-nonsense approach.

Megan tucked her tissue into her purse before meeting his eye. "One day, Nicole wrote a note to Benji, something about how she couldn't stop thinking about him, and so forth. And then she invited him to meet her in the janitor's closet—"

Logan unfolded his arms and thrust his hands to his hips. "The one where Gunner found the fake bomb?"

Megan jerked her head toward him as though she'd forgotten he was there. "I suppose, yes. There was only one closet, on the first floor at the end of the hall." She turned back to Sanchez. "When he got there, Nicole was waiting for him. She blindfolded him and… well, I don't know all that she did because the door was closed, but after about ten minutes, she opened the doors and there Benji stood with a scarf over his eyes and his pants undone..." Her voice caught and she dropped her gaze to her lap. "He was, well... exposed to all of us. Everyone took pictures and laughed. Kids posted the photos on Myspace and printed fliers that they taped all over the school. They humiliated the poor boy."

Silence reigned over the room.

Finally, Sanchez asked, "So, you think Benjamin Sykes might be getting his revenge?"

Mr. Carlson drew his wife close. "We don't know, Agent Sanchez. But when Megan told me the story, we agreed that we should share it with the FBI, just-in-case."

"Are there any other incidents that stick out in your mind, Mrs. Carlson? Any other kids involved?"

She shook her head. "No. At least none that I witnessed. There were some rumors, but I can't say for sure." Mrs. Carlson flushed and bit her lip.

Narrowing his eyes, Sanchez leaned toward her. "What rumors?"

"I don't remember much. Supposedly something happened between the boys on a class field trip to the State Capitol Building. Anyway, it was all just rumor—probably nothing to it." She fidgeted with her purse strap. "I'm sorry I can't be more help."

"You did the right thing, coming in today." Cameron reached out to squeeze her hand. "We'll add this to the other information we've gathered."

Sanchez stood, putting an end to the interview. "We'll assign a detail to you, Mrs. Carlson. They'll keep their distance, but they'll be there for your protection until we can find Sykes and talk with him. Call if you think of anything else."

Mr. Carlson offered his hand to Sanchez. "We will. Thank you." His gaze then included everyone in the room. "Before you judge too harshly, remember, they were just kids."

Acid burned inside Addison's chest and she crossed her arms. "Maybe, but even kids feel adult-sized pain."

The man nodded and guided his wife to the door.

She stopped before they left and, glancing back over her shoulder, she murmured, "I'm so sorry."

The agents waited until the couple disappeared down the hall before Sanchez spoke to Cameron. "Find this Benjamin Sykes."

"Yes, sir." He gathered his papers and left.

The dark eyes swung to Addison. "Does her story fit with the bombing evidence you have so far, Thorne?"

Addison bit her lip in thought. "The woman whom Mrs. Carlson referred to was indeed killed in the explosion. In fact, we determined that the storage closet of the shop Nicole Grey managed was the seat of the bomb."

Logan braced his hands on the table and leaned forward. "And the custodial closet at the school is exactly as Mrs. Carlson described it."

Sanchez reached for the suit coat hanging on the back of his chair. He slid it over his broad shoulders. "Okay, good. Looks like we may have a break in this case. I want you to keep me—"

Agent Cameron crashed through the door, interrupting him at the same time as Addison, Logan, and Miller's phones sounded an alert. "There's an active bomb threat at University Memorial Hospital."

Addison's heart skipped a beat, and her gaze flew to Logan. "Reed. Isn't that the hospital Harriet went to?"

He and Gunner sprang for the exit.

"Logan!" Addison's ribs compressed her lungs.

He shouted over his shoulder as he ran. "We'll meet you there!"

CHAPTER 21

Logan arrived to chaos unfolding at University Memorial Hospital. Because of the recent bombing, officials instantly considered the threat viable and ordered hospital personnel to evacuate the hundreds of patients and staff. Ambulances from all over the city arrived to help transfer the most critical subjects to other locations. Logan knew they placed healthier, more stable people at the back of the line, and figured he'd find Harriet in that waiting area.

Fear permeated the crowd. Some stared ahead in shock, while others cried. Police officers lined up to keep concerned loved ones away from the danger zone. People desperate to get information on family members panicked when they heard nothing. Pandemonium reigned.

Logan assessed the scenario as he checked in with the site commander. "Is there a master patient list? Have you accounted for all the patients?"

The officer shook his head. "Last I heard, they have only evacuated about 80 percent of the people. They're still working on it."

Logan searched the sea of people stationed at the back of the farthest parking lot. He choked down the desire to run there and look for Harriet. *This is exactly what I've been trying to avoid.* Helplessly, he ground his teeth and focused his mind on the immediate task.

Suited up in their protective gear, he and Gunner sprinted toward the patient wing. Other K9 units were already searching the ER and OR sections, so they entered through the main entrance and started with the stairwell.

"*Such*, Gunner. *Such*!" Gunner sniffed the cement flights as they bound their way to the highest floor. "It's a big hospital, boy." Fear pressed in on the back of Logan's mind, driving his feet faster. The top of the building was the last place he wanted to be. "Let's be quick."

Gunner seemed to understand the urgency as he ran, nose first, into each room systematically. Logan remained at his side every step of the way. The dog hesitated a few times, but eventually confirmed all the rooms were free of explosive materials. The hospital floors all had the same layout, and all were eerily silent in the void of human presence. Still, machines, unattached to patients, continued to whir and beep. Televisions droned on in empty waiting rooms. It resembled a post-apocalyptic scene where the population had vanished into thin air.

Hospitals all seemed to smell the same—antiseptic cleanser and the cloying scent of dying flowers mixed with canned, overcooked green beans. Gunner didn't notice. He remained focused on finding explosive scents while he searched. The duo ran behind the nurses' station and through the offices. In and out of each patient room, break areas, and waiting rooms. Gunner's nails slipped and slid across the gleaming tile floors, but he managed to keep his footing and race ahead.

With the top floor complete, Logan and Gunner raced

down to the third. They repeated the search pattern they had executed upstairs. Gunner dashed into the nurse's area and padded left into the office space. He stopped hard on his paws and barked furiously at what he saw. Logan was one step behind.

"What are you doing? You must evacuate the hospital." As he asked, he witnessed his answer. They caught the nurse standing in front of them red-handed as she stuffed pill containers of all sizes into her backpack. She stood before a locked cabinet that held all the controlled drugs on the floor. The glass door had been shattered and her fists overflowed with plastic bottles, and her eyes were as round as their safety caps.

Her gaze shot to a nearby exit directly behind Logan. "Don't think about it. Even if you could get by me, you'll never get past my dog. Put down the drugs. We need to get you out of here."

"Just let me go. No one needs to know about this, right?" The woman reminded Logan of a frightened chipmunk storing up for winter. Her eyes darted around the small room, and she tapped her fingers together in front of her chest.

"That's not how this is going to play out." Logan reached for the handcuffs clipped to his belt. "Put your hands behind your back." He pushed the button on the side of his radio mic. "I found a person in the building on the third floor in the nurse's station. I'm placing her under arrest, and I need someone to take her into custody and evacuate her."

"Officer Berg is on her way."

"Roger." Logan read the nurse her Miranda rights and escorted her to the stairwell door. Gunner continued doing his job on the way. "Look at it like this," he said to the woman as he passed her off to the local cop. "Now you can get the help you need."

The nurse glowered at him as the door closed behind them. "Let's go, Gunner. We're not finished yet. *Such*!"

As Logan and his dog ran through the hallways, he fought to keep images of Lobo from his mind, but they persisted, tearing at his heart. Visions of Lobo's warm brown eyes filled with excitement every time they had gone on a search hovered in his thoughts. He remembered Lobo's silly grin. He was the first dog Logan had ever called his own. He too was a Malinois like Gunner, but he had a darker coat and, unlike Gunner, his face was solid black.

Logan paused to catch his breath and figure out what had tripped his memory. He crouched down and curled forward, the painful thoughts taking a physical toll. Gunner cocked his head at him and stared. His tail wagged slowly as he padded back to Logan. He licked Logan's face again and again before pressing his nose into the fold at Logan's waist.

"Gun, I've tried not to care, but I have to admit, you're a truly amazing dog, and I love you, buddy." Logan threw his arm around Gunner's neck and hugged tight. Then he jumped up to his feet. "Come on, boy. Not the time for this. We've got to keep going. *Such*!"

Gunner barked excitedly and then ran back to work. In no time, they made their way down to the bottom floor. The patients' wing already received a tentative all-clear. Logan, still sick with concern over Harriet, darted toward the administrative building and the doctor's offices' complex. *Why didn't I ask her who her doctor was or why she was going to the hospital?*

But he knew why. He hadn't asked because he had been trying not to care. It was obviously too late for that, on all counts.

CHAPTER 22

Addison leapt out of the FBI bomb truck as soon as it came to a stop, its sirens winding down in a yowl. She scanned the crowds of people stationed in groups, glad to see the hospital's emergency evacuation plan was working as smoothly as they could hope for. The county's fire chief was barking orders into his radio, and Addison made a beeline for him.

"Addison Thorne." She flashed her badge. "FBI Bomb Tech. What's the situation?"

The chief checked her credentials and nodded, bobbing a steel-gray walrus mustache. "Glad to have you and your team. Currently, evacuations are still underway. This is a slower process than I'd like, but we don't want to cause more harm in a reckless race to get everyone out."

"Agreed, but if we can safely speed things up, we need to do that. Let's get the crowd pushed back another block at least. We have no way of knowing the reach of a potential blast wave. Same with the evacuees who are waiting for transport. Can you send some of your firefighters over to help move them farther away?"

"Will do." The fire chief spoke into his radio, repeating Addison's request before he continued with his report. "We have several K9 teams searching for explosives. So far, they've detected nothing. They just finished their sweep through the main hospital building and emergency room and are now moving to the admin complex and parking garage."

Addison nodded. "We'll require a second search pass to be sure after they're through with the first."

"Good idea. Otherwise, we have five trucks from surrounding counties and twice as many fire engines. Let's hope we don't need them all."

"If they find anything, we have robots on each bomb truck that can go in."

The chief gave her a thumbs up and took another radio call.

Addison scanned the emergency zone. Police cars, fire engines, and ambulances littered the area punctuated with federal response teams from the FBI, ATF, and Homeland. The amount of safety and rescue equipment and personnel sent a flush of pride through her chest. She squared her shoulders as her pulse slowed down a beat. These professionals knew what to do in the event the worst thing happened, but still she sent a silent prayer that they wouldn't have to prove it.

Until the K9 teams completed their searches, Addison was on hold. She walked back to the truck to find out if they'd heard from Logan. Firefighters, several police officers, and a handful of medical staff fought to move a large group of evacuees back another block beyond their current location. People searching for their loved ones cried and pleaded against a police barricade that undulated with their desperation.

Her heart ached for the frightened mass. Addison knew their fear and ran past the roped off area to help move people to a safer distance. At the same time, she searched the faces for Harriet. She checked in with the officer in charge.

He glanced at her ID without taking the time to read it. "Thanks for assisting. They have evacuated all the patients. The medevac helicopter took the most serious to other hospitals, and ambulances took the others. The people here are ambulatory for the most part. Just pitch in where you can. We're trying to get these folks over to the park two blocks west."

"I'll help until I get called back. K9 teams are still searching for signs of explosives. So far, they haven't found anything."

Addison gripped the man's shoulder in solidarity before she moved off toward the groups of patients. As she helped to move them away from the hospital, she asked random people, "Did any of you notice anyone who looked out of place? Maybe someone carrying a duffle bag? Did you see any bags, purses, or backpacks left on their own?" Shaking heads and eyes brimming with fear met her questions. All the while, she stayed alert for any signs of Harriet.

A half-hour in, Addison took a break for a quick check-in with her team at the bomb truck. When she got there, she climbed in through the back door. "Anything?"

Miller slid one side of his headphones off so he could hear her. "None of the K9 teams are reporting anything suspicious."

"Any word from Reed? Do we know where he and Gunner are?"

"No, but let me put a call out to him." Miller replaced his earpiece and spoke into his microphone. "Agent Reed, report in… Agent Reed, do you copy?"

"Reed here." The tension that had gathered at the back of Addison's neck eased when she heard Logan's voice.

"This is Miller. What is your location?"

"Just completed the patient wing search. Heading to Office and Admin complex."

"Roger. Stay safe."

Miller glanced at Addison, and she nodded at him. "I'm going out to talk to more patients and staff. Call me if anyone finds anything suspicious that we need to check out. I won't be far."

She hopped out of the truck and squinted in the bright sunshine. A group of gowned medical personnel, their green aprons splashed with blood, stood together behind one of the local fire trucks. Addison wondered if they'd had to interrupt procedures to evacuate. The number of lives the bomb threat alone put at risk astounded her—even if there ended up being no actual explosion.

Addison flashed her badge. "Is everyone okay?"

"We're fine, but they flew several of our patients, mid-procedure, to emergency surgery at other hospitals. I was in the middle of a rotator-cuff repair. Never thought it would turn into a life or death situation. I hate to think of how all the surgery patients are doing." The tall, thin surgeon peeled off her outer layer. "Have you found the bomb yet?"

"No one's found anything yet."

"If they don't find a bomb, how soon can we go back in?"

"It will be a long while, I'm afraid. The dogs are doing an initial run through right now, but even if they find nothing, they have to go through a second time. We can't be too careful. I'd hate to give the all clear only to have some hidden device detonate."

"Do we have to stay here?" Another surgeon checked his watch.

"Yes, I'm afraid so. Police must interview and clear everyone before they can leave."

"I have an appointment."

The tall doctor glared at the man. "A tee-time, you mean."

Addison shared a look with the woman before addressing the entire group. "You all should cancel your plans for the rest of your day. With this many people, I don't see you getting out of here until dinnertime at the earliest, and that's if you choose *not* to help."

What a jerk. How can some people be so self-centered? Addison moved off to query the next group huddled together. She went from one bunch of people to another. Some were patients, some nurses, others were administrative staff and doctors. No one remembered seeing anything out of the ordinary. Neither had anyone heard of a woman named Harriet Loomis.

As the hour pressed on, the excitement ebbed and the people forced to stay on site began getting grumpy. Police officers worked furiously to interview folks and get them connected with loved ones who could take them home. Addison slowly made her way toward the end of the line of evacuees.

There in a wheelchair, chatting happily with an elderly man sitting on the bench of his walker, was the woman she'd been searching for. "Harriet! Harriet Loomis!" Addison yelled and waved.

The woman held a hand above her eyes and scanned the crowd. Addison ran toward her. "Harriet! Thank, God! Are you all right?"

"Oh yes, dear. I'm just fine." She reached out to touch the man's hand. "Frank, this is my neighbor Logan's girlfriend. You know, the young man I told you about?"

Addison laughed despite herself. *Girlfriend?* She held her hand out to the man and shook his. "I'm Special Agent Addison Thorne." She smirked at Harriet. "And I'm actually *no one's* girlfriend." She crouched down in front of Harriet's chair. "Are you sure you're all right? We—Logan and I—have been worried sick about you."

"Where is Logan?" Harriet looked beyond Addison for him.

"He and Gunner are searching for signs of an explosive device."

"I hate his job. I worry every time he leaves for work." Harriet patted her new friend's hand. "Did I tell you; my neighbor is a secret agent for the FBI?"

Addison cringed. "He's an FBI K9 handler attached to the bomb squad," she explained. Then she squeezed Harriet's shoulder to reassure her. "He's one of the best at what he does, Harriet. Let me try to reach him on the radio. He'll be relieved to know I found you. He's worried about you too."

"He's such a dear boy."

Addison pressed the button on her radio. "Reed, do you copy?" She waited and smiled encouragingly at Harriet. "Reed, can you hear me?"

The radio crackled, and Logan's voice sputtered with it. "On my way into the second building. All clear so far."

"Reed. I've located Harriet. She's safe here with me now."

"That's terrific news! Give her a kiss. I'm entering. Out." Logan clicked off.

"See, Harriet, it's *you* who has Logan's heart." She reached over to embrace the older woman when the ground vibrated. A rush of hot air pressed her forward, and an ear-splitting blast assaulted her ears. Addison covered Harriet with her own body as a blast wave crashed into them. The pressure forced Addison's weight into Harriet. Ash and debris fell through the sky like snowflakes. She smelled the acrid black powder and spit its bitter residue from her tongue. They had been distant enough from the explosion to be out of danger, but…

"Logan!" Addison screamed.

CHAPTER 23

Relief poured over Logan, easing the weight of his painful memories. Harriet was safe—thank God. He didn't realize how much he had come to care about his neighbor until she was in danger. Logan patted his dog's shoulder. "Almost done, Gunner, then we can go see your favorite girl."

With more energy in his step, Logan followed Gunner down the wing of the doctor's offices. It was less likely someone left a bomb in this section of the hospital complex. A stranger leaving a parcel or bag would stand out among all the people who worked together every day and the patients they knew and treated.

The duo turned right into the first office in the corridor. Gunner sniffed each chair in the waiting room and the rows of magazines stacked in the rack. He padded past the fake potted plants and the long glowing fish tank, taking only seconds in the toy corner before he raced to the door leading to the exam rooms in the back. Gunner followed his nose in and out of three identical spaces containing cabinets and paper-wrapped exam tables. Someone had painted the primary colored walls with bright, friendly scenes. Together, Logan and his dog made quick work of the pediatrician's personal office and the administration bay before they returned to the outer hallway and moved on to the next set of offices.

All of Logan's breath sucked out of his lungs, and white-fiery light blinded his eyes. A searing gust lifted him off his feet, and sent him flying backwards, weightless on the edge of flames biting his skin. Debris pelted him. Something sliced his cheek and though his brain registered the effect as pain, it seemed remote and impotent. The blast crushed his soft tissue into his bones.

"Gunner!" he gasped. Or tried to, though no air passed through his vocal chords. Logan's spine slammed against something hard with no give. His head whipped back and crashed against the object. A piercing ring deafened his ears, and Logan felt rather than heard a sick crack. His vision went dark.

He floated in an empty, silent void. The high-pitched tone shrieked in his head, slicing into his brain. Feathers dusted his cheeks. His eyelids refused to open, and he drifted into the surrounding gossamer atmosphere.

The feathers sweeping his face grew damp… and rough. A firm stroke slid across his mouth. Logan blinked his eyes, trying to loosen his lids, but the deafening ring increased in decibel. He covered his ears with his palms.

Gunner's sloppy tongue made another swipe over his cheek and one eye.

"Gun?" Logan's lungs ached. They burned when he attempted to draw air into them. "Gunner? You okay, boy?"

Unbidden tears flooded Logan's eyes. Two firm hands gripped his shoulders. "Agent? Are you all right?"

Logan blinked repeatedly to clear his blurry vision. "I

think so, but I hit my head." He tried to rub the ache from his skull. Black powder and sulfur burned in his sinuses.

The police K9 handler who found him looked at his skull and chuffed. "Yeah, you could say that. I'm going to brace your neck until the EMTs arrive. Don't move, okay? Are you hurt anywhere else?"

"I… I can't tell."

"Okay, I've got you. We're going to get you checked out."

"Where was the explosion?"

"Down the hall. If you'd have gone another twenty feet, I don't think you and I would be having a conversation right now. You're damn lucky."

"My dog. Gunner!" Panic ripped up Logan's aching spinal column, and he tried to sit up.

"Whoa—don't move. Your K9 is right here. I checked him over. And he seems fine. He must have already ducked into the office doorway when the bomb exploded."

"Thank God." Logan's chest clamped tight against his efforts to breathe. "Anyone else hurt?"

"I don't think so, unless there was someone ahead of you searching this hallway?"

"No. Just me and Gunner in this hall. No civilians?"

"Not sure. We'll do a search and send the robots in to check it out."

Robots... Addison... Logan drifted off.

Dog tongue. A wet, sandpaper-sensation he knew well, slobbered all over his hand. Logan's mouth eased into a smile.

"Logan?" Addison's voice floated through his head. "Logan?" Louder.

Logan blinked his eyes open and tried to focus on the concerned hazel orbs staring into his face. "Addison?" It took a minute before reality sifted its way into his brain. He opened his eyes wider and glanced around his surroundings before he moved to sit up.

Two pairs of hands pressed his shoulders back. Men from the bomb unit team... *his team*. "Am I in the hospital?"

Miller answered, "Yes. Don't sit up. You need to take it slowly."

"Maybe, but I don't need to be taking up a bed. Get me out of here."

Addison's eyes rolled. "You'll be out of here in no time, but the doctor needs to check you out fully. They want to keep you overnight."

"The explosion. Was anyone hurt?"

"Besides you, you mean?" Addison smirked at him. "We don't believe so, but they haven't finished searching yet. The bomb went off two offices down the hall from where you were. K9 teams are checking for secondary devices now, so we thought we'd come check on you before our part of the investigation gets underway."

Logan's head screamed in pain. He closed his eyes against a wave of nausea. Saliva that tasted like rusty tin flooded the back of his mouth.

Miller held Logan's helmet up for him to see. "The collision cracked the back of your headgear all the way through. Good thing you had this on. This could have been your skull."

"Explains the headache." Logan tried to smile, but his mouth stretched into a grimace that jabbed his bruised brain.

Addison rested her hand on his forearm. "Doc says he thinks you're fine except for a serious concussion and some deep bruising on your back. You have a cut on your face, but it didn't need stitches. It's incredible you didn't break anything." She leaned close and studied his face. "Looks like you'll end up with an impressive shiner too. As I said, they're keeping you overnight. Then, if all stays well, you can go home. Harriet is making all sorts of plans to take care of you."

"Oh, no." He started to laugh, but he flinched at the movement and let the chuckle die in his throat. "So, she's okay? She wasn't in surgery or anything?"

"No. Harriet's fine. When I found her, she was making friends with an older gentleman with a walker. You might have some competition for her heart now." She squeezed his arm. "Listen, we're gonna get out of here and let you rest. Jennings is going to take Gunner to spend the night at the K9 facility. The vet has already checked him out, and he's one-hundred percent good-to-go."

Logan snapped his fingers, and Gunner's muzzle wiggled up onto the bed. Gratitude for his uninjured dog lapped at his heart. "That's because you're a smart dog, right Gun? You got out of the way just in time. I should have stayed closer to you." He ran his finger's over Gunner's head. A comforting warmth coursed through his chest. *Yeah, I'm way past not connecting with this pup.*

Addison moved away, and Logan grabbed her hand as it slid by his. "Thanks for being here."

Miller stared at them. First at Logan and then Addison. He mumbled something about the elevator, and he and the other agent left the room.

"Of course. You're part of our team."

"And thanks for watching out for Harriet."

A gentle smile graced Addison's lips. "See you tomorrow, tough guy. Be nice to the nurses."

"I'll try."

CHAPTER 24

Addison drove back to the explosion site. She pressed past the mob of news reporters, ignoring their questions. Shoving her hands into a pair of thin rubber gloves, she took up a clip-board and signed into the site. After slipping under the perimeter security tape, she checked in with the incident commander.

"Have they have completed the search for secondary devices?"

"Yes, ma'am. We have released most of the scene for search and rescue. All except for the part of the wreckage that is still standing. Structural engineers are assessing that section for stability now."

"Rescue? Did they find victims?" Addison's belly clenched. "I thought the hospital staff evacuated the building."

"There is evidence of human remains where we believe the seat of the explosion was. Possibly the bomber."

"Maybe." Addison didn't think so, remembering the woman searchers discovered at the center of the blast at the mall. "Where are you in the investigation?"

"The forensic specialist and the medical examiner are

at the location of the remains. Investigators have lined out the search grid across the rest of the site." The commander pointed to his left. "The evidence tents are over there."

"Is there a list of all the witnesses?"

"Yes, but so far no one seems to remember seeing or hearing anything unusual."

"I need a specific register of all employees working in the administrative wing. Not just today either. I want a full list of everyone who's worked there in the past week."

"I'll have it sent to you."

"Thanks, Commander. Where can you best use my help right now?" Addison held her hand above her eyes to block the sun as she surveyed the rubble. Several police K9 teams searched the area inside the grid, along with members of the FBI bomb squad.

"Best to check with the search team leader."

"Okay, will do as soon as I talk with the M.E." Addison picked her way over to the center of the bomb site. She detected nothing that appeared human-like at the scene.

"Agent Thorne, good to have you here."

"Yeah, sorry I left. An agent on my team was near the blast. He's in the hospital, but he'll be okay. I just got back from there."

"Glad to hear that. He's a lucky man. Unfortunately, we've found evidence of someone who wasn't so lucky."

The three of them crouched down, and the M.E. pointed out some splintered bone fragments among the shattered brick and framing. Addison took several photos with her phone.

"Amazing find, gentlemen. Does anyone know the identity of this victim? Are you sure there is just one?"

"The office belonged to a hospital administrator, named Jacob Price. We're assuming this is either him, or the bomber. We'll learn more after we get the evidence to the lab. We can hope for a DNA match."

"Will you please keep me in the loop if you identify the body?"

"Of course."

"Strange, though, don't you think?"

"What?" The M.E. glanced at her over his shoulder.

"There were hours between receiving the bomb threat and the actual explosion. Why didn't this person evacuate?" She tapped her lips with her fingertips as she considered the situation. "Thanks, guys. I look forward to seeing your reports."

Addison made her way across the site and approached the officer overseeing the grid search. After introducing herself, the cop directed her to a section that needed another searcher. She nodded to the official sketch artist creating his rendering of the scene before she took a video and several photos of her own.

She handed the artist her business card. "Will you be sure to send a copy of your sketch directly to my email?" She hoped to have at least that much to go on before they officially released the visually recorded evidence to the myriad investigative agencies, which could take hours—even days.

"Of course."

"Have they already taken all the official photos and video of this area?"

"Yes, and I'm just about through, too. I'll get out of your way."

"No problem, and thanks ahead of time for the copy of your sketch." They shook hands, and Addison continued on the path to her assigned grid section.

Her phone buzzed, and she answered. "Thorne here."

"It's Miller. Remember the lady who came into HQ the

other day worried that someone was targeting her group of high school friends?"

"Yeah?"

"Well, we just got a call from her husband. They heard about the explosion on Channel 9 News and wanted to know if there were any victims. The news is reporting that a person in the administration building was killed and, low and behold, one of Mrs. Carlson's high school friends is an administrator at that hospital. A guy named Price. Jacob Price."

"Incredible." Addison kicked a small stone aside. "I'm on my way to HQ. Notify SAC Sanchez and bring Megan Carlson in. Without a doubt, we can officially stop suspecting terrorists." Addison rubbed her mouth with the back of her hand and steadied herself before continuing. "Our unsub is a serial bomber. Searchers found remnants of a body near where the bomb detonated. The M.E. is studying the trace remains, and though he hasn't positively identified the body yet, the building's schematics show the seat of the bomb was inside the office of one Jacob Price."

The next day, Addison sat on the edge of the chair eating a turkey and Havarti cheese sandwich at her computer in the bomb squad office. Her desk phone rang, and she clicked on the speaker to include her team on the call.

Agent Cameron filled them in on the investigation from their end. "We've just received a phone call from a man whose son told him he got a hundred dollars from a random guy to hide the fake bomb in the custodian's closet at the high school."

Her pulse kicked up. "Can the kid identify the man?"

"No. The guy contacted him by text. The tech lab went through his phone and confirms the text came from a burner phone. They transferred the money and the package through a blind drop at a rec-center. We have a crew there now looking for trace evidence, but it's been too long and we don't expect them to find much. Tech analysts are scouring the kid's social media and email accounts just in case, but I doubt they'll find anything useful."

"Probably not." Addison closed her eyes and let her frustration roll off her shoulders. "What about the money? Does he still have it? Was it in an envelope?"

"No such luck. He spent the money taking his friends out and ditched the envelope." Cameron continued, "We did locate Sykes's apartment though, and called S.W.A.T. in to check it out. The guy lived in an apartment above a barn on the outskirts of Commerce City. We talked to the landlord, and the last time he paid rent was two months ago. She said she was in the process of evicting him."

"Has she seen Sykes lately? Was she able to give you a description?"

"She hasn't seen him, but she agreed to talk with the sketch artist this afternoon. We should have a likeness soon. When we got to the apartment, the place was deserted. Trash overflowed the bin, there was sour milk in the fridge—the place was filthy, but there was no sign of Sykes."

"Damn it. Was the landlord able to tell you where the guy works, or any other history?"

"When he signed the lease, Sykes used his mother as a reference. The address he provided for her is apparently the home he grew up in. It was where he lived while he was in high school.

"That sounds promising." She set her sandwich on her desk and licked a dollop of mayonnaise from her thumb.

"Except we can't find her."

"Have you checked out the house?"

"No one answered when we went. We're currently

waiting on a warrant, which is difficult if not impossible because the house isn't owned by the suspect. Anyway, we also found out that Sykes worked at a place called Fertilegenix. It's some kind of fertilizer manufacturer in northeast Denver."

"That doesn't sound good."

"No. And he stopped showing up for work about a month ago, too."

"What was his job?"

"He worked on the dock. The company swears they reported no missing inventory."

"It could be true. So far, Sykes has only used black powder and C-4. Of course, that doesn't mean that he won't escalate and involve chemicals in his next explosion."

"Let's hope there's not another event."

"Let's find him before he has a chance."

Benjamin sat back in his off-kilter recliner, sipping on a sour beer and staring at the television. He raised the volume of the broadcast. A woman with shiny brown hair stared out at him, reporting the tragic bombing at University Memorial Hospital. Video clips of the aftermath flashed onto the screen, and a smile wormed its way across his lips as he viewed the results of his assault. There was no mention of a victim, but Benjamin was certain that was due to the complete annihilation of the man.

He thought back to the terror radiating from Jacob's round eyes above the duct-tape covering his mouth and nose when he realized it was time to pay the piper, and he chuckled. After securing Price's arms and legs to his chair, he'd placed the bomb on the desk, mere feet in front of the man. Jacob could barely breathe from under the tape and

Benjamin hoped the bomb went off before he suffocated, but he'd never know for sure.

Benjamin's printer hummed and clicked as it printed a recent photo of Jacob Price. He taped the picture on his wall next to the picture of Nicole.

The TV screen filled with the pretty plastic face once again. "This, just in." Benjamin slid his hand down over his crotch, and his skin prickled in anticipation of the additional news. "The FBI has asked for anyone with any information regarding this man, to please call the number at the bottom of the screen." A 1-800 number scrolled repeatedly along the lower edge of the picture.

Benjamin's face—a photo of him in high school—flashed onto the TV. "What the fu—" His jaw dropped as he stared at his own younger image. "How the hell—?" His heart fluttered against his ribs like a frantic pigeon trying to escape a trap. His hand balled into a fist and he hammered his knuckles against his skull. *How did the cops find me? They haven't mentioned any of the gang, and I've been so careful. I left no trace!*

He was running out of time as it was, and this compressed his schedule. If they had his photo, the FBI could locate him easily. He had to finish his mission before that happened. Benjamin had to move up his plot for revenge. He pressed a few keys on his computer, and the printer groaned to life. When the figure of his most important target finished printing, he reverently touched the face with his fingertips. The image—the cocky expression—had dominated his thoughts for over a decade. "It's now time for my grand finale."

CHAPTER 25

It had only been two days, but Logan was weary of resting alone in his apartment. He hadn't realized how many screens he used until the doctors ordered him not to use any. That meant no computer, iPad, or e-reader, and no TV. They also restricted him from reading any text, playing word games, and working puzzles. *What the hell am I supposed to do all day?*

Sitting and staring into space gave him too much time to think, and that always took him to his time in the Army. In the last seconds of his dog's life, Lobo had been sniffing an area they had previously cleared that morning. Logan had let his dog off his leash to stretch and relax. That's when it happened. Logan's memory of the incident slammed into slow motion, pausing at the moment he heard the click. Lobo heard it at the same second. The best dog in the world froze in position and swiveled his head toward Logan, then calmly sat down in place. Logan had screamed for the unit to take cover and took two running strides toward Lobo when the land-mine blew. He never broke eye contact with his dog until the end.

The force of the explosion hurled Logan thirty feet. Along with Lobo, the blast killed two men who were closer than Logan had been. Days later, Logan woke in a German hospital. He'd never see Lobo again. There was nothing left even to bury, and it was all Logan's fault. He was the one who had cleared the area. He was the one who gave the go-ahead. Now two soldiers and a decorated military service dog were dead. The pain from their loss and his guilt were harder to overcome than any of the physical injuries he sustained.

Logan wished for months that the bomb would have killed him alongside his dog and the men from his unit. He missed their memorial services while his body healed, and he went through the motions of recovery. Though, his heart and mind were slower to mend. Eventually, the Army sent Logan home with a medical discharge. He hid out for half a year at his family's ranch in Wyoming, hardly eating, and drinking way too much.

One day, his sister brought him a package that came for him in the mail from the United States Armed Services. It was a photograph of him and Lobo together. His beautiful dog stared out at him from the frame with his quizzical eyes and goofy grin. Logan took a hard look at how he'd been wasting his life and was ashamed. After that, Logan got himself back in shape and applied to the FBI Academy. When they accepted him into the academy, Logan knew he had Lobo to thank, and even more so when the FBI offered him a spot in their K9 program after that.

The photo with Lobo became his most prized possession. The only personal belonging he traveled with. That and Lobo's spare dog-tags that he carried with him every day in his front pocket. The picture sat on the table next to his bed encouraging him to work hard and make their time together mean something. He'd received orders to Denver and there, Jennings paired him up with Gunner. Another remarkable dog, but Logan held himself back from bonding with his new partner. He wouldn't survive losing another dog. And in this line of work, it happened.

Logan had to do something to get his mind off his past, so he picked up his phone and called his sister, smirking to himself about how pissed she'd be if she knew she was his very last resort.

"What's wrong?" Caitlyn's straight-to-the-point greeting showed how rarely they spoke, but at least they *were* speaking—unlike Caitlyn and their older brother. Logan never understood exactly what happened between them. It was some misunderstanding that Dylan refused to rectify—something about property or inheritance. Caitlyn tried to talk to their brother about it several times, but finally she gave up.

Logan closed his eyes against the daylight that still induced headaches. "Why does there have to be something wrong? Maybe I just want to visit."

"Yeah, right. You only call when something is wrong. Are you okay?"

He chuckled. "Okay, you're right. I'm going to be fine, but a blast wave threw me against some bricks and I banged my head. I've got a concussion so they're making me lie around doing nothing."

"How bad?"

"I'm on sick leave. They'll restrict duty until I can prove I'm fine. Which I am."

"Hm." Caitlyn mumbled something Logan couldn't hear. "Sorry, just getting Ren into the truck. I heard about the bombings in Denver. I can't believe you didn't tell me you were involved."

"I'm telling you now. Anyway, how's Renegade's training coming?" Logan had helped his sister choose and begin training her German Shepherd-Malinois mix during the low time between the Army and going to the FBI Academy.

"He's doing great. He's so smart. Sometimes too smart for his own good." Her voice softened whenever she talked about Ren. "How's your new dog? Gunner, right?"

"Yeah. He's outstanding. Gunner is staying at the K9 facility while I'm in forced lock-down."

"Stop complaining. Be glad they want to take care of your brain and that you have the best care for your dog while you're down."

"I guess. How are things at the ranch?"

"Mom and Dad are traveling again. They're in Cancún, enjoying retirement and soaking up the sun. Otherwise, things are the same. Dylan is still being an ass."

"Still won't talk to you about why he's so mad?"

"No. I mean, I think I know why. I sent that email, and he read a bunch of crap into it that wasn't there. He's so stubborn."

"You can't hear the tone in an email, Cate."

"I know, I know. I've tried to talk to him in person too, but he just grunts and walks away." The engine of her F150 roared. "When are you coming up for a visit?"

"I don't know. I'm the new guy, and I won't have vacation until next summer."

"Have you met anyone?"

"Have you?" Logan snapped back.

"Whoa, defensive much? Must mean you have! What's her name?"

"There isn't anyone, Cate. I'm just sick of you asking me that all the time." Addison's image crept into Logan's mind, but he wasn't about to confess any feelings he might have to his little sister. She'd pester him all year about it. He reached for a t-shirt crumpled next to him on the floor and covered his eyes with the soft cloth to block out the light glowing through his eyelids. "How about you?"

"There are no interesting men up here in Hulett."

"You should come down here and visit me."

"In Denver? No way. Too much... too much everything."

Logan laughed. His kid sister had never been one for the city lights. He always figured she'd settle down with some rancher to raise beef and train dogs. "When do Mom and Dad get back?"

"Right before Thanksgiving. It's gonna be real chatty and nice having dinner with Dylan. Are you sure you can't come up? Even for the holiday?"

"I doubt it."

"Try."

"I'll let you know."

"I'm going to plan on you. So you better figure it out." Caitlyn laughed, and Logan's heart lifted a little with the sound.

Gradually getting back to work, Logan rested on a bench in the K9 training yard. Gunner sat next to him, panting. They'd completed a one-mile run. Usually a breeze, but after his head injury, it seemed more like a marathon. Logan was on a restricted training program until the doctor determined he had fully healed from his physical injuries and he attended at least one office visit with the Agency shrink. For now, he hoped to maintain some of his strength.

A shadow blocked the warmth of the sun on his back, and Logan turned to investigate.

"How're you feeling, Reed?" Clay Jennings's wide shoulders cast the cool shade. "Are you cleared for running?" Logan shielded his eyes from the sunshine blazing behind the agent.

"I'm good. Just waiting to get the pat on the head so I can go back to work."

"You probably shouldn't be jarring your brain against your skull by running."

"I'm taking it easy." Logan's head didn't agree as it pounded in time with his pulse. It was possible he might have started back a little too soon but sitting around was driving him crazy.

"Be sure you do." Jennings leaned his hip against the bench. "Sounds to me like you were a lucky S.O.B."

"Yeah, but Gunner was even luckier."

"Nah, he's just smarter." Jennings's teasing grin drew a responsive smile from Logan. "Listen, I'm getting married next Saturday. It's a simple ceremony. El, my fiancée, doesn't want a big thing. I thought maybe you'd like to come? We're inviting everyone in the K9 unit."

"Congratulations." Logan rose to shake Jennings's hand. "Where's the wedding?"

"On Flagstaff Mountain, up in Boulder. Just a casual service, then afterwards we're having dinner at the Boulderado Hotel. You're welcome to bring a plus one."

"Thanks, but don't feel you have to invite me just because I work here. I don't even know your fiancée."

"Don't worry, Reed. I'm only inviting you because I want Gunner to come, and you're his ride." Jennings clapped Logan's shoulder. "I had to get special permission to have all K9s at the hotel, but since they are police K9s, they gave me the okay."

Logan laughed and turned to see Kendra Dean with her long brown ponytail swinging from the back of an FBI baseball cap, and K9 Annie jogging next to her headed toward them.

"Hey! Welcome back. I heard you almost got blown up." She bent over and braced her arms on her knees, trying to catch her breath.

"Hi Dean, just about. How was your run?" Logan asked.

"Good." She guzzled a drink from a bottle of water.

Jennings stroked Annie's silky ears. "I invited Reed to the wedding."

Dean wiped her mouth with the back of her wrist. "Nice. Who are you going to bring?"

Logan shook his head. "I'll probably come on my own."

"No date?" Dean raised a dark brow.

"Besides Gunner, you mean?" Logan shrugged. "I haven't been in Denver long enough to meet anyone."

Jennings cocked his head. "What about asking Thorne?"

"Yeah. That's a great idea," Dean chimed in. "You guys are friends, right?"

Logan's phone buzzed, and he excused himself, walking with Gunner to the shade of a massive cottonwood tree dressed in yellow leaves for fall.

"Reed," Addison sounded excited. "Where are you?"

"I'm at the K9 facility, why?"

"I wanted to fill you in on the bomb investigation. Did you hear about the victim they found? There was trace evidence of a man in the office where the device detonated."

Logan gripped his phone. "I hadn't heard." The news hit him like a bag of bricks. If only he'd gotten there sooner. Maybe the guy would still be alive. He rubbed his eyes with his thumb and middle finger.

"Yeah, and the victim who was killed has been identified as Jacob Price—another one of the kids in the high school group that bullied Benjamin Sykes. The hospital personnel had plenty of time to evacuate, yet they found fragments of this guy all over the spot where his office used to be."

"Did Mrs. Carlson confirm that he was part of their group of friends?"

"She's the one who told us. She called in before we even had his remains DNA tested. She knew."

"Is she considered a suspect? She seems to know a lot about the victims."

"We're not taking the possibility off the table, but we don't currently believe her to be the bomber. We think it is the guy she claims her group bullied."

"I saw his picture on the news. You're sure it was him?"

"Not a hundred percent, but we have an A.P.B. out on him. We need to bring him in for questioning."

"Listen, I'm done here. I thought I'd swing by the squad."

"Not to do any work. You're on restriction."

"Yeah, yeah. I'll see you in a few." Logan clicked off the call. "I'm outta here."

Jennings tipped his chin toward him. "Let me know about the wedding. We need a count."

"Will do." Logan raised his hand in farewell and left Jennings and Dean discussing a missing person's case.

Logan and Gunner entered the squad room. Addison stood behind Miller, leaning over his shoulder as they both studied his computer screen.

"What's up?" Logan joined them.

Addison's dark spiky curls bobbed when she pivoted toward him. A brilliant smile brightened her face and caused an uncomfortable knot to form inside Logan's gut. He rubbed the spot with his fist.

"Hey. We're trying to figure out where the unsub purchased the bomb material he used at the hospital."

"Were the components the same or different from those at the mall?"

"Different. His bombs are escalating right along with him. First, the threat was false, but there was black powder explosive residue found on a fake bomb. Then, the second threat was false in one location and real in the other. That bomb was made with a liquid explosive inside of pipe bombs. This time, there was one very real threat, and the unsub constructed the bomb with C-4."

"Well, that explains my headache." Logan murmured, before peering over Miller's shoulder at the monitor.

"Exactly. The first set of explosives are easy enough to get ahold of, but C-4? It might be military ordinance. We called down to Ft. Carson. They're sending up military explosive investigators. If the bomber isn't in the Army, he may have purchased the plastic from someone who is."

Logan released a long breath. "And he's not done, is he? This could get even uglier."

"It will, unless we find him first." Addison peered into Logan's face. "Your black eye looks almost healed, just a little green around the socket. How are you feeling?"

"Like I should be back at work."

Miller chuffed. "Why don't you relax and enjoy the time off? Hell, you're getting paid."

"Paid to do what? Watch TV?" Logan straddled a chair and Gunner laid at his feet. "No, thanks."

"I thought you weren't supposed to be watching anything on a screen." Addison scowled at him. "Plus, I'll get my ass chewed if the boss finds out you're here. So…" She gestured toward the door. "Come on, I'll walk you out."

Gunner scrambled up to follow her. "Hey, you're my dog, remember?" Logan gripped the end of Gunner's tail and gave a gentle tug. He followed Addison and Gunner outside to the fresh autumn afternoon.

"You're sure you're doing okay? Your brain isn't too jumbled?"

"I feel fine. My head pounded a bit after I went on a short run this morning, so I'm taking it easy."

“Probably shouldn’t be running yet, you think?”

“Maybe. Hey, listen, um…” A wave of nervous jitters flowed through him unexpectedly. Logan’s pulse sputtered and kicked up a notch.

“What is it?” Addison’s brows bunched in a concerned expression.

Logan shook his head hard to clear it and regretted the move. His fingers flew to his temple.

“Logan, are you okay? What’s happening?”

“I’m fine, I…” Logan stared down at his boots. “Listen, you wouldn’t want to go to Clay Jennings’s wedding with me tomorrow night, would you? He invited me today and wants me to bring a plus one. Sorry for the short notice. Jennings suggested I ask you. It’s not a date or anything, just…” Logan peered up at her from underneath his lashes.

Addison stepped back, and her brows scrunched together. “You scared me, you jerk. I thought something was wrong with your head.”

“Sorry. I shouldn’t have shaken it so hard.”

She smirked at him. “Well, thanks for asking me. And since it’s not a date…” Addison laughed. “I’d love to go. Where is it?”

“They’re getting married up on Flagstaff. It’s a sunset wedding.”

“How romantic. Chilly—but romantic.”

“Jennings said it was casual—only a few people. Dinner at the Boulderado Hotel after.”

“Sounds perfect.”

His mouth curled into a smile and a thousand tiny bubbles tickled the inner wall of his chest. *It’s not a date, idiot.*

CHAPTER 26

Addison returned to the squad room, careful to erase any evidence of the silly smile she knew had tilted her lips. She wondered at her sense of giddiness. Logan was a friend—a co-worker. He'd only invited her to the wedding because Jennings told him to. That thought stung a little. Would he have thought to invite her if his boss hadn't basically ordered him to? Probably not. *I'm such a dork.*

Pushing back her shoulders, Addison lifted her chin and marched in to take her place behind Miller's shoulder. "Have you started tracking down the last guy on the list yet?"

Miller looked up at her from his seat with a knowing smirk. "Did you get Reed sent on his way?"

Addison couldn't prevent the heat creeping into her cheeks, but she could shut Miller down. She glared at him. "Did you locate Tyler Brookes yet? Or do I need to assign someone else?"

He almost laughed, but bit down on his lips in the nick of time. Still the merriment in his eyes danced on. "It took a while, but I finally found him. He works for Senator

Reynolds as a Communications Director. Only he's proving good at avoiding all of my communication."

"If he won't answer your call, then we'll go to his office. It's *his* life we're trying to save."

"I'm headed there now."

"Wait for me, I want to meet a guy who doesn't care if someone is trying to kill him."

"Let's go."

Miller drove and Addison worked his car's navigation system. It took a little over twenty minutes to get to the heart of downtown Denver. "Brookes is at the senator's office, right?"

"I think so, but either way I figure that's the most logical place to start." Miller clicked on the turn signal.

They parked in a multi-level garage on the same street as the government building that housed the senator's office. The building security guard lugged himself out of his chair behind the bamboo and chrome desk. He huffed over to them and demanded their IDs, then seemed to deflate when they showed him they were federal agents with the FBI.

"I'll call up to let his office know you're on your way."

"Don't bother. We'll let them know when we get there." Addison watched him from her position in front of the bank of elevators. Before they stepped into the compartment, she observed the guard lift the phone from its cradle—no doubt calling up a warning.

The bell dinged, and the stainless-steel doors slid open to an office suite that took up the entire fourteenth floor. They stepped out into a space with gleaming dark wood floors and floral-scented air. The receptionist, a young woman in her mid-twenties, wearing a suit that echoed back to Chanel, stepped around a tall desk boasting matching crystal vases filled with white roses—no doubt compliments of the tax dollars paid by the good people of Colorado. "Good afternoon. How may I help you?"

Addison and Miller flashed her their FBI badges. Addison said, "We're looking for Mr. Tyler Brookes. Will you please take us to his office?"

A Stepford Wife smile pasted itself onto the woman's face. "I'm sorry, Mr. Brookes is unavailable at the moment. May I have him call you?"

"No." Addison placed her hands on her hips "We are here in an attempt to save his life from a serial bomber. Hopefully, we'll end up saving all your lives at the same time, but we can't do any of that if he won't see us. Tell us where his office is. Now!"

The receptionist's face registered her alarm, and her eyes darted back to a row of offices along the outside wall. No doubt trying to decide whether facing an explosion was better or worse than her employer's wrath. She twisted her engagement ring around and around before she finally pointed them in the right direction.

Addison led the way. The minute she and Miller left the reception area, the young woman called Brookes's office to warn him they were on their way back. When they entered his office, Brookes deliberately set the phone receiver back in its cradle and raised an imperious brow at them.

He regarded them with a stony expression, but he did not stand. His blond, perfectly groomed, politico hair remained shellacked in place. He wore an impeccable Armani suit tailored to fit his athletic-club frame and a red power tie, both designed to intimidate. Neither did anything for Addison. "Is all this drama truly necessary?" he scoffed.

If it wasn't for the others in his building, Addison would have been tempted to leave this pompous ass to his own fate. "Yes, we believe it is, Mr. Brookes. Our investigation leads us to believe that you might very well be the target of a serial bomber. We are trying to save your life."

"Come, come. Why would a serial bomber be interested in me? The senator, perhaps, but me *specifically*?"

Miller edged his way forward. "Yes, you specifically. Do you remember a person named Benjamin Sykes?"

Tyler Brookes perched his chin between his thumb and forefinger, feigning a "trying to recall" expression, but a telltale flush reddened his neck above his snug collar and crept up to his ears. "No, I can't say as that name sounds familiar."

Addison leaned toward Brookes, bracing her hands on the edge of his desk. She lowered her voice. "Well, he remembers you. You and the group of kids who bullied him in high school. We believe he was instrumental in the recent mall and hospital bombings. Do your remember Nicole Grey?"

Brookes kept his expression bland, giving nothing away easily.

"How about Jacob Price?" Miller's voice rose from behind her.

Brookes shook his head and ran his fingers down his jaw, striking what he must have thought looked like an intellectual pose. He wasn't fooling anyone.

Addison leaned closer. "Come, come," she mocked. "Are you expecting us to believe you don't remember your best friend and your girlfriend from high school? Are you really that dense?"

Anger sparked in Brookes's eyes then, but he held his temper. "Now that you place them in context, I do remember them. But I have had no contact with anyone from high school since the day we graduated."

"Just because it was easy for you to forget, doesn't mean it was for others." Miller glared at him and lifted a framed photo of Brookes posed with the perfect young family from the desk. He tilted the picture for Brookes to look at. "You're willing to put them at risk?"

Addison grew weary of the resistance. "Look, Mr. Brookes. You may not think this is serious, but we know otherwise. We are here to warn you in an attempt to protect you. But not just you, you selfish son-of-a-bitch." She pointed at the frame Miller held. "Your family, along with everyone who works in this building, could be in danger right along with you."

"When do you imagine the bomber will attack?" Brookes glanced at the gold watch on his wrist.

"If we knew the exact time and place, we wouldn't need to warn you, would we?" Miller slapped the frame down on the desk face up in front of Brookes.

"I only ask, because my family and I are joining the senator in Washington for the next four weeks. We leave tomorrow afternoon. Does that help?"

"It might help you, but again, there are other people who work here to consider. Remember them?" Addison turned on her heel and stalked out of the office. Miller followed, slamming Tyler Brookes's door on his way out.

"What a prick." Miller murmured.

Addison pressed the elevator button. "Contact the building superintendent. Put him on alert in case we need to evacuate."

"On it. Should we assign a detail to Brookes and his family in Washington?"

"He'll be with the senator who has his own security. Alert the senator's team. But I doubt Sykes would go all the way to Washington. He's waited this long. I'm betting he'll wait until Brookes gets back to Denver."

"That's if he knows he's gone."

Addison chewed on her bottom lip. "He'll know. I'm certain that the other two victims were restrained at the bombsites. Why else wouldn't they have evacuated with everyone else?"

"Makes sense." Miller followed Addison into the elevator and waited for the doors to close. "They are definite targets. The bomber isn't interested in hurting people he considers innocent or he wouldn't warn us ahead of time."

"No. He's obviously targeting this group of high school friends, but he's doing huge damage to the locations as well..."

"What are you thinking?"

"It's just that he could blow up their cars or shoot them. Why is this guy bombing public buildings and basically destroying them? It's a bit overkill, don't you think? What is he trying to say?"

CHAPTER 27

Benjamin stood, tucked deep inside behind the coats hanging in the entrance closet of Tyler Brookes's mansion-like house. A thin layer of perspiration covered his body and his skin itched. The rich scent of leather emanating from the bomber jacket suspended in front of him filled the cramped space, making it hard to breathe. He'd broken into the home that afternoon when Mrs. Brookes left to pick up her children from their friend's. Tyler's wife had made it easy for Benjamin by leaving the sliding glass door open in the back, with only a flimsy screen barring his entry. When he snuck into the house, he counted six suitcases waiting near the front door. The family was obviously planning to travel somewhere soon. Benjamin would have to choose his moment carefully or miss his opportunity altogether.

Thirty minutes later, the Brookes children scampered into the house, chattering about their day. Their mother, following them in, hollered for her kids to stop running through the living room. The doorknob to the closet twisted. Benjamin held his breath and pressed his head back against the wall. His pulse spiked, sending sharp darts up through his scalp. She opened the door about six inches and Benjamin tightened his grip on the hilt of the hunting knife he'd brought with him. Her slender arm reached in for a hanger to slide her coat onto. With her face aimed toward the kitchen, she called out. "Get your homework done. Daddy will be home soon, and we have a flight to catch."

Without looking, she pushed her jacket inside, stabbing the darkness until the hook of the hanger caught on the rail. The soft woolen shoulder of her pea coat brushed across Benjamin's cheek as she closed the door. He let out a great breath, his heartbeat exploding in his ears.

Not long after that, Tyler's voice called out from the direction of the front entry. "I'm home! Everyone ready to go?"

"Hi honey. The kids are all packed. They're just finishing up their school work now."

Benjamin imagined her kissing Tyler during the pause in conversation. His mind slid to Tyler kissing Nicole and his stomach clenched.

"Can't they do their homework on the plane? We've got to leave."

Their voices faded as they moved to the back of the house; the sound deadened by the thick coats in the closet. Benjamin blinked as sweat trickled into his eyes. *How am I gonna get Tyler separated from his family?* He didn't want the whole family to pay for Tyler's sins. Especially the children. They were innocent. Benjamin flexed his fingers and re-gripped his knife. He chewed on his lip. *I might not have a choice.*

Tyler herded his kids from the kitchen to the entryway. "Get your coats on and take your luggage out to the car. I'll be out in a few minutes and then we'll take off."

"Can I get my teddy?" his daughter's small voice pleaded. "He's in my room."

"I'll get him and bring him with me. You two go get in the car."

Benjamin heard Tyler's heavy footsteps running up the stairs above the closet.

"Hannah, do you have everything?" Tyler called from upstairs.

His wife answered from the front hall. "We're all set. Meet you outside." She left, and the front door closed behind her.

Benjamin was alone with Tyler in the house. He opened the closet door and listened. Tyler was still upstairs. Benjamin crept behind the wall next to the staircase and waited for his enemy to descend. Heavy footsteps bounded downward, and Tyler paused to lift his own luggage. When he bent for his cases, Benjamin came up behind him and stuck the point of his knife into the skin above Tyler's kidney.

"Don't move."

Tyler stilled and slowly raised his hands. "Who are you? What do you want?"

Benjamin retrieved a wad of cotton material from his pocket and pressed it into Tyler's palm. "Stuff this in your mouth."

"Look, you can have whatever you want. Just—"

"I said stuff that in your mouth." Benjamin pushed the point further into Tyler's back, piercing the skin.

"Okay, okay." Tyler did as he was told.

Benjamin handed him a roll of duct tape. "Tape this over your lips and around your head, two times."

Tyler's eyes rolled to the side, trying to get a glimpse of his attacker while he wrapped his own gag around the back of his neck.

"Tighter!" Benjamin jerked the tape roll away and made

another rotation around Tyler's head. "Now, put your hands together."

Tyler hesitated, and Benjamin prodded him with the knife once again. He pulled a black knit hat over Tyler's head, down over his eyes before taping Tyler's wrists together, wrapping the tape all the way up over his fingers. Tyler tried to jerk away, but Benjamin rewarded him with a quick slice across his waist. The wadded cotton dulled his cry.

"Don't be stupid, Tyler." Benjamin whispered into the man's ear. "We need to go. If your family comes in looking for you before we leave, they'll pay the price. You don't want that, do you?"

Tyler shook his head and allowed Benjamin to guide him blindly out the back door. They crossed the yard to the gate Benjamin had snuck through earlier. His car was in the alleyway behind the grand house. He opened the trunk. "Get in." Benjamin shoved his captive into the hatch and slammed the lid. With as much calm as he could muster, he got in the car and drove toward downtown Denver.

It was dark when Benjamin drove into a parking garage near the Denver Capitol Building. He had to hurry. Timing was everything. In twenty minutes, they would lock the Capitol doors to visitors. He waited for a red compact car to drive past before he jumped out and opened the trunk. It stank like sweat and fear.

"Get out." Benjamin yanked on Tyler's arm to rush him. He draped an overcoat on Tyler's shoulders, buttoned it up the front, and stuffed the empty arms into the pockets. Wrapping a scarf around Tyler's neck and face, Benjamin disguised the gag. When he snatched the knit hat off of Tyler's head, the man stared at him, and his eyes rounded with fear.

"Remember me?" Benjamin sneered. "We're going into

the Capitol. Don't forget, I have a knife and it's long enough to stab you clear through, so don't try anything. Got it?"

Tyler nodded. Tears hovered on his lower eyelids.

With one arm around Tyler's waist and the other pressing the blade into his side, Benjamin guided Tyler toward the golden domed building. They entered through a staff door. A guard down the hall noticed them, but when he recognized Tyler, he waved.

"Good evening, Mr. Brookes," he called. "Go on through." The guard returned to his duty of escorting tourists out the front doors.

"Down the stairs." Benjamin pushed Tyler toward the stairway. His captor grunted and shook his head. "What's wrong? You're remembering what happened down there all those years ago, aren't you?"

Tyler resisted and swung his chin around to the guard, but he was busy and not paying any attention to the two men. Benjamin jabbed the knife into Tyler's lower back. He screamed, but the gag and scarf absorbed the sound.

"Go down the stairs, Tyler." Benjamin shoved him, and Tyler stumbled, desperately trying to stay on his feet. They descended to the basement level where the public restrooms were. "You remember this place from our high school field trip, don't you, Tyler?" Benjamin hissed in the man's ear. Tyler choked back a sob. "I do too. I've thought of this room every day for the past ten years. I brought you here to reminisce."

Benjamin wrenched the men's room door open and shoved Tyler inside. Tyler tripped and fell onto the floor. He pushed himself away from Benjamin with his feet until he pressed his back up against the far wall. Benjamin locked the door and strolled toward his captive. He yanked the hat from Tyler's head, leaving blond spikes poking out in all directions. The scarf and coat came off next.

. . .

In the rear corner of the room rested two lengths of a wooden broom handle Benjamin had cut and left there earlier in the day. He reached for the longer of the two pieces.

"Put your ankles together."

Tyler shook his head, his eyes brimming with fear. He kicked out at Benjamin.

Benjamin raised the wooden handle high and swung, cracking it against Tyler's shin. Tyler screamed into his gag. Tears and snot smeared together above the tape. "I said, hold your ankles together." Benjamin was wonderfully calm, completely in control. He'd dreamed of this moment—practiced it in his mind, over and over—and it was finally here. Everything was going just as he had planned. He raised the rod again and brought it down across Tyler's shoulder, eliciting another muffled yowl.

Weeping and trembling, Tyler held his ankles together and Benjamin bound them with more duct tape. Then he yanked Tyler's restrained hands down and taped them to his ankles, forcing the man's knees to bend up between his arms to his chin. Tyler struggled to breathe through his running nose.

Benjamin barked out a sarcastic laugh. "I know you'll enjoy what I'm going to do to you, Tyler. At least as much as I enjoyed it when you did it to me." He reached in and unclasped Tyler's belt and pants, then yanked them down. Tyler curled into himself, and Benjamin threaded the broom handle in through the crook of Tyler's left elbow, under his knees, and back out over the bend in his right arm, locking him in place. "Stay here. I'll be right back."

Decade old laughter echoed off the walls, making

Benjamin's skin crawl. He balled his fingers into fists and hit the sides of his head. "Shut up!" he screamed. Dragging his nails over his arms, he scratched furiously at what felt like hundreds of ants crawling on him. Benjamin struggled to unscrew the cover of a ventilation duct in the wall. He removed the supplies he'd hidden there earlier. Carefully, he lifted out a brick of C-4 rigged with a timer. He set the device on the floor five feet away from Tyler, but where he could easily see the digits tick by. Tyler's body jerked, and he moaned. Benjamin laughed, a high-pitched giggle lapping up Tyler's fear. "Time to pay the piper, Tyler. I'm sure you've heard... Karma is a bitch."

With his other supplies in hand, Benjamin unlocked the lavatory door and left the room. Outside, he laid his trap. He probably didn't need it, but he wasn't willing to take any chances. After he repaid Tyler for his abuse, he'd leave the man to contemplate his actions while watching the timer tick away the last hours and minutes of his life. He'd know exactly when the bomb would detonate and erase his existence. But just in case Tyler somehow got loose, he'd end up tripping the booby-trap at the door and blow himself up, anyway.

After Benjamin set the trap, he re-entered the bathroom. He glanced at himself in the mirror, almost not recognizing his own face with the wild, feral look hovering in his eyes. Feeling powerful, like he'd never felt before, he picked up the shorter end of the broom handle. He flailed it across Tyler's back and exposed buttocks, leaving red welts in his wake. Tyler screamed with each blow, and the muted sound was a symphony to Benjamin's ears.

Benjamin beat the rod against skin and bone over and over before doing to Tyler the unspeakable thing that Tyler had done to him in this very room ten years before. The day Jacob had held him bent over and Tyler assaulted him with the end of a mop handle. Their evil laughter bounced off the walls and echoed in his mind.

He meant every whip of the rod to be a retribution for the hundreds of degrading moments he'd had at Tyler's hand. Instead, with each stroke, vivid images of his personal humiliation played out in his mind. His memories stirred back to life, taunting him rather than bringing him relief.

Benjamin finally exhausted himself with his violence. His arms ached from the exertion and he dropped to his knees. Both men fell still. Tyler lay on the floor, whimpering, but not moving. His eyes staring at nothing. The glorious vengeance Benjamin expected to feel never came. His pulse didn't surge with the victory he craved. Instead, his heart was hollow, and he felt tragically unsatisfied. He pulled himself to his feet and threw up in the sink, his stomach acid sour in his mouth. His hand trembled as he wiped tears from his eyes.

He had become his own nightmare. Tears streamed down his face, and he wiped them on his sleeve. He peered down at Tyler and no longer saw a monster, but a scared boy. He saw himself.

"Goodbye, Tyler," Benjamin muttered. His head pounded—he failed to accomplish what he had come here for. He didn't feel any better. *Stupid, stupid, stupid.*

Tyler's eyes widened as they took in the timer attached to the explosive. He gained new energy as he wriggled on the floor and tried to cry out against his gag.

Benjamin dropped the wooden weapon, and it clattered against the tile. Stepping through the rigging on the door, he left Tyler to his ultimate fate. There was clearly only one thing left to do.

CHAPTER 28

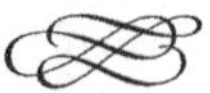

Addison took all the dresses out of her closet. There were four. None of which were the type of dress she could wear to a wedding—a lot of black with buckles and chunky boots. *Why did I wait till now to decide what to wear? I don't have anything that will work!* She threw a skirt with suspenders on the floor and kicked it. "This is what I get for not having any friends who are girls!"

That thought triggered her memory. She'd been a bridesmaid in a wedding years ago. *Where the hell was* that *gown?* Addison marched into her closet and rammed hangers back-and-forth across the bar. Sure enough, deep behind her winter coats was a plastic wrapped dress. If memory served, it was hideous. But it might be more appropriate than the others. She tore the thin musty covering away and held the gown out for scrutiny.

The fabric on the sleeveless fitted bodice was a midnight blue-on-blue damask with a broad scoop neckline. Addison liked the elegant top that hung to her mid-thigh, but the underskirt was ridiculous. The seamstress made it with yards of navy tulle covered in sparkles. Bling was not her thing.

She tossed the dress on the bed and went down to the kitchen to pour herself a glass of wine. It was only noon, but she needed the boost and savored the rich taste of black currants.

Logan told her the wedding was casual. The sparkly gown was too much, but her long belted sweatshirt dress was too little. Frustration pressed down on her, tensing the muscles in her neck and shoulders. She never went anywhere nice. Jeans and leggings were her go to. Why did she care what anyone thought, anyway?

Logan.

At the thought of him, a tickly sensation bloomed low in her belly and wriggled through her body until it caused her to shiver. Emotions she didn't want to think about flared inside, and she downed the rest of her wine to douse them. *I am SO not going there.*

Addison stomped back up her stairs, determined to figure out something to wear.

She stood in the doorway to her bedroom and stared at the blue dress tossed on the backside of her bed. Only the bodice was visible. The ballerina princess skirt hung off the far side, hidden from view. An idea wound its way inside her mind, and a smile curled her lips. Addison snatched the dress up and held it in front of her body before the full-length mirror on the bathroom door. The tulle gave the gown a demented mermaid look but, *maybe...* She pressed the satiny textured fabric of the top against her leg. *It might be a little short, but I bet I could pull it off.*

Addison bounded back down the stairs to the utility drawer in the kitchen and rummaged around for a pair of scissors. *That fairy princess crap is coming off!*

Dissembling the dress was easier than she'd expected. Addison glanced at the clock. If she ran, she'd have time to zip to the department store for some new heels, hop in the shower, and be ready for Logan when he came to pick her up. Her nerves made her jumpy, and she dropped the scissors on her way to return them to the kitchen. They bounced and clattered down the stairs, landing point first into the wood floor. *For God's sake, Addy. What is the matter with you? Calm down!*

The thought of Logan seeing her in the altered version of her dress sent heat flashing through her blood, and it bloomed in her face. She hadn't felt like this since her high school prom. Addison laughed out loud at herself as she grabbed her keys and dashed out the door.

Logan tugged on a pair of pressed jeans. He never wore creased jeans anywhere but at his family's ranch in Wyoming and maybe church when he went with his mom. But the dark-blue jeans were dressier than his everyday Levi's. He'd bought a new white dress shirt to wear under his gray-chalk lined blazer. The wedding was casual, so no need for a tie, but Gunner wasn't so lucky. After his dog bath, Logan replaced his collar with a bowtie.

"Let's go get the girl, Gunner. Ready?"

His dog barked in response and wagged his tale. Logan wondered once again if his partner understood English. He ran his hand from Gunner's muzzle to his tail and opened the door. On their way down the steps, Harriet called out her door to him.

"You two look very handsome. Are you going on a date?" The old woman's eyes sparkled.

Logan chuckled. "A wedding."

"Are you taking Addison?"

"She's riding with us. Yes."

Harriet opened her door the rest of the way and stepped

out, her house dress blowing in the breeze. "Don't give me that. Riding with you—indeed. Taking a woman to a wedding is a date. In fact, it's more than a date. And it's about time."

Logan grinned despite himself and looked down at Gunner. "Well, we better get going." He hadn't wanted to get involved with anyone. Not his neighbor, not his dog, and certainly not Addison, but the gooey way his insides felt at the thought of picking her up told him his intentions were not proving to be his reality.

"Wait!" Harriet disappeared inside her apartment for a minute and returned with a bouquet of daisies. "You should never show up for a first date empty handed."

"Where did these come from?"

"My niece sent them over, but I've looked at them long enough and they're still fresh, so take them."

Logan bent down and kissed Harriet's cheek. "Thank you."

When he stood, Harriet's eyes were glassy, and she swatted at him. "Go on now. Have fun. I'll want to hear all about it."

"Good night, Harriet."

Logan and Gunner pulled to the curb outside Addison's turn-of-the-century house. He took a deep breath to settle his nerves and fingered the ever-present dog tags in his pocket. "Now or never, Gun. Let's go." He let his dog out of the car, and they went to the front door and rang the bell.

"Come on in!" Addison's voice floated through the screen, so they stepped inside. "I'll be right down."

Logan occupied himself with the framed photos on the mantel. He lifted one with a younger Addison standing between a woman who looked exactly like her, and a tall dark-haired man. He turned at a creak on the stairs. His mouth dropped open. Stunned at the sight of Addison in her short, midnight-blue dress, he coughed to cover his obvious delight. "Wow."

A shy smile graced her face. "Really?"

Logan stared. She was incredibly lovely, but he'd never seen her uncertain. He smiled up at her. "Really." He held his hand out to her, then remembered he was holding the flowers Harriet gave him.

"Are those for me?" The color of the dress made Addison's eyes a deeper blue. Her black hair glistened in shiny curls. His gaze traveled from her red lips down her curves, accentuated by the snug dress above her impossibly long legs. "Logan?"

He snapped his gaze back to her face. "Uh—Yes. Actually, they're a gift from Harriet."

Addison laughed, tossing her chin up and tempting him with her graceful neck. "She's such a dear."

"Uh—huh."

She took the bouquet from his hand, and he was enveloped in the beguiling musky scent of her perfume. "No one has ever brought me flowers for a date before." Her smile fell, and her eyes flew open. "Not that this is a date. Right? I mean... you know what I mean."

Right. Not a date. Not a date. Remember that, you idiot. "Sure. And they're not from me, they're from Harriet."

Addison's shoulders dropped slightly as she went to the kitchen to find a vase. "Right."

That wasn't the reaction he'd expected. Had he disappointed her? He was out of practice with reading between a woman's lines. He shoved his hands in his front jeans pockets.

Addison returned. "Gunner sure looks handsome." She bent to hold Gunner's face in her hands. She glanced back at Logan. "You both do." He didn't want to consider why that small compliment made him stand a little taller.

"Are you ready to go? Do you have a coat?"

The hour-long drive to the foothills of Boulder was strange. He'd never been awkward around Addison before, but tonight he was nervous about saying the right thing—wanting to be interesting or funny and not coming across like a jerk. Addison acted differently too. She kept her hands folded in her lap instead of her usual demonstrative gesturing.

By the time they descended into the valley, the topic of work came up, and they fell into their familiar rhythm. They wound up the tight hairpin turns on the face of Flagstaff Mountain, and when they arrived at the wedding, the only awkwardness remaining was inside of him—in the way he was reacting to Addison in that dress. Logan had to force his eyes away from her, and he dutifully kept his hands in his pockets, his inner voice shouting at him. *She's your boss. She's your boss. She's your boss!*

The amphitheater where they held the wedding overlooked all of Boulder Valley. Behind them, the sun-drenched the horizon in peach and periwinkle as it nestled against the mountains. Jennings, a cocky smart-ass by nature, stood fidgeting at the front, nervously searching the back of the crowd for his bride. Next to him sat Jennings's all black Belgian Malinois, Ranger. He too appeared to be anticipating the woman his handler waited for.

Addison wobbled on her heels as she turned on the dirt path to find a seat on the stone benches. Logan shot his hand out and clasped her elbow to steady her. She smiled her thanks, and he kept his fingers on her skin as long as he could, reveling in its silkiness and the electric energy that pulsed up his arm from touching her.

Logan recognized many of the faces in the crowd. The K9 staff all had their dogs with them, which seemed fitting. A string quartet started playing, and the congregation stood.

Logan had never met El Clark, the woman Jennings was marrying, but he'd heard she was a social worker and that they'd met on a human trafficking case. A pretty teenaged girl with long brown hair, wearing a white flowing dress, carried a bouquet of sunflowers down the path. She smiled up at Jennings, and he beamed.

Next came a classic beauty in a simple white form-fitting silk gown. Her red curls were back lit by the sun and glowed like fire. She walked down the aisle on the arm of SAC Sanchez, who winked at Kendra as he passed by. Logan returned his attention to Jennings. The hard-as-nails former Marine was a puddle of mush as he reached for his bride's hand. Logan chuckled. *We all have our weaknesses.*

The pastor spoke about the meaning and wonder of marriage. The couple said their vows to one another and exchanged rings. Hoots and hollers from several of the K9 handlers punctuated their kiss. The crowd applauded as Jennings and his bride made their way back down the aisle as an officially married couple.

Logan's pocket vibrated. Addison's small velvet handbag buzzed. Several others in the group retrieved their cell phones from various locations on their persons, all staring at their screens.

Addison's eyes locked with his. "Another bomb threat! This time it's the Capitol Building."

CHAPTER 29

"Let's go!" Addison bolted up the dirt pathway a mere ten feet behind the newlyweds. Her heels slowed her down, so she kicked them off on her way to Logan's SUV.

"Sorry, man." Logan shook Jennings' hand. "It was a beautiful wedding, and you have a gorgeous bride. Congratulations. But there's a bomb threat at the Capitol Building in Denver." Logan explained their quick exit.

Jennings hollered, "Be safe."

Logan ran past Addison to open her door before sprinting to the driver's side. Gunner loaded up and Logan retrieved a black duffle bag from behind his seat. Seconds later, Logan crammed his civilian clothes and jacket into the pack and tugged an FBI-K9 shirt over his well-muscled torso. Addison blinked her admiring gaze away as he leapt into the car. He pointed to the emergency light switch on the dash. "Light us up."

Addison flipped the toggle up and blue and red light bounced off the darkening pine trees as they drove as fast as possible down the twists and turns of the mountain and then sped toward the highway. Addison got on the radio to ask for the details of the situation. Both FBI and ATF bomb squads had been alerted. The Denver PD was onsite organizing the evacuation, which on a Saturday night primarily included the homeless people that camped out around the Capitol Building and across the street in Civic Center Park.

"I can't go to the Capitol in this dress." She gritted her teeth, angry at herself for not bringing her own go-bag, and she smacked the dashboard.

"Drop me and Gunner off and then you can drive home to change."

"Damn it!"

"The dogs will have to clear the area before you enter the building, anyway. You'll be back in time."

"Maybe. It's taking forever to get there."

"We're almost there. Ten more minutes." Logan took the Speer Boulevard exit. As soon as he was on the city street, he clicked on his sirens to accompany the flashing lights. They screamed through the night toward the historical gold-domed building in the center of Denver.

Logan came to a screeching halt near the cordoned off entrance to the Capitol. He hopped out of the vehicle and opened Gunner's door. He fitted a K9 flak jacket over his dog and then, as he glanced up at the gold-plated dome of the Denver Capitol, he shoved his own helmet onto his head. Addison ran barefoot around the front of the car and jumped in, ready to go.

"I'll be back in a flash."

Logan leaned into the car and stared at her for a weighted second before he kissed her hard and fast. "Be careful. I'll see you when you get back."

"Be safe, Logan." He nodded and slammed the door.

Addison took off toward her house, which was only a little over a mile away. She ran her fingertips over her lips where he'd kissed her. No time to think about that now.

~

Logan and Gunner found the Site Commander and checked into the scene. He assigned Logan a quadrant of the building to search.

"Come on, Gunner, let's go to work." As the partners jogged up the steps of the Capitol, Logan glimpsed the words, "One Mile Above Sea Level" etched into a marble stair, marking Denver as the Mile-High City. Two more steps and lights glinted off a round, brass emblem set into the stone depicting the mountains and stated, "5280 Feet Above Sea Level". Logan clenched his jaw, determined to save the old building itself from being leveled.

It was a Saturday night, so the place was mostly empty, making the evacuation an easy step. Logan made his way to their designated search section. "*Such*, Gunner!"

Gunner ran through the corridor of the grand structure to the left of the entrance. Their assignment was the south end of the first floor and the corresponding area in the lowest level. Someone had unlocked the office doors for the search prior to their arrival, which increased their speed. Down one side of the hallway, and Gunner had yet to hesitate. Logan jogged with him up the other side. Together, they searched the reception areas and the back offices behind each door.

Returning to the center of the building, Logan glanced up at the inside of the 180-foot-tall dome. *Who would want to destroy such a magnificent part of history?* Gunner yanked on his lead, snapping Logan back into the focus he needed. They raced along all the walls, offices, and alcoves in their section, Gunner sniffing the whole way. Nothing there.

Logan guided Gunner down the stairs to the lower level. *If I was going to set a bomb, this is where I'd do it.* Not much occupied the basement floor. The building's utility room was next to two custodial closets. Logan and Gunner ran through those first. The compact rooms normally remained locked at all times unless one of the janitorial staff was using them. It didn't surprise Logan that Gunner found nothing there.

They pushed through the door to the women's bathroom. Gunner checked each stall, the row of sinks, and the trash cans. Nothing.

Back out into the corridor, they dashed toward the men's room. Gunner was two feet in front of Logan when he stepped on a floor mat at the entrance to the restroom. A click sounded. The particular sound was one neither Logan nor Gunner wanted to hear. Gunner, meticulously trained to respond, halted instantly. Ice water splashed along Logan's nervous system, and his muscles contracted and froze. His heart thudded hard against his ribs, echoing in the hallway.

Here he was, in the very place he struggled with all his might to avoid. Logan's dog was a mere breath away from being blown to pieces—again. Logan stared at Gunner, but saw Lobo's face. "No," he whispered, his body wanting to collapse. Then he spoke to Gunner, "*Zustan,* Gunner. Don't move."

Gunner had stepped on a pressure pad trigger. The bomber had hidden the pad under the floor mat. Logan scanned the area for wires that led to the device. Long, thin black wires snaked from the mat up along the doorframe of the restroom. Logan held his palm up as if to stop Gunner from moving and clicked his radio with the other.

"I've got a live one here. Downstairs, lowest level, men's room."

"Evacuate. We'll send in the robot."

"Can't. We've tripped a pressure pad."

"Shit. Okay. Don't move. A bomb tech is on the way."

"Roger, that." Logan stepped slowly toward Gunner, who whined but knew better than to move. "It's okay, Gun. I'm gonna get you out of this." Logan got down on his knees and gently lifted the corner of the mat. It appeared there were three pressure pads, all with wires running up the heavy door. He couldn't let his dog get killed. Not this time.

Logan scrunched his eyes tight, forcing images from a different explosion, years ago, out of his mind. He needed to focus. Lobo had been killed on Logan's watch. This time, if at all possible, Logan would make sure Gunner survived, or he'd die trying.

Logan took hold of Gunner's collar to steady him, before sliding his hand under the mat. Millimeter by millimeter, he edged his way to the lip of the pressure pad. Sweat dripped from his face. A rivulet trickled into his eye, stinging with salt. Logan blinked it away and forced himself to breathe. The tips of his fingers slid over the edge of the pad.

"*Zustan*, Gun. Good boy. Just don't move." Gunner clearly interpreted the intensity of the situation. He sat unmoving, soft whines floating on his breath.

Slowly Logan edged his hand under Gunner, between his dog and the pressure pad, gradually replacing Gunner's weight with his own. Logan estimated the pressure-weight ratio, and when he was as sure as he could be, he nudged Gunner off the pad, removing his dog from his deadly position. He carefully replaced the pressure of his hand with his own body weight. He sat on the pad knowing as long as the pressure was greater; he was safe. The explosive would blow only when the weight was removed. Logan's shirt was drenched in sweat, and tears clouded his vision.

"Go on, Gunner. Get out of here!"

His dog sat on the floor by his feet. Logan reached behind him and unclipped Gunner's reward toy. He tossed it to the stairs. "*Aport!* Go get it, Gun."

Gunner lived to play with his toy, but this time he watched it fly through the air and land on the lower steps. His gaze returned to meet Logan's. He cocked his head and laid down, tucking his nose flat on the floor between his front paws. He looked up out of the top of his amber eyes at Logan and whined.

"No, Gunner. Get out of here!" Logan's pulse surged with fear and adrenalin. "Get! Go on!"

Gunner refused to budge.

Logan's mind flooded with the guilty images from long ago. He and Lobo had checked the area the hour before. He had been certain there was nothing there, that they were safe. But Lobo knew. The second he'd stepped down from the personnel carrier, he knew. His golden eyes met Logan's less than a breath before the explosion disintegrated them forever. Logan was blown backward into the vehicle, but he alone had survived. The others weren't so lucky, and it was all his fault. He'd lost the best dog imaginable, along with two men from the unit he was attached to. How could he have been so careless?

The official report came back holding Logan blameless. The investigation uncovered that Taliban soldiers had taken out the lookout guarding the area, slipped in and planted several cellphone activated landmines at the perimeter of the safe zone. There was no way anyone could have known.

Still, he should have sensed it. He should have been the first one out of the vehicle. He should have... Logan broke down. Tears covered his face, and his shoulders jerked with sobs that had wanted to come for years.

"Lobo!" he cried. "Lobo! No!" The images in his mind as

clear as if he stood there in the scorching desert once again. "I'm sorry…"

"Logan?" A soft voice called out to him, but he couldn't focus on it. Refused the undeserved comfort it offered.

He hid his face in his hands and murmured, "I'm so sorry…"

CHAPTER 30

"Logan, it's me. Addison." She came down the steps and lifted the bomb suit's helmet off her head. "We're going to get you out of this." Gunner padded over to her, bumped her fingers with his nose, and then returned to his vigil, sitting and facing Logan. He whined before licking Logan's hand.

Logan sat on the mat, covering the pressure pad in front of the men's restroom. He had drawn his knees up and wrapped his arms around them. Muttering words she couldn't hear, he remained unresponsive. Logan seemed to be in a dream state of some kind as he stared into the space before him. Addison's heart pinched. "Gunner's here, and so am I. We're right here with you. But I need you to focus on me."

He didn't acknowledge her. Instead, he wiped his eyes on his sleeve and repeated an apology to someone only he could see. To Lobo.

"Who is Lobo, Logan?" As the question crossed her lips, she remembered the single photo she'd seen in Logan's apartment. A dog. His dog—the one he lost in Afghanistan.

Addison realized then that whatever happened must have been traumatic, and it was rearing its debilitating ugliness. Her gaze fell to the mottled skin on his forearm and the pieces clashed together.

She raised her voice and sharpened her tone. "Logan!"

One dark eye peered up at her from behind a fold in his sleeve.

"Logan, it's Addison." She gripped his arm. "What happened? Why are you talking to Lobo?"

He tucked his face into the crook of his elbow and didn't answer.

"What happened to Lobo?"

Logan muffled a response into his arm. "He died because of me. Don't you see? I can't let that happen again."

"I'm here with you. You're going to be okay."

"Gunner!" Logan's eyes sparked wildly, and he startled her with his sudden outburst. He stared at her. "Get out of here and take him with you! Now!"

Addison stroked the soft fur on Gunner's back. "It doesn't look like he's willing to leave you, and neither am I." She made a quick assessment of the wires. They didn't have time to deal with Logan's ghosts right now, no matter how painful they were. If she could get them out of this mess, she'd listen to his pent-up agony for as long as he wanted her to. For now, she had to focus on getting them the hell out of there in one piece. "You radioed in that you tripped a pressure plate?"

"There are three. One under me and two on either side."

"Okay. The door looks like it pulls open. You'd have to move for us to get inside, so we're hopefully going to diffuse the explosive component by detaching the pressure plates on this side of the door." Addison lifted the edge of the mat to see what she was dealing with. It appeared straightforward, and that made her nervous. "Why would someone rig a men's bathroom?"

"Especially since no one is in the building." Logan cleared his throat, seeming to regain some of his composure. "Anyone working here would use the restrooms upstairs. And if the bomber wanted to bring down the Capitol, why not just set a remote-controlled device?"

"Maybe he did. We don't know what we're dealing with on the other side of the door. Pressure plates would prevent someone from finding the explosive before the bomber was ready for the blast to occur."

"True, but so would hiding the bomb where no one could find it."

"Stop talking for a minute. I need to think about this." Addison stared at the black chords, appraising the configuration. It should be as simple as cutting them from the pads. The simplicity of it made her as nervous as a handful of jumbled wires would have. She clicked the button on her radio. "I'm on location with Agent Reed and K9 Gunner, preparing to snip the wires connected to three separate pressure pads. Thoughts?" Addison directed the body camera attached to her suit at the wires so the other techs in the bomb squad truck could see what she was dealing with.

"I agree." Miller's voice squawked over the line. "Looks like your best option."

"Roger. I'll cover Agent Reed and Gunner as well as I can, just in case. Confirm that everyone is out of the building."

"Already done. You should send the dog out too."

Addison shook her head. "He won't budge."

"Good dog." Miller clicked off.

"Great dog." Logan's voice tripped on his words.

"Okay, Logan, I'm going to step back here behind you, between you and the bathroom door. I'll clip the line on the right side and then the one on the left. If we don't blow the door off the hinges by then, I'll cut the wire to the pad you're sitting on. Got it?"

"No, Addison. You will not put yourself in this position. I want you to leave me with the wire cutters and get out of here. If I snip them without incident, good. If not, then only one of us dies. That's the logical decision, and you know it."

Addison's eyes pricked. She touched his cheek, wiping her finger through his drying tears. "I'm the one in the suit. So, it isn't the logical decision. Plus, there is no way I'm leaving you here alone."

"Why? Why would you risk two lives instead of just one? I need you to leave and force Gunner to go with you. *Please,* Addison."

The fist gripping her heart squeezed until her entire chest ached and a lump jammed up her throat. "We don't have time to think about why right now, Logan. I'm doing this my way, and that's final. So sit still."

Without giving him a chance to respond, Addison shoved her helmet back on her head and stepped one leg over the mat, careful to avoid the wires, then the other. Her suit was hot and heavy on a good day. Now it was a prison of heat, and sweat trickled down the column of her spine. It was difficult to crouch down in the bulky armor, but she finally sank low enough to reach the strands.

She closed her eyelids and breathed in. Opening her eyes with an utter focus on the job at hand, she let her breath out in a gush and slid the clippers over the first wire. "Ready?"

CHAPTER 31

The room compressed with a heavy silence. Addison clipped the wire. Nothing.

Logan released the breath he'd been holding. "How do you do this for a living?"

Addison snickered behind him. "I'm secretly an adrenaline junky."

"That's not a secret."

"Okay. Here we go again." She snipped the second wire. Again, nothing happened. "Good sign. Now for the pad you're sitting on. Ready?" Clip.

Logan's muscles released all at once, drained from the continuous flex they'd held for the past hour. He collapsed onto Gunner and gripped his fur. "You stupid, wonderful dog! Why didn't you go? You're supposed to do as you're told!"

Gunner responded by bathing the dried sweat and tears from Logan's face. Then he bounded to the stairs to retrieve his toy. He ran it back to Logan and deposited it in his lap. Addison's melodic laugh echoed behind him, soothing his raw nerves.

"I've never seen that kind of loyalty before, Logan. That dog is your best friend."

"I..." He pulled Gunner's furry shoulders into his chest. "Thanks, Gun. I love you, boy."

Gunner's tail swept back and forth through the emotionally charged air.

Addison squeezed Logan's shoulder. "Okay, you two need to get out of here. I have a job to do."

A noise sounded from the other side of the bathroom door. Logan's eyes shot to Addison. "Did you hear that?"

"Sh."

They both canted their ears toward the door. There it was again. "Sounds like someone's crying."

"Hello?" Addison pressed her ear against the door.

A grunt echoed in response.

"Someone's in there." Addison stood back and hit her radio. "We've got another person down here inside the bathroom. Sounds like they're gagged. I can't make out what they're saying. I'm going in."

Miller answered, "Send Reed and the dog out, first."

"Roger."

"And be careful. The door might still be wired."

Logan shook his head at Addison. "Not on your life. I'll stand behind the wall, but I'm not leaving."

The grunting grew frantic.

Addison sighed and searched the seam of the entrance. "I'll check for anything that looks like a tripwire before I open the door, but this is dicey. I wish you'd leave, Logan."

"You don't have time to argue with me. We need to save whoever is on the other side."

Addison relented and continued her search. She looked over her shoulder at him with a grim expression as she reached for the pull handle. Logan turned away, covering

Gunner with his body as they both took cover behind the brick wall.

The door opened with ease, and Addison stepped inside. "What the hell are you doing here?"

Logan sprang to his feet and followed her to see who she'd found. He ran into the restroom to find Addison staring at a half-naked man bound and gagged laying on the tile. His wrists were duct taped to his ankles, and he was bent over a wooden stick, his body bloody and bruised. A section of a broom handle lay on the floor beside him. One end was covered in blood. The man sobbed incomprehensible words into the cloth taped into his mouth.

"You know this guy?" Logan reached for the Leatherman he carried on his belt. He opened the blade to cut through the man's bindings.

Addison called for paramedics. "We've found an injured man in the downstairs men's bathroom. There is a bundle of C-4 wired to a timer on the floor next to him. We have five minutes and twenty-nine seconds to get him out of here and diffuse the bomb. Make that five and twenty-one. Go, go, go!"

"On their way," Miller responded.

Logan cut through the tape, and the man curled himself up into a ball. He screwed his eyes shut tight and moaned. "You're safe now. We're going to get you out of here." Logan peeled the silver tape from the man's face, and he coughed when Logan removed a wadded-up piece of bloody cloth. "What's your name?"

The man kept his eyes closed, his head lolling on the floor. Logan removed his FBI jacket and covered him.

"His name is Tyler Brookes."

Logan's gut bunched. "A friend of yours?"

"Hardly. Mr. Brookes was the ringleader of the mean high

school kids the bomber has targeted in the current spree of bombings."

"You mean the group of school friends Mrs. Carlson told us about?"

"The very same." Addison crouched down near the plastic explosives whose timer continued to click away the seconds in red digital numbers. She glanced at Tyler. "Why are you here? I thought you were supposed to be in Washington?"

Tyler only sobbed harder. Two paramedics entered the room. Their eyes darted around and landed on the bomb.

Addison perched her hands on her hips. "Focus, guys. We don't have much time. Get this man out of here, now. You can assess his injuries outside." The medics stood frozen, unsure. "Do it NOW, gentlemen!"

Addison's command jolted them into action. They gently lifted the man on to a stretcher, covered him with a light blanket and took him from the room.

"Now you." Addison spoke to Logan and pointed toward the door.

"I'm not going. The time is ticking. How can I help?" Logan's pulse throbbed at the same rate as the timer. He could live every day for the rest of his life without this level of adrenaline, but he was determined to stay.

Addison glared at him but said, "Get my tool kit. It's by the door."

Logan, relieved to have some way of assisting, ran to grab her bag. He handed it to her as she knelt by the gray bricks of clay explosive. "If I can separate the components, I should be able to diffuse this sucker." Gingerly, she touched the timing device, loosening it from the C-4. "Hmm." She drew a pair of heavy-duty scissors from her kit and cut through a nylon strap holding the clock to the bomb. She let out a sigh.

Logan lifted the gray brick half an inch from the floor, and Addison unwrapped the strap, releasing the timing mechanism except for the red and green wires that plugged into the timer and ran through the C-4. His gaze darted to the red numbers blinking the seconds away. Fifty-two.

Addison's breaths became shallow pants as she concentrated. Logan forced a gulp of air into his own lungs. She stared up at him. "This is the moment of truth. I'm going to clip a wire. I want you and Gunner in the hallway."

"I'm not leaving you in here alone."

Addison gritted her teeth. "I have a protective suit. You don't. At least get on the other side of the wall. You owe that to Gunner."

Her words stabbed into him. He glanced down at his incredibly brave and smart K9 partner.

"I mean it, Logan. Please."

He swallowed and nodded once. "Clip the right one, Addy."

Her expression softened at the use of her shortened name. "I will. Don't worry." A brief smile brushed over her lips. "We have a certain kiss to discuss."

He reached for her face, cupping her jaw. "We have a certain kiss to continue, you mean." The intensity in their eyes clashed. "You saved my life, Addison. I'm going to make it up to you."

"Good. That's a promise I'll hold you to. Now get out of here."

Twenty-three seconds, twenty-two...

Logan stood and took hold of Gunner's lead. "*Kemne.*" Together, they moved toward the door. He looked back to see Addison poised over the bomb with a pair of wire snips in her hand.

Thirteen seconds, twelve...

Logan and Gunner ran into the hall and took cover behind the stone wall. He was thankful for the solid structure of the century old building. With his own body, Logan covered his dog and whispered the count out loud. "One-one-thousand, two-one-thousand," on up to fifteen-one-thousand. He loosened his grip on Gunner.

"Addison?"

His hero ambled her way around the corner from the men's room in her bulky armored suit. She'd undone the top portion of her protective gear and let it hang upside down over her hips with the arms trailing. A broad grin spread the width of her face as she held up the timer in one hand and the bomb material in the other. She leaned against the wall and slid down its length till she sat on the floor.

"Call it in, will ya?"

Logan was next to her in three strides. He pressed the radio on his chest. "All clear! All clear!"

CHAPTER 32

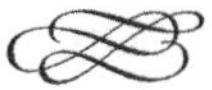

Weak-kneed, Logan rushed to Addison and knelt beside her. She let out a breathy giggle—a nervous laugh likely fueled by the adrenaline saturating her blood. He stroked the side of her face, amazed at the brave and wickedly smart woman before him. "You did it."

"Thank God. I love this old building."

He bent to kiss the top of her head, her hair damp from her helmet.

"Logan, don't. I'm soaking with sweat."

"You just saved Gunner's and my life, the life of that man in the bathroom, and a historical building. I don't care if you're bathing in sweat. You've never been more gorgeous in my eyes than you are right now." He cradled her face between his hands and kissed her with tender reverence. Her lips were warm and inviting. Logan looked into her eyes.

Her soft gaze held him for a moment before she lifted the timer. "I'm hoping for more of that, but we need to get these components up to the truck."

Logan stood and hauled Addison to her feet. "Yeah, and I want to talk to the naked guy."

Addison smirked. “I’m not sure I ever want to hear you say that again.”

He laughed and shook his head. “You know what I mean —Tyler Brookes. I want to talk to him. He’ll be able to confirm the identity of the person who tied him up, assaulted him, and set the bomb.”

“Right. He’s the only victim who’s survived. If it was Benjamin Sykes, we’ll know for sure and can bring him in.”

“I can’t imagine what those people did to Sykes that was so bad he held a grudge for ten years and is now on a mission to kill them.”

“Do we have any other leads?”

A clambering on the steps interrupted them, and a group of investigators descended into the hallway. One CSI photographed all the components before Addison took the explosive parts up to the bomb truck. Her team… *their* team, would dissemble the device to make sure it was completely safe before sending the parts to the crime lab.

Logan lifted the top section of her armor. “Why don’t you climb out of your suit? I’ll carry it up for you.”

“Thanks.” She shook her legs out of the heavy material. Addison had encased herself in black spandex, and she shivered in the thin, wet fabric. Logan put his arm around her for warmth. They climbed the stairs together on their way to join their squad.

The physical let-down from the intensity of the event she’d just navigated had Addison’s body feeling like it was eighty-years-old. She was grateful to have Logan carrying her heavy gear. As they ascended the steps, she told Logan what she knew of Benjamin’s high school experience. “The group of kids humiliated Sykes and bullied him during a sensitive time in his development. If he had any mental instability at the time, their nasty behavior could have triggered all sorts of issues."

"Lots of kids get picked on, though. Most don't blow up buildings and murder people."

"True. He was probably already a ticking bomb in his own right. But kids don't think about these things." Addison and Logan walked out of the Capitol Building and down the marble steps together, with Gunner leading the way. She breathed in lungs full of the fresh night air. Her team stood in front of their truck waiting for them and applauded as they appeared. She twisted her limbs into an awkward version of a curtsey. "Thank you, thank you." Addison laughed then shouted, "Okay, now someone get Agent Cameron on the phone."

Burke Cameron's voice came over the speaker inside the bomb truck. "We felt bad abandoning Clay and El at their wedding dinner, but we're on our way to the hospital to interview the man you and Reed found in the restroom. Should be there in about ten minutes. Is everyone on your end okay?"

"Yes. Some of my team is inside now with the CSIs investigating all the miscellaneous components left there and searching for any other evidence. I've locked the actual explosive device safely away in the containment vessel." Addison combed her fingers through her curls. "Listen Cameron, I'd like to be there when you guys talk to Tyler Brookes since I was the one who warned him in the first place."

"Fine with me. We'll see you at the hospital." He clicked off.

Seconds later, Addison's phone beeped with a texted photo of the newlyweds' first kiss. They appeared happy, even though most of their wedding guests had been called away. She tilted her phone for Logan to see. He nodded and grinned, but when his eyes met hers, his expression held desire and promise. Addison clasped his hand in the shadows. Now wasn't the time to explore their growing feelings for each other, but she looked forward to it—maybe tomorrow, after all the dust of the night had settled.

Addison gave her team a few instructions before Logan drove her to the hospital to interview Brooks. When they entered the parking lot, they saw Sanchez, Dean, and Cameron huddled together with a blonde woman she figured was Susan, Cameron's fiancée. They pulled up next to the group.

"We'll find a place to park and be right with you." Logan maneuvered into a spot nearby. He left his engine running when they got out of his SUV, then he locked the doors.

"Will Gunner be alright out here alone?" Addison grabbed his arm.

Logan smiled at her. "Don't worry. They design K9 vehicles for the dog's comfort. There are sensors that ensure the interior temperature is comfortable for him. If it's too hot, the air-conditioning comes on. Too cold and it blows heat, and his water bowl is an auto-fill when he nudges the lever with his nose."

"Wow." Addison was impressed.

"Yeah, the bureau treats its dogs better than its people."

"As well, they should. He is completely dedicated to his job, and I've never heard him complain." Addison sent Logan a wink. The backs of their hands brushed and their fingers reached out, acknowledging the touch without making it obvious to anyone else.

Leaving Cameron's future wife in the waiting room, the agents converged on the fourth-floor nurse's station asking where they could find Mr. Brooks.

A young, dark-haired nurse held a file folder against her

chest with crossed arms. She came around the semi-circle shaped counter in front of the nurses' work area to meet them. "I'm sorry, but Mr. Brookes is not seeing anyone right now."

"We're not friends of Mr. Brookes," Sanchez peered down at her name tag, "Nurse Tellamar. We're FBI." He opened the leather wallet that held his badge and ID.

She took her time reading his identification card and checking Sanchez's face against the photo. "I see." The nurse glanced over her shoulder before squaring up to him. "Unfortunately, you're still not going to interview him tonight. Mr. Brookes has been through an extremely emotional experience. He is with a psych nurse now who is sedating him—he needs to sleep. I'm sure you'll be able to visit him first thing in the morning."

"Is there a police guard on his door?"

"Yes."

"Okay, thank you." Sanchez left the nurse with his business card. "Please, call me if there are any changes."

She accepted the card and returned to her work behind the desk.

Frustrated, the group joined Cameron's fiancée downstairs, and they shoved chairs together to discuss their next move. Giving the agents their privacy, Susan left to get everyone coffee. Addison and Logan were filling the others in on the events at the Capitol Building when she came back carrying a tray of hot drinks. Addison enjoyed her first soothing sip when both Sanchez's and Cameron's phones buzzed simultaneously. Both men checked their screens.

Sanchez answered the call, and Cameron stood. "We've got to go. The warrant came through for Sykes's mother's house. S.W.A.T. is on their way. We'll meet them there." Susan shrugged and set the tray of coffees on the table.

"Honey, you'll have to ride along. Unless you'd rather call an Uber?"

"I don't mind. I'll stay out of your way." Susan clasped her hands together.

Cameron pressed a quick kiss on her cheek before they all ran out the automatic sliding door.

As Addison and Logan sprinted to his car, he clicked the fob to unlock it and they jumped in. "Put the address in the GPS."

"Got it." Addison typed the information into the dashboard computer. She flipped the switch for lights and sirens and they were off. Five minutes into the drive, a message blared across the radio. "Bomb squad requesting K9 assistance." The dispatcher stated the address.

"K9 Unit 5973 in route." Logan responded to the call, then glanced at her. "Sounds like we've got something at Sykes's residence. First time the bomb threat isn't at a public building."

Renewed energy coursed through Addison's body as she rose to the occasion. She wiped her clammy palms on her thighs. "Drive faster! I don't want anyone getting hurt." The Explorer surged forward as Logan reacted to her command.

They skidded to a stop next to the bomb squad truck with Sanchez's car parking right behind them. Miller leaned out the back door of the rig. "The S.W.A.T. team is in position and waiting for you two."

Addison leapt out of the SUV and waited for Logan to unload Gunner. She overheard Sanchez ordering Susan to stay in the car. "No matter what, Susan. I mean it. Do you understand?" Addison peered over the top of Logan's car and saw Kendra rub Sanchez's back before Susan nodded and he shut his door.

Cameron bobbed his head in agreement, kissed his girl, and followed Sanchez. Together, they all donned their flack vests as they approached the S.W.A.T. staging area. In a well-choreographed routine, the agents surrounded the house. The breach team, each touching the shoulder of the officer in front of them, mounted the steps to the front entrance with Addison, Logan, and Gunner following behind them.

"Stop!" The word echoed through the darkness as the lead agent held a fist up in the air. "This door is wired!"

CHAPTER 33

Logan and Gunner made their way along with Addison to the front entrance. Everyone froze in position when the lead agent announced someone had wired the doorframe with explosives. Sanchez ordered the S.W.A.T. team to back away from the building, and he called dispatch and told them to issue a reverse 911 call. "I want the people in the surrounding houses to evacuate before the S.W.A.T. and bomb squads proceed. Is there a house phone? If so, find this guy's number. Let's see if we can get him talking.

Agents ran to do Sanchez's bidding. Once all the neighbors were at a safe distance, Sanchez rested his hand on Addison's shoulder and said, "Time to do your thing."

Addison stepped into her bomb suit. "Will do, sir, but anyone not in my squad needs to retreat behind the danger line. That includes S.W.A.T."

"This is a live event, Thorne. I don't want you near the house without backup."

Logan stepped toward Sanchez. "Gunner and I will provide cover for her, sir."

Sanchez nodded slowly as he considered the situation. "Okay, and we'll get a sniper in position." He spoke into the radio, ordering the specialized team to stand down and take cover.

Addison knelt before Gunner. "Are you ready, boy? You're the one with the magic nose. See what you can find." She stood and gave Logan a meaningful look before taking his hand. "Be careful and prepare to duck for cover at any second."

Logan wove his fingers through hers. "Will do. You do the same. We have a date to keep after all of this."

A gentle smile softened the hard line of her mouth. "I'll be there." She squeezed his hand once and then moved up the walk.

Logan bent down and held Gunner's muzzle in his hands. "It's been a long night, boy. Let's get this done. *Such,* Gun. *Such.*"

Gunner bolted toward the house and dotted his nose around the perimeter. He checked the rear door, which didn't appear wired, and ran across the back of the residence, pausing at windows or various scents that interested him but weren't the goal. They searched along the dark side of the single-story structure where no street light shown. Logan noted a flickering glow shining up through a basement window.

He reported into his transmitter. "There is some light in the basement and possible movement. It could either be the glow of a TV or a person moving. Unknown at this time." He and Gunner continued the perimeter search. After finding nothing to cause an alert, Logan led Gunner up onto the porch. They checked the picture window and the old dilapidated couch that slumped under it. Finally, they approached the front entry.

Gunner sniffed the seam of the door. He sat down on the

warped floorboards and whined. Logan clicked on his radio. "We definitely have explosive on the front door. But only here." Logan unclipped Gunner's toy from his belt and handed it to the dog. "Yesss. Good dog. Good boy, Gunner!" He led his dog into the yard to enjoy his reward while members of the bomb team approached the wired door.

Miller dispatched the robot, which they carried up the steps and set in front of the entrance before abandoning it there.

Sanchez shouted into his transmitter. "All personnel, take cover!"

Logan and Gunner joined Addison inside the bomb truck to watch the robot's movements. They stared at the computer monitors as Gorty rolled up to the door. Extending the camera from its arm, the robot gave the bomb techs an up-close-and-personal view of exactly what they were dealing with.

Addison cocked her head. "That doesn't look right."

"I'll move in closer." Miller maneuvered the robot. Its arm reached forward, revealing a piece of paper stuck in the upper corner of the door. "Does that say—"

"Gotcha," Addison murmured. In that second, a blinding white light lit the computer screen and an ear-splitting boom rocked the truck. A secondary monitor viewing the full scene from a camera on top of the rig revealed Gorty catapulting off the porch, sailing through the night air, and landing in a mangled heap of melted metal on the front lawn. The smell of burnt black powder hovered in the air and stung Logan's throat.

"Holy Shit!" Miller yelled as he slammed backwards into his chair.

Addison gasped. "Thank God, that wasn't one of our people!"

Iron bands squeezed Logan's chest as he ground his teeth

together.. *Thank God, that wasn't you, Addy.* How was he going to deal with her facing this kind of danger all the time? He'd ignored his plan not to care about anyone on his team, and now it was too late. If something happened to Addison or Gunner, it would crush him. He'd never be able to recover.

Miller spluttered, "Rest in peace, Gorty."

Addison pushed by Logan. "Help me with my suit. I'm going in."

Logan jumped from the back of the truck. "Not without us, you're not." He stared at the missing face of the house. Half the wall was gone, exposing splintered lumber, a wad of ruined furniture, and shards of glass. The front porch took the greatest punch. "Let's enter through the back. Gunner didn't detect explosives there."

Addison agreed and led the way. Logan and Gunner followed her, and the S.W.A.T. team was right behind them. Gunner again did not indicate explosive material in the back, so the breach team rammed the flimsy door off of its hinges. They entered, each step taken with caution. Logan tapped Addison's shoulder and pointed to Gunner. She nodded, and Gunner took the lead. The dog made his way through the kitchen, sniffing each cupboard and closet. When they cleared that room, Gunner led them down the hall toward the living room.

A horrible odor barred their entrance, and Addison knew at once what it was. She grabbed Logan's arm and he turned to her and nodded.

"There's the body." He pointed to a chair in the corner of the room. What used to be a person sat tied to the chair. The entire head was wrapped tight in silver tape. The person most likely died from suffocation.

"My God." Addison shuddered. "Is this the mom?"

Gunner sat down next to a closed door in the hallway and barked. Logan lit up the space with his Maglite.

"Stop!" Addison grabbed his arm and pointed to the top of the door frame. A thin clear strand, perhaps fishing line, stretched across the opening. Logan looked back at Addison.

"Trip wire," she said. "Take Gunner out now. We've got it from here."

He considered arguing with her. He hated leaving her inside, but when he glanced back at the S.W.A.T. team waiting on him, he did as she ordered and returned to the truck.

By the time he and Gunner made their way back to the truck, Addison and her crew had disabled the trip wire and had crept almost to the bottom of the basement stairs. Logan watched Addison's actions from the view that her body camera provided. There, she faced another closed door. Addison flashed her light around the edges. It didn't appear that anything was rigged to the opening. She stood to the side of the door and knocked. Logan's stomach knotted into a steel fist, and he had to remind himself to breathe.

"Mr. Sykes, FBI, we're coming in."

There was no response. Addison knocked again and tried the knob, but it appeared locked. She signaled to the breach team, and they moved forward, smashing the flimsy door aside with their ram. The S.W.A.T. team entered the room before Addison to provide cover. When she stepped into the space, a thin man with stringy hair and bulging eyes faced her from the center of the room. He wore a vest strapped with bricks of what looked like C-4 and held a pushbutton mechanism in his hand. Addison raised both of her palms. "Mr. Sykes? We're here to help you and at the same time, keep your neighbors safe. Is that alright with you?"

The man shook his head. "I think you better leave."

CHAPTER 34

"Okay." Addison gestured to the S.W.A.T. Team. "You guys get out of here. Go on up. I'll call you if I need you."

Logan's stomach dropped. "What is she doing?" He leaned closer to the monitor, trying to make sense out of the scene playing out before him.

Miller wiped his forehead on his sleeve. "She's trying to talk Sykes down, but first she has to get him to believe she's cooperating with him. That she's on his side."

"No!" Logan's stern voice caused everyone in the bomb truck to turn and stare at him. "That's foolish. There is no good reason to risk her life to save a murderer. Get her out of there!"

"This is her job, Agent Reed." Miller stood up and stepping close, took Logan's arm. "It might be better for you to wait outside."

Logan yanked his arm away and pushed against Miller's chest to keep him from coming any closer. "I'm not leaving."

Miller leaned to Logan's ear. "This is why it's not good to

get involved with another agent," he hissed. "She's the best at what she does. We need to let her do it."

Logan jerked his chin in acknowledgement and stepped back, his intestines churning with what felt like cement. Miller returned to his seat at the monitor. By then, Addison was alone in the room with a wired to blow, Benjamin Sykes.

"Mr. Sykes. Is it alright if I call you Ben?" Addison took a step backward, giving Sykes a little more room.

"Benji."

"Okay, Benji. Why don't you tell me what's going on? You're very upset. Is there anything I can do?"

"There is nothing anyone can do. It's done." The man scratched at his arm.

Addison directed the camera on her suit to a wall covered with photos, a then-and-now portrayal of the people Sykes had killed. There were pictures of the janitor's closet, the mall, and hospital. Above those was a larger photo of the Denver Capitol Building, its golden dome glinting in the sun.

"Why now, Benji?" She took a step in his direction. "Did something happen?"

The man stared at her with his protruding eyes. "My mother…" He gulped "I have nothing left."

"Is that your mother, upstairs?"

Sykes closed his eyes. "She kept telling me how stupid I am." His eye popped open in a flash of mania. "I had to make her shut-up!"

Addison raised a hand. "Okay, Benji. She can't say that to you anymore. It's over."

Cameron watched the monitors from the back door of the truck. "Sykes must have murdered his mother. Her death was probably what triggered his bombing tirade."

Logan nodded his agreement, but couldn't take his eyes away from the screen. "He wrapped her whole head in duct tape to stop her insults." He glued his focus to Sykes's fingers wrapped around the detonator.

"Awful way to die," murmured Cameron.

Sykes cried out. "They all needed to die, but I had mercy on Megan. She never knew what was going on, anyway. But Tyler… I heard on the news that he's still alive—that the FBI diffused my bomb. Why didn't you let him die? He needs to die!" Benjamin hit the side of his head with his fist.

"Tyler will be brought to justice, Benji, but you can't take that into your own hands."

"He's an evil person. They all were… so cruel. I've tried for years to let it go. Mama always said I was stupid for allowing people to treat me like that. That I deserved it if I didn't stand up for myself."

"People can be really awful, but that doesn't mean it was your fault." Addison took another step toward Sykes, and Logan clenched his jaw, holding his breath.

Sykes raised the hand holding the trigger. "Yes!" He yelled at Addison. "My mama said."

"Okay, okay. I understand." Addison raised her palms in a conciliatory gesture. "But, why blow up buildings? Lots of other people got hurt besides the ones you wanted to pay."

"Those places are a constant reminder. Every time I drive by them, they mock me. The mall where they all hung out after school, the hospital where what Tyler did to me was exposed, the Capitol where the worst happened. It all had to go. Don't you see?" Sykes grew more agitated, and his fingers twitched on the device.

"I get it, Benji, and you've punished them all now, you've made them pay. But why have you strapped yourself with explosives?"

An eerie gleam flashed in Sykes's eyes, and he scratched his forearm so hard blood trickled down toward his wrist. "You're right. I *have* punished them. Even Tyler. I gave him just what he gave me. That day, on our class trip to the Capitol, they'd been including me, acting like my friends. I thought finally, they'd accepted me. Then Tyler and Jacob told me they had a joint they wanted to share, so we snuck away from the field trip. They took me to the basement bathroom, and—" Sykes's eyes streamed tears for a hurt that was still very present to him. He closed his eyelids, and his chest heaved with a sob. He scrubbed his running nose with his free hand.

Logan shuddered, remembering the scene at the Capitol Building—the bloody broom handle laying on the floor next to Brooks.

"He deserved what I did to him, and he deserves to die," Sykes screamed. "But I failed! Stupid, stupid, stupid." Sykes hit himself in the head with his free fist each time he uttered the word.

"No, Benji, you're *not* stupid. You're hurting. We can help you. Will you hand me the trigger? Please, Benji. I want to help."

Logan couldn't stand still any longer, and he bolted from the truck. He headed toward the house, only to run into the unyielding grips of Sanchez and Cameron.

"You are not going in there, Reed," Sanchez insisted.

Logan struggled against them with all his strength. "Let go of me!" Gunner growled and barked at the men. He could attack any minute, even without the command, if he believed his handler was in danger. "*Lehne*! Down, Gunner." Logan ordered. Gunner laid down, but continued to growl.

Blinding light seared into Logan's retinas. His arm shot up to cover his eyes, milli-seconds too late. Sound waves crashed into his eardrums, squeezing his still bruised brain. He dropped to his knees, instinctively covering his head with his arms. Scorching air sizzled past him, bringing scalding sparks in its wake. The boom echoed in his bones and vibrated out through the top layer of skin. He flew backward onto the ground. Pieces of ash and stone flitted down through the re-darkened sky.

"Addison!" Her name tore through his throat and propelled him forward to the demolished house. The burning building wavered in his vision as he scrambled on hands and knees toward the destruction. Fingers reached for him, tried to grab ahold of his shoulders, but he blasted through. "Addison!"

He sprinted into the rubble and flames, holding his head with both hands against the excruciating pain. Gunner stayed with him every step of the way. "Addison!" he screamed again.

"Logan!"

He stopped mid-stride and held perfectly still. Had he heard his name?

"Logan!" He heard it again, followed by coughing.

Frantically he searched to his right and then to his left, though daggers pierced his eyes. Where was she? "Addison, where are you?"

A large chunk of gray rubble shifted in front of him, and like a transformer it slowly became Addison Thorne—defender of his universe. He stumbled over to help her up.

"Addison? What happened?"

Squad members ran to carry her to the truck. After she'd shed her armored suit, was checked over by the medic, and had guzzled two bottles of water, Addison told them what happened. "Sykes made me turn my camera off. He confided in me that the boys had raped him in the bathroom that day and he'd never recovered. He asked me to make certain Tyler paid for what he did, and then he announced he was going to blow himself up. He gave me the count of ten to get out of there, before he released the trigger. When he started counting, I ran as fast as I could up the stairs, but this suit is so heavy it slowed me down." She covered her face with her hands for a second before she continued. "I was sure the bomb would go off before I could escape. I made it to the front entrance when the house exploded behind me. The blast threw me out about twenty feet."

"You're lucky to be alive." Miller handed her another bottle of water.

Her hand trembled as she reached for it. "For sure, but the suit saved my ass, just like it's supposed to." Addison laughed, as was her way in the aftermath of a crisis. Logan couldn't find any humor.

His vision swam, and he shook his head to clear it. Then everything went black.

CHAPTER 35

"Logan, can you hear me?" Addison leaned over him as the paramedics strapped him to a gurney. "Logan Reed, wake up!" Her voice wobbled as she sought the medic's face. "Is he going to be alright? What happened? It's not an aneurism, is it? There was blood coming from his ear!"

"He'll have a complete examination at the emergency room, ma'am. I can say with certainty it wasn't an aneurism, since he's still with us. I'm guessing his eardrum burst. He might have a concussion. His pulse is a little thready and we need to get him to the hospital. The doctors will take good care of him." He nudged her toward the doors at the back of the ambulance. "Ma'am, please step out so we can go."

"I'll follow you there." Addison patted Logan's pockets for his car keys. Finding them, she kissed his cheek. "Wake up, damn it, Logan." Then she sprang from the emergency vehicle and ran to Logan's SUV. Gunner was never more than a foot away from her side.

Cameron looped an arm through her elbow, bringing her up short. "Where are you going?"

She glared at him. "Hospital."

Red and blue flashing lights gave his face a ghostly hue. "Well, you're not driving. Give me the keys." He held his hand out.

Addison's body trembled in response to her own traumatic experience on top of the concern she felt for Logan. It had been one hell of a night. She handed Cameron the keys. "You better drive fast, Agent Cameron." Addison loaded Gunner in the back and ran to the passenger's side. Sirens blared into the dark sky as the paramedics rushed Logan to the ER.

"I will, but first I have to check on Susan and see if Rick and Kendra will give her a ride." Cameron leaned into the car. "Hey, Reed's going to be okay. It's probably just a blast concussion."

"Yeah, but he's still healing from a previous concussion."

Cameron's brows knit together. "Then why was he working?"

Addison tossed her head back against the headrest and sighed. "Because he's Logan."

They found him in an ER exam room. Logan's eyes were open when they entered. That was a good sign. "Hey, you. You fell asleep on me, right when I was telling the most exciting part of my story." Addison rushed to Logan's side and slid her hand over his.

He blinked several times in slow motion, and a smile kindled on his lips.

A nurse followed them in. "The paramedics told me Mr. Reed would have visitors soon." She smiled and checked Logan's IV. To Logan, she said, "The doc has ordered a CT scan. That will tell us exactly what's going on inside your head." She patted his shoulder.

Addison swallowed to press down the rising ache in her chest. "That sounds serious. Is the doctor concerned? What caused Logan's ear to bleed?"

The nurse adjusted the pulse ox device on Logan's finger. "Is it alright with you if I answer your friend's questions?"

Logan gave her a nod, but then grimaced.

"Hold still." She situated a cold pack on the side of his head before answering Addison's questions. "We're always cautious when someone loses consciousness. That and the bleeding from his ear could mean a serious diagnosis, so the doctor wants to be absolutely certain about what's going on inside Mr. Reed's skull. However, he is responsive and his pupils are normal." The nurse fluffed Logan's pillow. "He will most likely be fine with plenty of rest, though double concussions are no laughing matter and a burst eardrum isn't fun." The nurse tutted at Logan, and he offered her half a smile.

"How soon can he go in for the scan? When will we know the results?" It irritated Addison how calm medical personnel always were. Like they had all the time in the world. It gave her a desperate, helpless feeling she despised.

The woman smiled patiently at her. "The doctor is admitting him overnight. We'll know more in the morning. If all goes well, the doctor might release Mr. Reed tomorrow. He must rest completely this time, however. No work, in fact, no play either." She leaned over the bed and patted Logan's chest. "You hear me now? No work. Bed rest for at least two weeks, maybe more." She glanced over at Addison. "He'll need someone to be with him the whole first week. We can't risk another fall."

"I…" Addison's gaze moved to Logan.

He cleared his dry throat. "I'll be fine."

"No, Logan. You should come stay with me. I can take care of you while you're in bed."

Logan had the nerve to smirk, and Cameron chuffed on his way to the door. "I'll be in the waiting room."

Addison rolled her eyes. "You know what I mean."

Logan squeezed Addison's hand. "Honestly, I'll be fine at home. I promise I'll rest."

Addison raised her chin and looked down her nose at him. "Well, it's your choice—home and Harriet, or my house and me. Whichever you prefer, but one of us is going to watch over you, either way."

Logan scratched his jaw as though he had to think about the decision.

Laughing, Addison pinched his arm. "You're lucky you have a concussion, or I'd smack you upside the head."

He grinned. "Where's Gunner?"

He's in the car. We parked in police parking, and I left the engine running with the doors locked, just like you showed me.

"That's my girl." Those silly words wormed themselves deep inside her heart and nestled in with joy. Addison rolled her eyes to cover her pleasure.

"Do you want me to take Gunner to my place or over to the K9 facility?"

"I'm sure he'd rather be with you, but would you mind running him by the facility's vet? Just to be safe?"

"No problem, if you promise to call me as soon as you get the results of the scan."

Logan held up his hand in the boy scout three-fingered salute. "I promise."

"I'll see you in the morning, then. Do you want anything from home?"

"I'll need some clothes. We can swing by my place on the way to yours."

"No. I'm not kidding, Logan. I'm putting you straight to bed and you will not move. I'll run by your apartment on my way back here in the morning and get you a few things. I have your keys." She dangled the key chain above him.

"You're not going to be like the nurse in Stephen King's book, *Misery* are you?"

"Yes, probably." Addison stuck the tip of her tongue out at him.

"Then I guess you'd better prepare to keep me locked up forever."

"Maybe I better." She bent down and kissed him softly on his forehead.

~

Addison went in search of Cameron. She found him standing in front of a vending machine. "Ready?"

He pushed a button causing a granola bar to fall to the bottom of the machine, and he reached inside the flap to retrieve it. "I am now."

They made their way to Logan's car. "Thanks for driving me to the hospital." Addison claimed the driver's seat.

Cameron clicked his seatbelt. "No problem, but can you drop me off at HQ? I'm meeting Susan, Rick, and Kendra there."

"Sure. Wow, what a crazy night. I feel bad for Clay and Eloise. Everyone abandoned their wedding celebration."

"It's been a night they'll never forget. I don't suppose they minded everyone ditching them, though. They got to start their honeymoon earlier."

Addison searched for the words to bring up the horrors of the night. "So, at least there's no doubt that Benjamin Sykes was the serial bomber. Right? I mean, tons of evidence blew sky-high when he released the trigger on his vest."

"We got your conversation with him on tape, and we have the video from your body cam until he made you shut it off."

"Do you think Tyler Brookes will give a full statement?" Addison flicked the turn signal on with her fingers. "I mean what he did to Sykes in high school…"

"That will ruin any political aspirations he had."

"I guess that's another part of Sykes's revenge."

Cameron eyed her, his gaze appraising. "You think Sykes's actions were justified?"

"No. I don't believe revenge is justifiable, but I can't help feeling sad for the teenaged Benjamin and his ruined life."

"Sure, but there was a lot more going on in his brain than his abuse at school. It sounded like the relationship he had with his mother was dysfunctional."

"Do you think her death triggered Sykes's bombing spree?"

"Sure could have. It makes sense, but in truth, we will never know for certain." Cameron reclined the seat a little and stretched his legs. "What I don't understand is why Sykes didn't target Megan Carlson. She said herself that she was friends with the bullying crowd."

"Yeah, but I think she was on the peripheral. Sykes said he chose to show her mercy. Maybe he figured she showed him mercy at some point—simply by not taking part."

"Maybe. Sykes certainly sought revenge for Nicole Grey, Price, and Brookes."

"It's as though he put each of them through what he felt they'd put him through—especially Brookes."

"Hm." Cameron closed his eyes. "I'm sorry this all turned out the way it did, but I have to say, I'm glad it's over."

Cameron dozed until Addison said, "We're here." She rolled up to the side of Cameron's car. He got out and thanked her for the ride. She waved at the others and drove off on her way to the FBI K9 facility to meet the unit's vet.

~

Addison paced the walkway outside the vet's office. Gunner's head swiveled with her movement. They'd been waiting for the animal doc to make an evaluation of the effects of the explosion on Gunner. She considered Logan's dog, who was sitting tall and fully alert. Gunner seemed fine to her, but she'd promised to bring Logan's dog in for him.

"Agent Thorne?" An older gentleman stepped out of his car. He stuck out his hand, "I'm Doctor Riggs. Thanks for bringing Agent Reed's K9 in. The effects of a blast, even one from a distance, can often be subtle, so we like to do an exam right away."

"Happy to. Can I help?"

"Yes, please. Since I don't have any staff here at this time of night, I'd appreciate your assistance. Follow me." The doctor unlocked the office and led the way into a small room with a dog-sized exam table. Posters on the wall warned of heartworm and the different chew-toys that vets considered dangerous for dogs. "I'll just give him a quick physical examination, paying particular attention to his vision and hearing. Has he behaved normally since the blast?"

"Yes. He seems the same as usual to me."

"Good. That's good." He patted the table. "Up, Gunner." Gunner sprang to the tabletop with ease and lay down. "Good, boy." Dr. Riggs listened to Gunner's heart and breathing. He peered into his eyes with a light and performed a hearing test that involved sounds that Addison couldn't hear.

"Very well. I think our pup here is just fine. Watch for strange reactions to loud noises. He may develop an aversion to intense sounds or fireworks. If you notice nervous or frightened behavior, let me know right away. We can offer him some de-sensitization training to ease his nerves."

"Thanks, Doc. I'm taking Gunner home with me until Reed gets out of the hospital. Does he eat a special food?"

The vet grinned. "Yes, in fact, he eats beef. Agent Reed

should have plenty in his freezer. Give him a meal once in the morning and once at night. Leave it frozen. It slows him down."

Addison shrugged her shoulders. "Whatever you say." She took ahold of Gunner's lead, and he jumped off the table. "Ready to go get some dinner, Gun?"

He gave her an open-mouthed, tongue-hanging grin, then licked his chops and barked.

CHAPTER 36

The next morning, Addison and Gunner drove to Logan's apartment. On their way up the stairs, Harriet came out onto the landing, the scent of fresh baked goods surrounding her. "Where's Logan? The news reported the bomb threat at the Capitol, and the house that exploded, and Logan never came home last night. Now you're here... without him. What happened? Is he..." Concerned wrinkles webbed out from her worried eyes.

Addison clutched the woman's hand. "Logan is okay. He's at the hospital, but he's going to be all right. In fact, they're releasing him this morning."

Harriet's rounded shoulders relaxed. "Why did he have to spend the night there?"

"The blast wave from the explosion concussed his already bruised brain. But he's had a ton of tests, and the doctor said he'd heal fine, as long as he rests for a full three weeks."

"He won't though." The crease between Harriet's eyes deepened. "You know how he is."

"Don't worry. He'll rest this time because I'm taking him to my house where I can keep an eye on him. In fact, that's why we're here—to get him a change of clothes and a few things he might need."

Harriet didn't bother to hide her pleased grin. "Oh, well… that sounds like a wonderful plan."

Addison laughed. "We'll see how Logan likes being nursed with an iron fist."

"He'll hate it, but it's the best thing for him. I baked cookies this morning, I'll pack some for you to take to him while you're getting his things." Harriet shuffled back inside, humming to herself as she closed the door.

Addison and Gunner ran up the remaining flight and let themselves into Logan's apartment. She checked the refrigerator for food that might spoil and found two plastic dishes half-full with mystery casseroles, a gallon of milk, and several bottles of beer. She tossed the leftovers and left the beer. She'd give Harriet the milk on her way out.

An empty backpack hung on the bedroom doorknob. So, she used that to pack his things. On the floor across from the unmade mattress, were two piles of clothes. She could tell which was the clean stack because he'd folded those, and they smelled fresh. From there she chose gym shorts, sweats, and a handful of shirts. In the bathroom, she gathered his toiletries, then she glanced around the room looking for anything else Logan might need. Her gaze stilled on the framed photo of Logan with the dog. Addison picked it up and stared at a younger Logan kneeling next to a dog that resembled Gunner, but had a black face. *This must be Lobo.* On impulse, she stuffed the frame into the pack.

"Ready to go get him?" she asked Gunner. The dog bounced on his front paws and scampered to the front door.

On the way out, they traded Harriet the milk for her cookies, and Addison promised to keep her posted on Logan's recovery. Seconds later they were back in the car on their way to the hospital.

~

Logan smiled at Addison as she held her front door open for him. She carried a backpack filled with clothes for the next few days. His head still felt like a massive vice was squeezing it between its steel jaws, and he looked forward to stretching out in bed. Addison's bed. Change of plans.

"You know, I'll be fine on the couch. In fact, I'd rather lie there because then I can watch TV."

Addison raised a dark brow and adopted a salty expression. "No TV or any other kind of screens for you for at least a week."

"You *are* going to be like Nurse Wilkes, aren't you? Doctors always overstate their recommendations. You know that, right?"

"No. I don't know that. Logan, this is your brain we're talking about. I want to be able to have long interesting talks with you for years to come, maybe play chess—not feed you gruel because your brain turned to mush."

Years to come? Logan considered the impact of her words. Their comfort surprised him, considering how hard he had tried to avoid attachment with anyone—especially Gunner and Addison. What a chump. What he tried not to do, he ended up doing in spades. He didn't want to imagine his life without either of them next to him every day. *I really did damage my brain!* "Years to come, huh?"

An alluring blush pinkened her cheeks, and he reached out to brush his fingers across the color. Addison leaned her face into his hand. "I'm so thankful you're going to be okay, Logan."

"Not as thankful as I am that you're alive. I thought you were in the house when it blew. The explosion yanked my heart right out of my chest." He swallowed hard at the memory. "I wouldn't have recovered if I lost you."

Addison smiled and kissed his palm. "Will you tell me something?"

He tilted his head in question and then winced at the pain caused by the shift.

"Here, let's get you set up on the couch for now. You need to rest." Addison busied herself with collecting blankets and getting him a pillow.

Logan eased himself down and rested his head on the downy cushion. "What is it you want to know?"

Addison knelt next to the couch and took his hand. "Why did you put yourself on that pressure pad in place of Gunner?"

A black shadow fell across his mind. "Because he's my partner."

"No, Logan. Please, don't do that." Her gaze, the color of the sea, seeped into his soul. "Talk to me."

He squeezed her hand and pulled her up to sit next to him on the couch. He took a moment to consider his words. "It's a long, dark story," he murmured. "One I've never talked with anyone about. Not even the FBI shrinks."

Addison used the remote to turn on the gas fireplace. She covered their laps with a quilt and snuggled into the nook under his arm. "I'm here."

Logan leaned his head back and closed his eyes. "Once upon a time, there lived the greatest dog the world has ever known. His name was Lobo…"

They sat together for hours, quiet after Logan's sad story about the senseless, tragic loss of his dog and his fellow soldiers. Gunner had climbed up onto the couch on Logan's other side. Logan never allowed him on furniture, but today was different. This dog Gunner, his new best friend, understood him. Logan couldn't guess how, but Gunner knew. He rested his head on Logan's leg and lapped occasionally at his hand, especially when the words caught in his throat; when they jammed against the aching lump of guilt, making it difficult to speak.

And there was Addison. Addy. How did he end up here holding pure love, devotion, and acceptance in his arms? He didn't deserve it. He shouldn't accept it. Yet here he was, greedily grasping at a second chance. He reached for Addison's chin and tilted her face to his. "The doctor said nothing about this." He brushed his lips across hers, and she pressed up into him.

"That's the other thing we promised to discuss... That kiss."

"Let's talk about it for years to come." Logan drew her into his chest and planned to never let her go.

EPILOGUE

Over the following week, Logan slept a lot. When he woke, Addison was always there somewhere in the house. She'd taken vacation time to care for him, and her presence was comforting. It filled him with contentment in a way he hadn't expected. Logan remained on the couch, but Addison hid the remote so he wouldn't be tempted to watch TV. He wasn't. Logan found that he would much rather talk with her than do anything else.

She came in from the kitchen with a mug of hot Earl Grey. He didn't like tea, but wasn't about to turn her offering away. "Thanks." He reached for the cup and blew across the steaming surface.

"There are a few of Harriet's cookies left, do you want some?"

Logan patted the cushion next to him. "No. Why don't you sit?"

She snuggled up under his arm. "You know what's weird?"

He closed his eyes and leaned back against the cushion. "What?"

"I haven't gone anywhere since you've been here, other than for a run, and I don't feel edgy at all. Usually, I get fidgety when I hang out anywhere for too long." She glanced up at him. "I feel… calm—peaceful. It's nice."

Logan gave her a squeeze. "It's nice for me too. Thanks for taking such good care of me." The truth was, he could sit like this, together with her on the couch forever and not feel the pull of other things.

"Oh! By the way." Addison sat up and faced him. She reached into her sweatshirt pocket. "I found these in your jeans when I ran a load of laundry." Addison slid Lobo's dog tags out and dangled them in front of him.

Logan swallowed a gulp of too hot tea and coughed. "Thanks." He held his hand out for them. Gunner sat up from his position at Logan's feet and sniffed.

Addison kept the tags in her hand and wrapped her fingers around them. "Can we talk a little more about Lobo?"

He shrugged and absorbed a sigh. Logan didn't like to talk about Lobo, but he couldn't refuse Addison. "What else do you want to know?"

"I'd like to talk about your… reaction… to the extreme stress you were under at the Capitol. What happened that night? When I came downstairs, it seemed like you were in another world."

Shame pressed down on his shoulders and heated his face. "I'm not sure, Addy." He patted his dog's head. "Gunner wouldn't leave, and I kept seeing Lobo when I looked at him." Logan set his cup on the table and braced his forearms on his knees. He stared down at the carpet. A fresh ripple of guilt and grief slithered around his heart and constricted like a snake. His breathing grew shallow. Gunner rested his chin on Logan's arm and flapped his tail once against the floor.

"You believe what happened to Lobo and the other soldiers that day in Afghanistan was your fault. But how could that be?" She stretched her hand to his thigh and rubbed up and down. "You told me that something happened with the guard posted to watch over that area. Right? Don't you think maybe he's the one to blame?"

"No, the Taliban attacked him, Addy. And I was complacent. I should have sensed there was something wrong."

"How was it complacent to trust that you'd already cleared the area and that there was a guard stationed to guarantee no one had been there? How could you know that the guard was a traitor?"

Her words slapped him and he peered up at her. "What do you mean? Why do you say that?"

Addison looked abashed. Her face flushed, and she swallowed, but she met his eye. "When you first came to the bomb squad, I tried to get to know you, remember?"

Logan's limbs went cold, and he nodded.

"Well, you wouldn't open up, so I pulled your military records to learn more about you."

He reminded his lungs to pull in oxygen and stared at Addison.

"Most of your last mission was redacted. I couldn't find out anything." She moved off the couch to kneel in front of him. "So… please don't be mad… I went to Sanchez. I told him I was concerned."

Logan closed his eyes and waited for the flash of scorching anger to pass. "You talked to Sanchez about me?"

"I didn't know you then, Logan, and I was worried that you were a loose cannon. I had an entire team I needed to keep safe. Besides, that was then. I didn't know you like I do now."

Logan pulled away from her and sat back against the couch cushions. "So, you got Sanchez to poke around into my past? I didn't realize he had that kind of clearance."

Addison nodded. "He found out that the Taliban didn't kill the guard. Instead, he was a traitor, loyal to them. Apparently the investigation took some turns into top secret territory, so they blacked out any mention of the details in your jacket, and sent you home believing that the guard had been killed and that you missed a bomb on your initial sweep."

Tears stung Logan's eyes. The dark secret he'd held all these years was that he'd missed the landmine. That he'd screwed up and his best friend and some outstanding soldiers died because of him. He couldn't speak. One maverick tear bailed over the edge of his eyelid and galloped down his cheek.

"Logan, I'm sorry I dug into your records without your permission, but you need to know Lobo's death was not your fault." She placed her hands on his knees and peered up at him. "You took Gunner's place on that pressure pad at the Capitol so you'd be the one to die if it blew, and not Gunner. Am I right?"

Logan forced a harsh whisper. "I couldn't lose another dog."

"But Gunner refused to leave you. He loves you and is loyal beyond measure."

Gunner whined, uncomfortable with the tension, and lifted a paw onto Logan's leg.

"It's time you let yourself off the hook and let Lobo rest in peace."

What was she saying? "Why can't you leave this alone, Addy? It has nothing to do with you."

"Yes, it does Logan—both professionally and personally." She climbed back up onto the couch and faced him. "You need to forgive yourself and you probably ought to see a therapist who can help you deal with the truth and untangle it from the lies they allowed you to believe. We have stressful jobs, and you must deal with this if you're going to be a solid member of the squad."

Logan knew she was right, but the thought of digging through all the emotions was daunting. "And personally?"

"Personally, I care about you, Logan. More than you know. So it hurts me to see you in such pain. I was thinking it might help you if we had a memorial service for Lobo, to honor him and give you a chance to say goodbye. What do you think?"

His grief was still so raw, even after the years that had passed. But he sensed she was right. "Okay. That would be nice." He held out his hand for Lobo's tags, and Addison placed them in his palm. He rolled one of the tags across his knuckles.

"Will you teach me how to do that?"

"It's easier with a quarter."

She smiled and retrieved one from a loose change jar by the front entry.

"Maybe I could bury these." Logan jingled the tags. "But it would have to be somewhere permanent."

"Where?"

"The ranch."

"In Wyoming?"

Logan nodded and gripped the dog tags tight in his fist. "Want to take a road trip with me?"

"When?" Addison cocked her head, liking the idea of seeing the place Logan grew up. "While you're supposed to be resting?"

"Yes. It's the perfect time." Logan sat forward, his obvious enthusiasm for his idea growing. "If you don't mind driving, that is. There's no reason I can't sit in a car and rest as easily as I can here on your couch."

Addison usually loved spontaneous adventures, but this one included his parents. That was a different dynamic altogether. "We should check with your doctor—see what he says."

"Come on! We could go up for Thanksgiving." Logan stood up, energized by his plan. "It's the perfect time."

"Thanksgiving is for family." A sudden case of nerves skittered across her skin. "I'm sure your mom doesn't want extra mouths to feed. Especially with such short notice."

Logan gazed at her a moment and then grinned. "You're nervous. Why? About meeting my family?"

"Well," She looked around for something to do with her hands, and tidied up the coffee table where Logan's things were. "I just don't want to be a bother. Don't you think you should wait until after the holidays?"

He continued to consider her, making her jitters more jittery. "My family will love you. Especially my sister."

"But, this should be about you and Lobo. I'm not sure I should even be there." She picked at a few lint balls on the blanket.

"Of course you should be there. It was your idea." He took her hand and pulled her into his arms. "I want you to be there."

"And Gunner?"

He chuckled. "Of course."

Addison slid her arms around his neck. "It's just that meeting a guy's family..." She stared into his dark eyes, looking for an answer to the question she didn't want to ask.

He drew her closer and kissed her forehead. "Yeah, it's a big deal. I've never taken anyone home to meet my family before. So... will you come?"

She pressed her cheek into his neck and tightened her

embrace before nodding. "Okay. But check with your mom about Thanksgiving and find out what we can bring."

His low laugh vibrated against her ear. "You don't know my mom. She'll be thrilled we're coming, and she won't allow us to bring anything but ourselves."

"Just ask, okay? I don't want her to think I was born in a barn."

It was a little over a six-hour drive from Denver to the Reed Ranch in Wyoming—if you weren't traveling with a high energy K9. Addison and Logan stopped every couple of hours to let Gunner out to run. After adding stops for gas and food breaks, they ended up pulling into the long gravel road leading to the homestead near 7:00 p.m. Their headlights flashed on the face of a sprawling log cabin home with a broad front porch that stretched across the full length of the house. All the windows were ablaze with a cheery light, and as they drove in, the front door swung open, and a woman came out waving at them. Logan reached over and tapped the horn.

Addison parked next to a ranch truck, and by the time they exited Logan's Explorer and let Gunner out, three other family members were down the steps making their way toward them.

"Logan, my little cowpoke, it is so good to see your face." His mother pulled his head down to kiss his cheeks and hugged him hard.

He returned her exuberant embrace. "You look beautiful, Mama—you're so tan. How was your vacation?"

"Thank you." She held her arms out as if displaying herself. "It was wonderful. Though, I'm not sure your dad enjoyed himself as much as I did. You know he doesn't like to take off his boots or his hat." She laughed and tapped Logan's nose.

He rolled his eyes and then gestured toward Addison. "Mama, this is Addison Thorne." He bent to pat his dog's head. "And this is my new partner, Gunner. Gunner, *Sedni*." His dog parked himself next to Logan's left leg.

Addison took a steadying breath and held out her hand in greeting. "It's nice to meet you, Mrs. Reed."

The woman smiled, but her eyes were appraising. She shook Addison's hand with both of hers. "Call me Stella. Glad you could come. I hear we owe you a debt of thanks for taking such good care of our boy."

"Not at all. I didn't do anything but make sure he rested."

"Knowing Logan, that was a hard job." Mrs. Reed kept Addison's hand in hers and led her toward the others. "This is Logan's daddy, John, and this is Dylan and Caitlyn, his brother and sister." They each shook hands with her in turn.

"Hi." Addison's limbs felt long and gawky in her black spandex. These were sturdy people who dressed in denim and flannel. She rubbed her arms for warmth.

Caitlyn stroked the head of a big beautiful dog that sat next to her. He resembled Gunner in form, another Belgian Malinois, though the fur on his back and head was tawny, his underside and the back of his legs were solid black. "This is Renegade. Logan helped me train him."

"He's very handsome. Hello, Renegade." Addison held her hand out for him to sniff.

"I call him, Ren."

"Let's get you two inside by the fire." Stella slipped an arm around Addison's waist and guided her toward the door. "Dylan, you get their bags. I don't want to see Logan lifting a finger, you hear?"

"Yes, ma'am. Wouldn't want your baby to break a fingernail." Dylan grinned and playfully shoved Logan's shoulder before they embraced in a man hug and slapped each other's backs.

Caitlyn took her turn greeting her brother by throwing her arms around his neck. "It's so good to see you, Logan. I'm glad you're having a memorial for Lobo. It's time."

"Yeah, it is. I'm surprised you're here." Logan lifted her off her feet in a hug. "I thought I'd have to catch up with you tomorrow."

"I'm only here because I wanted to see you."

Logan rubbed the top of her head with his knuckles, messing up her hair, and she swatted at him. He then stepped over to his dad and shook the man's hand. "Dad. Thanks for having us."

"This is your home, Logan. I'm glad you're here." They all followed Stella up the steps and into the house, with Dylan bringing up the tail-end with the luggage.

The large, rambling, two-story home glowed inside with honeyed light saturating the golden log walls. A huge elk's head stood guard above a massive stone fireplace, and colorful Indian blankets lay scattered on the backs of chairs and couches. The effect was warm and welcoming, its rustic design as far away from city architecture as one could get. Something was baking in the oven that caused Addison's mouth to water. Her stomach rumbled and made Stella smile.

"I'm glad you're hungry. I cooked all of Logan's favorites."

Addison glanced over her shoulder at Logan, who raised his eyebrows and smiled. "Thanks, Mama. I can always count on you."

"Well, you're looking a bit thin to me. You're not eating those frozen meals, are you?"

"No, ma'am. Well—not all the time."

The dogs behaved as though they were long-lost friends and were soon curled up together in front of the fireplace. Stella shuffled the family into the dining room. John took his place at the head of the table, and Logan pulled out a chair for Addison. Caitlyn followed her mother into the kitchen to help serve the meal.

"Sorry to sit you right down to eat, but Dylan has been griping for the last hour about starving to death." Stella hollered from the other room.

Logan faked a punch at Dylan's stomach. "The last thing Dylan is, is starving."

Dylan laughed. "You got that right. Not starving, but hungry as a bear. What took you so long?"

"Dogs are like kids, man. You gotta stop every hundred miles for a potty break and snacks." Logan's gaze rested on Gunner, and Addison recognized a deep love for his dog shining in his eyes. She had high hopes that this trip would put Logan's ghosts to bed, once and for all.

After a filling country dinner with everything covered in a rich brown gravy, Stella showed Addison upstairs to her room. While she was unpacking her few things, Logan came in and shut the door behind him.

"Got everything you need?"

"I think so." She noticed he'd added a long-sleeved flannel over the top of his T-shirt. "Except I didn't bring any plaid." She winked.

"You laugh now, but when you're freezing your skinny butt off up here, you'll be wishing you did. I bet Caitlyn has something you could borrow."

"I'll be fine. I have jeans and a sweater."

Angry voices filtered into the bedroom from downstairs.

A moment later a door slammed, vibrating through the walls. Logan sighed. "Well, that didn't take long."

"What?"

"That was Catie, storming out the door after getting into it with Dylan. Those two have always fought like wildcats, but it's worse these days. They've had a mis-understanding and can't seem to resolve it. Sorry you have to witness it."

"I don't have siblings, so I can't imagine. Will they make up, do you think?"

"Not likely, but either way they'll always have each other's backs."

"What happened?"

Logan stepped closer and put his arm around her. "I don't want to talk about them right now. I've got about five minutes—tops—to get the goodnight kiss I came in here for."

Addison leaned into his solid chest. "Yeah?" Their lips met, softly at first, but a flame ignited in her belly and she raked her fingers into his hair, pulling him closer. She opened her mouth to his, and a muted groan escaped from Logan's throat. His hands moved over her back, drawing her in. He adjusted and made room to slide his hand up her ribs to cup her breast. Lights of longing flashed behind Addison's closed eyelids.

Tap. Tap. Tap. "Logan, you let that girl get some sleep. You're supposed to be lying down, too. Say, goodnight, now."

He chuckled into their kiss. "Told ya." He backed away and bent to give her one last peck. "See you in the morning."

Logan was out the door in the next second, leaving Addison stunned by the sudden extinguishment of their passion. Obviously, she wasn't in Kansas anymore. Logan was a grown man—a soldier... an FBI agent—but it was clear whose orders he followed when he was in his parents' house. Addison smiled to herself. *This explains a lot.*

~

Logan's mom poured forced cheer on the morning, thicker than the syrup on his pancakes. He knew she was trying to help in her way, but there was nothing joyful about the day. It was the morning Logan was going to honor Lobo and then put him to rest. He'd already picked the perfect spot out under a massive cottonwood at the edge of the eastern pasture. The same tree Dylan, Caitlyn, and he had swung from as kids. Their swing still twisted in the wind when it blew, and if he tried, he could almost hear their childish laughter bubble by on the breeze.

Addison joined him at the breakfast table. "Good morning." She ran her fingertips across his shoulders, sending coils of heat racing through his blood as she walked behind him, stepped over Gunner, and took the seat to his right. Gunner got to his feet and stretched before greeting her with a few slobbery licks. She patted his shoulder.

"Hope you're hungry!" His mom called from the kitchen.

"Just coffee for me. Thanks."

Logan shook his head and chuckled. "Good luck with that."

In seconds, Stella floated into the room carrying a plate stacked high with pancakes in one hand and a steaming cup of coffee in the other. She placed both before Addison. "Breakfast is the most important meal of the day, and even more so on a ranch." She eyed Logan's dish. "Ready for more?"

"No, ma'am. Thank you, but I want to get on with the memorial." He didn't risk looking his mother in the eye for fear of the sympathy he'd find there. This was hard enough without bearing her sorrow, too.

"Okay. Let us know when you're ready to go. Your dad and I want to drive out and be with you."

"Thanks, Ma."

When Stella returned to the kitchen, Addison placed her hand on his. "How are you doing this morning?"

Logan shrugged, not trusting his voice. He sipped his coffee and let the hot, bitter liquid soothe the ache in his throat. "I'm okay."

She whispered. "What am I going to do with all these pancakes?"

"The easiest path is to just eat them. Food is not a battle you'll win with my mom."

"But..." With wide eyes, she made a sweeping gesture at the five plate-sized cakes smothered with butter and syrup. "You're gonna have to help me."

After they launched a decent joint attack on Addison's breakfast, they put on their jackets and went outside. Logan opened the hatch on his SUV to retrieve the simple white cross he'd made that resembled the ones for fallen soldiers at Arlington. He loaded it along with a shovel into the back of a ranch truck, then patted the open tailgate and said, "Load up, Gunner." His dog sprang onto the bed.

"Do you have Lobo's tags?" Addison rubbed his back between his shoulder blades.

He answered by patting his pocket. "Ready?"

"Whenever you are."

Logan wondered if he'd ever truly be ready, but he knew this was the right thing to do. "Let's do it."

His parents followed them to the pasture in his Dad's truck. They parked at the fence and stayed inside the cab, respecting Logan's wish to be alone. Logan snapped Gunner's lead on his collar so Addison could keep him with her while Logan had some time at the burial site by himself. Gravel crunched on the road, and Logan looked up to see his sister's F150 rolling toward them. After shutting off her engine, she and Renegade joined Addison and Gunner.

"Logan, I made something for you. I thought..." She held out a pouch made to look like an American flag.

Logan took it and rubbed the soft fabric between his fingers. She'd stitched Lobo's name on the side in dark blue beads. Tears clouded his vision, and he kept his head down.

"I thought you could bury Lobo's tags inside it," she murmured.

He reached for his sister, and they embraced. She spoke into his shoulder. "I know this is hard. But we're all here for you. Lobo was the most amazing dog. He was your friend."

His throat thickened, and it hurt to breathe. Logan gently tugged Caitlyn's long braid, kissed the side of her head and released her. "Thanks, Caty. It's beautiful and fitting." He needed to get on with it before he broke down. "Stay here with Addy, will you?"

"Of course." Caitlyn gave Addison a sad little smile, and the women stood side by side holding leashes. Gunner and Renegade sat stoically, reflecting the mood of the morning.

Logan clenched his jaw and reached for the shovel and the wooden cross. He trekked across the meadow to the tree that held such fond memories. It still would now, with Lobo's marker. After pounding the cross into the soil, Logan dug a hole and knelt by it, gripping the tags inside the patriotic bag. The dirt he'd turned smelled like home.

He placed the bag softly at the bottom of the space and stared. "Lobo, every day we worked together, you were willing to lay down your life for mine. You asked nothing in return. You saved countless lives with all the explosives you found. You're the bravest dog I ever knew. I'll never forget the look in your eyes in the seconds before your death. You knew it was the end, but you weren't afraid. Your eyes were filled with love. I will never forget you. Never." An agonizing sob escaped his chest, and he filled the grave with loose dirt and tears.

A whinny echoed from the hill overlooking the pasture. Dylan sat mounted on his horse, holding an American flag on a pole. His horse reared up as Dylan urged him forward, and they loped down the hill, Old Glory fluttering behind them. He came to a halt next to the tree.

"I thought this decorated patriot deserved his flag." He dismounted and planted the post next to the cross. "It's the one the Army sent home after Lobo's official military memorial. It came after you left for the academy and we waited to give it to you in person."

Tears clogged Logan's throat. "Thanks. I didn't know. It means everything."

Dylan nodded and gripped Logan in a fierce embrace, holding him for a long moment before he remounted and took off. Logan stepped back and looked upon the grave with its cross and flag. He popped into a stiff salute to his K9 brother-in-arms. With tears coursing down his cheeks, he remained at attention with his hand stiff against his brow.

Behind him he heard Addison call, "Gunner, no."

A second later, Gunner was at his side. He sat straight and still next to Logan and didn't move until Logan finally released himself from the salute. Logan dropped to his knees to say one last farewell to Lobo, and Gunner laid down, inching his nose onto Logan's lap. He knew. Somehow, he knew.

Eventually, Logan's parents drove back to the house. Caitlyn spoke quietly to Addison before taking Ren home, and Addison approached Logan. "Mind if I sit with you? Or would you rather I left you alone?"

Logan closed his swollen eyes and stretched a hand out to her. "I'd like you to stay."

She took his hand and sat on the ground next to him.

She ran her fingers through Gunner's coat. They sat together in silence for a long while until Logan finally spoke.

"Want to hear some stories about one of the best dogs the world has ever known?"

"Yes, I do." She tucked her fingers under his arm and leaned on his shoulder.

"His name is Gunner, and he refused to leave me when we thought we were going to get blown up. Then he helped me say goodbye to my best friend. He honors me with his loyalty, compassion, patience, and love. I promise to do my best to honor him in return."

Addison squeezed his arm and laced her fingers into his. They sat together, with Gunner at their feet, in silence for over an hour. A chilly breeze rolled off the ridge and she shivered in its wake.

Logan slid his arm around her shoulders. "Ready to head in?"

"I'll stay as long as you want to. This is important."

He bent his head to look at her and smiled in a way that glowed in his eyes. "Thanks for this. And for being here—staying with me. All of it." He got to his feet and pulled her up with him. Gunner stood, stretched, and shook his coat. A deep sense of peace surrounded them.

She touched Logan's cheek. "Thank you for trusting me with your grief. And for bringing me up here to meet your family and see where you grew up. It means a lot to me." She took a deep breath. "*You* mean a lot to me." Her heart fluttered like moth wings against a lantern.

Logan took her face in his hands. His warm gaze holding hers, he kissed her. He shifted, and closing his eyes, he kissed her again, more insistent this time. Addison slid her arms around his neck and opened her mouth to him. He took command of her senses and she let herself fall into the euphoria of the moment. Her body expanded and contracted all at once, and she pressed herself into him.

Gunner bounced on his front paws and barked, wagging his tail. Addison laughed into their kiss and Logan pulled back, chuckling.

"The thing is," he kissed the tip of her nose, "Gunner thinks you're *his* girl." He kissed her temple and then her ear. He whispered, "I keep telling him, you're mine."

Addison's heart overflowed, and her eyes mirrored the emotion. "I am?"

"I love you, Addison." He kissed her with such tenderness that her knees almost failed her.

"Logan, my heart is yours. It has been since I saw you with those boys downtown. You are a good man—brave and giving. I love you."

His cheeks grew ruddy, and he kicked at some leaves on the ground. "I think I've loved you since I first saw you in your bomb suit. When you took your helmet off and there you were, the most beautiful woman I'd ever seen. I was stunned… I still am. You are an incredible woman, Addy—strong and brilliant."

They held each other until Gunner barked at them again. Laughing, they walked together, hand-in-hand, with Gunner leading the way back to the ranch house. Addison looked forward to an afternoon sitting with Logan and his family, enjoying the beauty of northern Wyoming. She felt peace, at last.

~ The End ~

Thank you so much for reading *Mile High Mayhem*. I hope you enjoyed it!

I would be absolutely thrilled if you would take a minute to leave a review on Amazon. Thank you so much!

~ Jodi

Review Mile High Mayhem

Look for my next series: **Tin Star Partners**

Order Book 1 Now!

Renegade

Renegade

Tin Star Partners - Book 1

Small Town Thriller!

Caitlyn Reed and her dog, Renegade, are thrown into the midst of murder and intrigue when they discover a dead body while on a trail ride in the black hills of Wyoming.

The local sheriff is hell bent on a conviction, and Caitlyn's brother, Dylan, is in his crosshairs. Desperate to prove his innocence, Caitlyn turns to Deputy Colt Branson for help, but she must grapple with their rocky romantic past to gain his aid.

As Caitlyn and Renegade pursue the killer, the investigation catapults their lives in a dangerous new direction, one with mysterious strangers, convoluted clues, and deadly violence. In a whip-cracking turn of events, Caitlyn finds herself under suspicion. When all the chips fall, Caitlyn uncovers shocking evidence that rocks their small-town community to its core.

If you like twist and turn plot lines woven with danger,

mystery and suspense, you will love Renegade — Book 1 of the Tin Star K9 Series.

Stay up-to-date on all my new releases and other news. Join my mailing list!

or

Visit my website at Jodi-Burnett.com

ALSO BY JODI BURNETT

Flint River Series

Run For The Hills

Hidden In The Hills

Danger In The Hills

A Flint River Christmas (Free Epilogue)

A Flint River Cookbook (Free Book)

FBI-K9 Thriller Series

Baxter K9 Hero (Free Prequel)

Avenging Adam

Body Count

Concealed Cargo

Mile High Mayhem

Tin Star K9 Series

RENEGADE

MAVERICK

CARNIVAL (Novella)

MARSHAL

JUSTICE

BLOODLINE

TRIFECTA

ACKNOWLEDGMENTS

During the writing of this novel I had the wonderful experience of attending the Douglas County Sheriff's Citizen's Academy. The deputies who ran the class were top notch professionals who were also kind. They shared their knowledge of the law, their experiences, wisdom, and wonderful senses of humor. I learned a great deal I was able to insert into my novels.

As always, I would like to acknowledge and thank my beta-readers and editors for helping me to polish this book and get it ready for publication. Any success I enjoy is largely due to you! Thanks to my best friend and husband, Chris. You are the very best (and most patient) sounding board I could ever hope for. Thank you for your unending love and support. You are everything. I'd also like to thank all of my readers. Art is never complete until it is shared and interpreted by another. Thank you for reading and for the encouragement you send my way. You make writing such a joy!!

Mostly, I thank the good Lord who blesses me with an imagination, a love for stories, and the opportunity to write them down to share.

ABOUT THE AUTHOR

Jodi Burnett is a Colorado native. She loves writing Romantic Thrillers from her small ranch southeast of Denver where she also enjoys her horses, complains about her cows, and writes to create a home for her imaginings. Inspired by life in the country, Jodi fosters her creative side by writing, watercolor painting, quilting, and crafting stained-glass. She is a member of Sisters In Crime, Rocky Mountain Fiction Writers, and Novelists Inc.

Made in the USA
Monee, IL
09 August 2024

63530058R00152